C0-ATF-965

The Amboy Duchess

Vicki Moss

HORSETOOTH
PRESS

horsetoothpress@optonline.net

Copyright © 2007 by Vicki Moss

ACKNOWLEDGEMENTS

Quotes from Jack Newfield articles in
the *Village Voice*, New York, NY,
originally appeared in 1973

Moss, Vicki

Amboy duchess: fiction, 2007 / Vicki Moss – 1st ed.

ISBN 978-0-9787095-2-5

This is a work of fiction. Any resemblance to events,
establishments or persons living or dead is coincidental.

Cover design: Gerry Burstein
                 David Mera

horsetoothpress@optonline.net

For all who fight back

". . . the public and the private worlds are inseparably connected . . . the tyrannies and servilities of the one are the tyrannies and servilities of the other . . ."

". . . to help women to earn their livings . . . is to help them . . . to have a mind of their own and a will of their own . . ."

Three Guineas, Virginia Woolf, 1938

Prologue

Avi
1941

The 1938 Ford sedan was parked on a deserted Coney Island street overlooking the ocean, just blocks from the Half Moon Hotel, in the predawn hours of a windy November morning. Avi leaned back in the driver's seat, the window next to him open. He enjoyed feeling the brisk air on his face, hearing the waves break against the shore, one of his favorite sounds, and he let his thoughts roam randomly. He pictured his eight-year-old daughter asleep in their small Flatbush apartment, thought about sports, about how he missed the baseball season each year when it ended. He worried about the bad news from Eastern Europe, war wreaking havoc in what he still thought of as his homeland even after two decades in New York. The salty sea air dampened his brow. He pulled his handkerchief from his jacket pocket and pressed it against his forehead. He hummed softly to himself, a song he had learned only recently, "Bei Mir Bist Du Shein." As a boy in the Romanian side of the Bucovina he had loved to sing. He was the Tannen family's entertainer, telling his brothers and cousins stories and jokes, singing songs for them.

1

The Amboy Duchess

Now he often crooned to his little girl, Winnie, sometimes sad songs, feeling sorry for her because her mother had died when she was so young. He flicked on the radio to see if he could catch some music or maybe some breaking news.

* * * * *

A few blocks away, another man also listened to the radio. As Avi daydreamed, worried, pondered life, a short, squat man with huge hands and spatula-like fingers rested on a bed in a sixth-floor room of the Half Moon Hotel, a half-finished bottle of Canadian rye on the table beside him. That night, a ten-room suite on the sixth floor of the Brooklyn beach hotel housed some of the country's most notorious gangsters. In room 623, facing the ocean, one of them, Abe Reles, the head of the Brownsville gang that had called itself the Amboy Dukes, but which newspapers were calling Murder Incorporated, had for the past few months been busy informing on some of his better-known cohorts. He was at that moment getting drunk while listening to the European news. Six of New York City's crime detectives sat just outside the door of his room, protection from the threatened racketeers who might want to do Reles harm. The window was open and Reles, like Avi, was lulled by the sound of the surf, the clanging of a buoy. He closed his eyes.

For some reason, the news reports later speculated, Reles got up, pulled the sheets off the bed, knotted them and tied them together. He twisted a four-foot length of radio lead-in wire to the sheets and tied the free end of the wire to a steam valve under the window. Then he let the sheets down the hotel's east wall, two windows north of the hotel's boardwalk front and climbed out on the window ledge and lowered himself to the fifth floor. He clung to the sheets with one hand while tugging at the screen and the window with the other. He managed to raise both about six inches.

As he worked, the knot on the steam valve upstairs loosened. Reles kicked toward the fifth-floor window ledge as if he wanted to land there, but all he managed to do was scuff his shoes. The wire broke loose of the valve, the sheets gave a jerk out the sixth-floor window, and the 160-pound gangster plunged to a concrete roof forty-two feet below.

* * * * *

As Avi waited a few blocks away in the car, still listening to the radio, the hotel's occupants continued to sleep or listen to radio broadcasts or play cards. No one at the Half Moon heard the noise of Reles falling to his death.

Minutes later, a man in dark clothing came up beside Avi, leaned against the car and casually pulled a gun from inside his jacket.

"What . . ." The startled Avi had no time to wonder what was happening. The gun exploded five times, blood splattered on the seat, the window, and Avi slumped forward over the wheel of the vehicle, dead before the second shot hit its mark.

The car sat on the deserted beach street as a dim light glowed in the east, the sun beginning its rise. All around, on more populated streets, sounds of the November day began, people coming out of their houses, clattering down steps as they ran for buses, the hotel staff a few blocks away getting the day started. Reles was found, sprawled full length, dressed not for bed but rather as if ready to leave, in a gray suit, white shirt, blue-gray sweater, and black scuffed shoes. Meanwhile, crowds of reporters jammed the lobby, the hallways, streamed through the beach streets.

But the street where the lone car sat remained deserted as the chill November dawn set up the day. An hour later, a figure approached the car. He reached inside his jacket, pulled out a gun—but didn't fire. Instead, he slowly pulled open the car door, saw Avi drenched in blood, and then walked the few blocks to the hotel to make a phone call. In a few minutes, the police arrived, along with a coroner who declared Avi dead.

Part One

The Amboy Duchess

One

Winnie
1974

It was eight a.m. and I was waiting in the driveway for Steven to come out so I could cart him to school when a huge moving truck rumbled into the street and blocked my way. I would have jumped out and yelled at the driver—I was in no mood to be impeded—when this blond muscle-man leaped out to direct the driver to the vacant house across the street.

"A little more to the right, Yossie." The man waved his arms and yelled in broken English laced with Hebrew as the driver maneuvered the truck.

Not that I could leave yet, anyway; nine-year-old Steven still had to gather up his books and the lunch I left for him on the kitchen counter, and he wasn't in any hurry. Paul, twelve, and more independent, had already left, his junior high within walking distance.

I turned the key and the ancient Toyota engine began its soft gravelly hum. As I thrummed my fingers on the seat impatiently, I wondered how the movers were going to get the furniture into the locked-up house; no one had been there in weeks. Maybe they've got a key, I figured. Just then, a dark blue Buick drove up, parked in front of the Frankels' house up the block, and a tall, slim woman in sharply pressed khaki shorts and a blinding white T-shirt jumped out and loped toward them, every perfect blonde hair on her head staying right in place as she bounced along, even though a breeze was producing a whisper among the young May leaves overhead.

"You beat me here!" the lanky woman yelled to the movers, waving her keys at them as she got to the vacant house and headed toward the front door.

I pulled my short trench coat up around my lap and pressed my nightgown under my thighs. I usually did everything—woke everyone, fixed lunches and breakfasts, made the beds, drove Steven, even picked up groceries—before showering and dressing. Now I was self-conscious. I didn't want that perfect-looking woman to judge her new neighbor as slovenly. I glanced at my hair in the mirror, the wild reds streaked now with unruly grays; of course, wouldn't you know, I'd forgotten to comb it. I pulled out the brush I kept in the glove compartment and did a quick, imperfect patch-up job.

The Amboy Duchess

Just then Steven flashed out, his fine black hair a dishevelled version of a Beatles do. "Come on, Mom! Let's hurry! I'm going to be late!"

I leaned toward him as he yanked the door open and jumped into the passenger's seat. "Kiss?" I asked him, amused at his sudden burst of conscientiousness. He shoved his head toward me and pecked at my cheek, then used the back of his hand to wipe off my more energetic buss. "Don't get all hot and bothered, Stevie, we can't get out of here till they straighten out the truck."

He squirmed to face the rear window. "They're not in your way, Ma. You can do it."

"Another minute." I squinted out the rear-view mirror. "He's not done yet."

"You can get around him, no sweat."

"For a nine-year-old, you're a hotshot driver."

He shrugged and grinned, evidently taking the remark as a compliment. Nothing ever throws this kid. I slowly backed out around the truck.

"So, what've you got planned for today?" Steven asked as we glided out of the cul-de-sac.

"Don't know. A lot of errands, shopping for your dinner, for starters. Got to look in the paper, see if today's want ads are any different from yesterday's." Maybe I'll shove my head in the oven, I thought, feeling the pressure of suddenly being the sole supporter of my family.

"How come you're not going to teach summer school while you look for some other kind of job?"

I snorted at that. "When the department divvied up the summer courses, there weren't enough to go around."

"Can you do anything besides teach French?"

"Ay, that's the rub, m'lad. Your mom is a washout in the skills department." I took the turn into Oak Lane with a screech. "Sorry." The elementary school in this part of town was on a heavily bowered street, its stone walls nearly invisible under a sheet of ivy. Admiring it, I resolved again, as I did every morning lately and at least a hundred other times each day, that I would not move from Archer Road or away from Blue Wood; the kids and I loved this New Jersey town, so close to the George Washington Bridge we could almost walk to the city, if we wanted.

I wanted my children's lives to be as stable as possible. I was determined to keep the house, determined to see to it that their day-to-day activities continued pretty much as always—at least for the six months they spent with me. If only Richie hadn't decided to take off for the Florida Keys before the ink was even dry on the divorce decree, leaving me with all the bills: mortgage payments, orthodontist, car loan, music lessons for the kids, taxes . . . everything. We hadn't heard from him in nearly three months and now, with the Hunter College semester just about over and the boys champing at the bit for summer to begin, my money was running out. I was glad I had months ago managed to get summer camp paid for. I only hoped Richie would be around when camp was over; he was supposed to pick them up and take them to their new school for his half of the year.

I'd cross that bridge when I had to, but meanwhile I was panic-stricken most of the time, unable to sleep nights and barely able to function well enough days to keep the children's lives normal. I had no idea what kind of job to look for, or even how to begin.

"Okay, kid, knock 'em dead." I leaned toward Steven and kissed the air in his direction, as he pulled the car door open and jumped out.

"Are you picking me up later or should I walk?" he asked, slamming the door and peering into the open car window.

"You're walking today. I don't know where I'll be."

On the way home, I stopped at the supermarket. Back on Archer Road, my driveway was now flanked by two cars; someone had moved the blue Buick and a red Jaguar was facing it. The moving truck was neatly parked alongside my new neighbor's front lawn, littered now with cardboard cartons. The movers were hauling chairs and armoires and mattresses from

11

the back of the truck, just managing not to trip over the two children who insisted on helping them, a girl and a boy about the ages of Steven and Paul.

I got out of the car and opened the rear door to get the groceries from the backseat. As I leaned in, a tall man emerged from the interior of the no-longer-vacant house. Not unattractive; severe-looking, rather, his hair clipped so short I couldn't even tell what color it was.

I hauled out first one sack, then another, tried to balance the third in my arms, but slipped on my way up the walk, causing my coat to come unbelted and my nightgown to flap up around my legs.

"Damn!"

Cans of juice, plastic bottles of cola, and a large package of paper napkins danced onto the lawn as I tried to catch them. Glancing up, I saw him, framed in his front doorway, watching me, unsmiling, hands tucked into the pockets of his rumpled chino slacks, shoulders slightly raised, bony shoulders, giving him a look of barely contained energy, or tension.

Two

There I was, moping on my front steps, watching the shape-up of the volleyball game in my new neighbor's driveway across the street, when he yelled to me to join them.

In the nearly two months she had been living on Archer Road, that Marilyn Lewen, the dazzling blonde in the perfect pressed clothes, had started a Friday night book discussion club, organized a community group to plan a block party, and become a member of the nearly defunct Blue Wood Peace Committee, formed a few years ago to protest the Vietnam War, and was rejuvenating it by drawing up anti-nuclear and save-the-earth petitions. Now the woman was running up and down the street trying to persuade her more lethargic neighbors to face off against one another on either side of the net that her ex-husband Stu was setting up. The two were divorced, but he lived only blocks away, having bought a second house in town and moved into it the same week Marilyn and their children moved across the street from me. Every weekend, and many weekday evenings, he was at her house, helping her fix this or that, playing with his children. If they got along so well, I wondered, why couldn't they have stayed married? The truth was, I was jealous. I wished Richie had stayed closer to home and taken a more active part in raising his children. My kids had left for camp a week ago and were due for their first visit to their father as soon as camp ended. I was very anxious about their spending six months in a strange town, in a strange school—with their strange father. But that was the final agreement; I had no further say in it.

Marilyn had been to my front door twice this morning, but I had begged off, as I'd begged off all of her eager-beaver social activities. Socializing with neighbors didn't seem to match up well with the dispiriting quest of shaping a new life, at least not until I could bolster that new life with an income.

I'd gone on a number of job interviews in the past weeks, but potential employers were viewing me as unemployable—not only because of my dismal lack of any saleable skill, but also, and maybe more so, because all my education made them think I would be too expensive, or dissatisfied with what they were willing to pay. If they only knew!

I dangled my keys at the furry ball of a kitten doing flip-flops at my feet. Steven had walked in with the tiny thing in his arms a few days before leaving for camp, announcing, "It followed me home, Ma. It has nowhere else to go," and I had empathized with the poor little orphan. When it came time for the boys to leave, though, I realized I was the one who would be in charge of caring for it. But I didn't mind; it kept me company at night. And in the morning, it was a comfort to hear another creature in the house.

"Ah, well, cutie, time to go in for my morning coffee." I lifted it to my lips to take solace from its pulsing warmth. As I stood, Stu Lewen waved at me again.

"Come on," he yelled. "My side needs another player."

I waved back, but shook my head, no.

Inside, I peered into the refrigerator. It was nearly empty; this morning I had finished all the English muffins and the rest of the cheese. I was out of fruit, out of donuts, out of bread. What could I *nosh* this time? I figured I'd better make a trip to the supermarket; I hadn't bought food in more than a week. When the kids were home, I kept the kitchen well stocked for their pre-teen appetites. But now I was trying to conserve money.

"Oh, well," I mused out loud, reaching for the milk container and bending down to pour the last of it into the kitten's bowl. "It'll do me good to eat less. Maybe I'll lose some weight."

"You don't need to lose weight. You look perfect the way you are."

I whirled around, startled. Stu was standing just outside the screen door.

"Eavesdropper!" I couldn't help laughing.

"Come on. Play with us," he repeated. "Why do you want to sit here by yourself? We need you."

"I don't really feel like it, Stu. I'm too depressed to play ball."

He pulled the screen door open and, though we hadn't yet established this kind of neighborly bond, he let himself in. Once in the kitchen, though, he stood awkwardly, shoving his hands down into the pockets of his shorts, then yanking them out, putting them behind him, and letting them drop to his sides. I considered helping him out, maybe even asking him to sit, but I was annoyed at his casual assumption of friendship and decided to let him endure a little discomfort.

"Why are you depressed?" he asked, finally.

"Oh, maybe you don't know." I leaned back against the counter, crossed my arms over my chest. "I'm out of work."

He cocked his head, scrutinized me, his expression even more serious than usual. I'd been avoiding the Lewens and didn't know him at all; but I could see that he wasn't the easygoing, full-of-fun guy he seemed to want everyone, maybe even himself, to think he was.

"Well, you're not going to find a job here in your kitchen," he said, grabbing my hand and trying to pull me toward the front door. "Instead of nursing a depression, come out and get some exercise and get rid of those blues."

I laughed, but pulled my hand away. "No! No, really, Stu. I don't want to."

He stopped and peered at me so intensely that I felt as though I'd better run somewhere to hide. It would be very hard to keep a secret from this man.

"What *do* you want to do today?" he asked; it was clear he really wanted to know.

I didn't know what I wanted to do. I supposed I would lie on the couch and play sad music again until it got dark and I could go out for the portion of the Sunday *Times* that got delivered on Saturday night. But I wasn't going to tell him that.

I shrugged, tipping my head from side to side. "I don't know. Maybe you're right. I guess it wouldn't hurt me to have a little fun."

I used to be an athlete, but it had been years since I'd played any kind of ball. This day, I tripped over my feet and continually banged into everyone else, knocked people down a few times and fell twice myself. But batting the ball back and forth with my fists, getting caught up in the competitive fervor, was exhilarating, a good outlet for all my pent-up whatever:

17

frustration, anger, despair. I was actually sorry, two hours later, when it was finally over and the small crowd Marilyn had managed to pull together began drifting away to their own houses after cleaning the munchie-littered lawn and helping Stu take down the net.

I lingered at the end of the driveway, talking to the mother of one of Paul's buddies.

"I haven't seen you in weeks," the woman was saying. "We've been wondering how you are, but I didn't want to intrude. Are you managing all right?"

I felt better now than I had earlier when Stu dragged me out of the house; after the physical exertion, the word "depression" didn't fall as easily from my lips as it had a few hours ago. Besides, I didn't want to complain to the woman. The attitude toward divorce here in Blue Wood was less cosmopolitan than one might expect from a New York bedroom community. Since Richie and I had split up, I'd become the neighborhood pariah. At a dinner party I'd gone to a couple of months before, the women had treated me like I was some kind of celebrity, each one coming up to me somewhat surreptitiously and asking what "it" was like, the tones of all their voices betraying what could only be construed as awe tinged with envy. The men, on the other hand, seemed to regard me as dangerous. Before my divorce, they had always tried to draw me into their discussions, as if their talk would be sure to interest me more than their wives' conversations did. But now they kept away from me. They stood in groups of twos and threes, the smoke from their pipes wafting in my direction, though I could see they were trying not to look at me. They seemed to be on guard against me; as each one's wife approached me, that man kept his eyes glued to us. It was as if they were afraid that their own wives might take it into their heads to forsake their marriages, too—even though it was Richie who'd left *me*, many of them blamed me for wanting a career, a life away from home. I wasn't going to let any of them, the women *or* the men, know I was brooding.

"Oh, yes. We're fine. Everything's fine."

"Well, it's good to see you. Stop by one evening and let's get caught up." The woman peered at her watch. "Now I'd better get back. Jack will be starved. The poor man doesn't know how to open the refrigerator door himself." She laughed, edging away from the driveway and up the block, waving goodbye.

I gave the volleyball a good, hard kick toward the Lewen's garage and started walking slowly back across the street.

"Winnie!" Marilyn called from inside the garage, where she was tucking the net up onto a shelf. "Wait! Why don't you stay awhile? Let's get acquainted," she said, coming out to the driveway. "We're going to have some home-style pizza for lunch. Why don't you join us?"

Her kitchen was stark white, white cabinets, white tile floor, white drapes framing the floor-to-ceiling glass doors that looked out on the patio, the only relief the brilliant green shrubs that shined through, making the glass look tinted.

Marilyn set three places on the center island, white dishes, white-handled forks and spoons, white lace doily-like placemats, the whole thing contrived to create a casual atmosphere; but perched on the stark-white stool, I felt as if I were under orders to relax.

"How long have you been living in Blue Wood?" Marilyn asked as she bustled around from refrigerator to counter to oven.

"It will be five years next month." In my head I counted back to the day Richie and I and the boys had moved in, me under protest, not wanting to leave the city where I had just entered graduate school. "A lot has happened since then," I added, more to myself than to Marilyn, thinking about the irony of how I was left here now without Richie, having to give up graduate school, and he was god-knew-where, doing god-knew-what.

"You're divorced?" Marilyn asked, not taking her eyes off the green and red peppers in the chopping bowl, as her hand made small automatic movements, up and down, up and down, chop-chop-chop-chop, chop-chop-chop-chop.

"That's right."

"We hardly had a chance to get to know your children before they were off to camp," Marilyn said. "I think they're the same ages as Abbie and Jason, nine and twelve?"

"Mmmm-hmmm."

"My kids just left yesterday," Marilyn said, as she dumped the pepper mixture into a sizzling frying pan and threw large slices of onions and mushrooms into the chopping bowl. "They went down south to their grandparents. My parents really miss them. We've been up here since before my divorce. I considered going back home, but Stu and I thought it would be better for the kids to stay near him and I agree. Now, of course, we all miss each other. They'll be gone the whole month of July. How long will yours be gone?" Finished chopping, she finally looked up.

"They'll be gone for six months. Till the beginning of the new year. Two at camp, then four with Richie in Florida. Our arrangement is they spend four months with each of us. I'm worried it'll be hard on them, switching schools back and forth that way. Switching *lives*, really. But we figured it would be better for them to have relationships with both their parents— and Richie was hell-bent on living in the Florida Keys. He told the judge his work took him there! Yeah, right. He took his work there, is more like it. He's a shrink and he's on the staff of a research center that moved there. He does a lot of his work right on his boat! But I am a little sorry I sent the kids to camp. Maybe it would have been better to keep them home with me so we'd at least be together for our whole six months. They couldn't wait to get back to camp, though. And I do need this time to find a job."

"Still worrying about job-hunting, are you?" Stu sauntered into the kitchen, smelling like baby powder, his hair and neck damp. He bent over the chopping bowl, picked out a mushroom chunk and threw it back into his mouth. Marilyn slapped his hand and he backed away, pulling one of the stools out from under the island, turned it backward and straddled it.

"I can't help it. It's a bitch, looking for work."

"What kind of work are you looking for?" Marilyn asked.

"Good question." I picked up a fork and ran my fingernail across the tines as if it were a musical instrument.

"Well, what do you do?"

"Until now, I've been studying for a doctorate in Romance Languages and teaching French at Hunter College. But that's useless experience in the so-called real world."

The silence that followed this was too much.

"What—uh—what do *you* do?" I aimed the question at Marilyn.

"Me? Oh, I don't do anything! I mean, um, I'm still a housewife, just a housewife. I guess when the kids get older, I'll look for work again."

I wished I'd asked the question differently, or directed it to Stu, anything that would have avoided that particular answer. But I turned, gracefully I hoped, in Stu's direction, and said, "And you?"

"Oh, Stu is president of a bank." Marilyn answered for him, the pride in her voice adding to the humiliating "just a housewife" for herself. "He just started there a couple of weeks ago. Before, he was a vice president with Continental Federal and we lived in Manhattan, and before that he worked for the State Banking Commission in New York. Now—it's so exciting!—he's president of Allerton Bank . . ."

"Oh, I know that bank! I think I do. It's a small bank? Three or four branches? Some of them in Brooklyn?" I knew I'd heard or read the name, but now I couldn't think of where. "Now how do I know that? Where did I hear of Allerton Bank? I know I know it. Seems to me I just read about it . . . in one of the New York papers, I think. Now, what did I read . . .?"

"Did I hear you two comparing notes about children as I was coming down the stairs before?" Stu broke in so unexpectedly, I had to strain to recall what we were talking about before he joined us.

"We, uh, Marilyn and I were just talking about, that is, she was telling me her, uh your, children are down south. Down south, was it, Marilyn? At their grandparents?"

Stu grunted as he got up and turned the stool around, sat on it, and tilted all the way back, his long legs stretched in front of him, his feet providing leverage. Once again, I felt I was being perused.

"Stu, you'll fall that way." Marilyn pronounced the warning as if she were talking to one of her children.

"So—you're from the South?"

"Marilyn is," Stu replied. "I'm from Brooklyn. Originally."

"Really!? Me too."

"No kidding? Where?"

"Flatbush."

"You're from Flatbush? That's where I grew up. My dad was a cop there."

"Your father was a cop?"

"Yup, the only Jewish cop in the borough, I always thought. Moe Lewenthal, famous Moe. What street did you live on? Maybe you knew him."

I caught my breath. I had a sudden flash of Moe Lewenthal's face under the blue cap, a face I would never forget, the burly Moe, sliding along Kings Highway from store to store. I was only a small child at the time, but I could still see him in a huddle with some neighborhood punk, pocketing what I only later came to understand was probably a payoff for looking the other way when some deal or other was going down.

Moe Lewenthal. God!

Now I was the one to do the scrutinizing, studying Stu, sitting across from me, his arms crossed over his chest, waiting for me to answer. Stuey. Stuey Lewenthal, the boy with all the Band-Aids, the kid who always had scarred elbows and patched-up knees. I had a fuzzy memory of him always getting into scrapes with other kids. My memory of his father, though, was vivid. I could never forget Moe. Moe, the cop-on-the-take. Nor could I forgive what he had done to my father. I knew it was only suspicion, but Uncle Dovid and Auntie Golde had exchanged knowing looks a couple of times when Moe Lewenthal's name was mentioned. They'd never answered my questions about who might have shot Avi, but I grew up with the impression that the cops, and this cop in particular, might have had something to do with it.

Nearly choking on the memory, I started to cough. "Oh, God . . . get me some water . . ."

"Here . . ." Marilyn ran to the sink, pulled a glass from the cabinet and turned the tap on. "Stu, get some ice!"

Stu got up and tugged the freezer door open, pulled two cubes from the box on the door and threw them in the glass Marilyn was holding out to me.

"Are you okay?" Marilyn asked, as I took a sip of the water.

"What happened?" Stu wanted to know when I finally stopped coughing.

"I don't know. I just, I must have swallowed, my saliva, I guess, down the wrong pipe."

"Stu, the pizza's ready," Marilyn said. "Get the cola from the fridge and let's sit down. Maybe you're hungry, dear. All that exercise. I know I'm not used to all that jumping around, either."

"But you organized the game!" I laughed, grateful to Marilyn for changing the subject.

Marilyn brought the food to the table, chattering on about how she hated New York and missed the small Mississippi town she grew up in where everyone knew everyone else. "When we got divorced, I convinced Stu to live in the suburbs, and then we found the two houses so close to one another, so perfect for joint custody. And Stu is glad we're here, too, aren't you, honey?"

Honey? What kind of divorce *was* this?

Stu nodded, as he pulled a bottle of wine from the wine rack on the counter. "Chianti," he said, holding the bottle up so I could see it. "Would you like some?"

"Oh, yes!" Marilyn chirped. "That's a good idea! I never even thought of it. Wine in the afternoon. But so what?"

"Yes, I'd love some!"

Stu pulled out three wine glasses, set them on top of the island, and poured. Then, waiting until Marilyn was seated, he turned toward me again.

"So," he said. "We were talking about Brooklyn. Where did you say you lived in Flatbush?"

"Oh, I really wasn't there very long," I hedged, sipping the sharp, red wine as I tried to think of how to avoid answering Stu's questions.

"But you said you grew up in Flatbush," Stu persisted. "Which school did you go to?"

"I only lived there for a short time, when I was a very little girl. I hardly remember it. I never went to school there." What was a little lie? Later, when we knew each other better, I could remember details I'd "forgotten" before.

"Do you remember what street you lived on?"

"No," I lied again, shaking my head, slowly, back and forth. "I have no idea what street we lived on."

"How long did you live there?"

"We moved—that is, I did—after my father died. I—I had no mother. She died when I was very little. I went to live with my aunt and uncle when I was . . . oh, very young. I stayed with my grandparents a lot even before my father died. And then I grew up with my aunt and uncle. In Canada. That's really where I grew up. In Canada."

Mostly, it was all true enough. I wasn't even nine when my father died. And I *had* stayed with my grandparents once in a while before going to live with Uncle Dovid and Aunt Golde in Montreal. But I remembered plenty.

I remembered, for example, that we had lived on Avenue P, Avi and me, the same street the Lewenthals lived on. For some reason, I couldn't have said right at that moment exactly why, I didn't want to tell Stu that I remembered very well how I used to crawl out onto the fire escape of the tiny third-floor walkup we shared, and peer, like a peeping tom, into the Lewenthal's kitchen across the street, and watch Stu's mother reciting things I couldn't hear as the woman tried to shove food into little Stuey's mouth. Stuey was a few years older than me, and I could remember thinking that his mother treated him like a baby. I also remembered being jealous, because sometimes I wished I had a mother who would treat me like a baby, too.

The Amboy Duchess

I remembered other things, too, about my life on Avenue P before I went to live in Canada, things that had nothing to do with Stuey Lewenthal.

I was proud of how Avi treated me; he talked to me as if I were one of his pals and he encouraged my independence. I was proud I had my own key and could get into the house by myself after going to the grocery store for milk or pot cheese, even on the days when Avi got home late and left me there alone; proud, too, that I could fix sandwiches for us both even when I was only four and the housekeepers stopped coming.

Besides, I thought, still defensive, I had nothing to complain about; Avi was the tenderest of loving fathers. He would read to me before I went to sleep every night and sing songs, even though sometimes they sounded so sad; he was always there in a flash when I woke with one of my bad dreams. And we had fun together; I remembered riding on his shoulders through the streets when he went out for his newspaper, or on a wonderful train when we visited my grandparents on my mother's side, or my aunt and uncle in Montreal for every Jewish holiday.

I also remembered conversations I used to overhear when Uncle Dovid and Aunt Golde came to visit us. I wouldn't really eavesdrop. But I couldn't help hearing. And I certainly

29

remembered. Especially later, when I was starting to realize some of what it meant.

But mostly that was much later. After it was too late.

After that night, the night that was no bad dream.

Uncle Dovid and Aunt Golde had come from Canada to stay with me because Avi was going to be out all night, though I didn't know why. They were asleep in Avi's bed when the sirens woke me. It was so late the only sound in the apartment was the harmony of their snoring duet. I lay there in my cot and watched the beams of the headlights dancing across the walls like spastic shadow puppets. I knew something was wrong because earlier that night something else had awakened me; it must have been a dream, but it had seemed like a warning.

I had opened my eyes and there, in the doorway, was my mother, a filmy transparency, trying to tell me something. I recognized her, "the lovely Stella," as Avi always called her, from all the photos he'd shown me. I was too terrified, though, by the warning she was trying to convey to acknowledge the apparition, or even to call out to Aunt Golde, as I usually called out to Avi when I woke up scared; instead, I hid my face under the covers. Then I must have fallen back to sleep because the next thing I was aware of was the wail of the sirens and the dancing lights.

Of course, I didn't know until later that what I heard and saw were the ambulance and police cars rushing by on their way to the Half Moon Hotel. Only moments before, the kitchen rooftop had broken the fall—and the spine, as well—of one of the most notorious of Brooklyn gangsters, Abe Reles.

I didn't know either that my father's body would be found, too, just hours later, a few blocks from the Half Moon.

I remembered.

But I didn't want to tell this stranger who was Moe Lewenthal's son Stuey, this Stu *Lewen*, what I remembered. At least not until I could sort it all out, and find out what kind of man he'd become.

And what he knew about my father's death.

The Amboy Duchess

Three

Sarah
1904

In the summer of 1904, my grandmother Sarah foresaw what was coming and tried to save my father's life. Or anyway she knew something bad was going to happen to Avi. She had had a vision, one of her uncanny portents. She knew, knew, that Avi's death would be premature. She couldn't bear to lose another child. But more than that, she also knew the death would be brought about somehow by Asher, her husband, and by her eldest boy, Label. She didn't know anything more, not when it would happen, or where. But it was enough. She knew she had to save Avi from this destiny.

That morning, after Asher went to *shul* for the morning prayers, Sarah dressed Avi and the baby, little Dovid. She left the small hut the family lived in and she left Roznov, the tiny *shtetl* in which Asher commanded so much respect, and she walked the nine miles home to her parents' village.

She walked in sweltering heat, clutching Avi's hand, Dovid slung on her chest, convinced that if she kept Avi away from his father and his brother—forever, if she had to—she might save him.

Her steps across the field were long and deliberate; four-year-old Avi, whose tiny hand she gripped, trotted next to her, having all he could do to keep from stumbling. The infant was held securely next to her heart, swaddled in Sarah's own tattered shawl. The glint in her eyes as she strode flashed copper, as though lit by the stray wires of coppery hair that escaped from the shawl, but those eyes glowed mainly from within, lit by rage. Saving Avi's life was only one reason she had decided to leave.

She would not stay in that man's house another hour. Let him return from the synagogue and call for his dinner. See how he'd like it with no one there to cater to him. She was not a servant. She was from a fine family, educated people, well-spoken; her sister, Gitel, had learned seven languages from Uncle Jacob. She, herself, had not learned, but that was because the family thought her qualities lay mainly in her beauty. She would bring a better marriage, they thought, if she were not too learned. And she had, just seven years ago, when she was fifteen. Wouldn't they be surprised to find out that her husband was a *gölem*, a demon.

Oh, yes! On the outside, he was a good match: tall, handsome, smart, his blue eyes twinkling with shrewdness and humor, a respected member of their *shtetl*. But others didn't see him as she did. She felt a twinge of guilt for having left four-year-old Label in Roznov, but she wasn't worried about him; Label was Asher's pride. And anyway, her fear was for the future. She'd had the dream again last night, and she wished she knew what it meant. There was a death, Avi's, she knew, in a strange, violent, faraway place. The baby, little Dovidl, the one she held across her chest now, was also in danger. Asher loomed over them, Label beside him. She would save the younger children from them.

For herself, she could handle her husband, though she had to watch him carefully, because if she let her attention flag, if she daydreamed about the dancing she used to do or the flower chains she and the other girls used to weave, she would find herself receiving such shouts and insults you would think she was the most lazy, the most stupid woman on earth. Unlike Chana, her good friend from her home village. Chana's husband, Heshy, knew how to speak to a wife gently and with kindness.

This morning, before Asher left for *shul*, he threw his silver wine cup across the room, nearly hitting Avi, who clutched at her now as she walked even faster, remembering. And why? What was the cause of that outburst? She had forgotten to sew the small rip in Asher's yarmulke, his skullcap! He wore it under the black hat, anyway. She would sew it later. But she wasn't permitted even a few words of annoyance, or any of explanation, either. She must cut his toenails, bathe him on Friday nights, be there for him when he wanted to use her, no matter how! So she had cleared the table this morning, put away the breakfast bread, fed the baby, wrapped some food for Avi, gotten herself dressed, and walked out of the house and to the path that led away from the tiny hamlet. She would show him he couldn't throw things or shout at her. She was not his property. She was his wife, to be respected.

But the man respected no one. Anyone in the *shtetl* might fall into his mouth or be coerced into doing something the rabbi might disapprove of. Like the time he decided, on his own, without a *minyan*, the ten men necessary to make village choices, that he would sell the new baby goat to a peddler passing through the village. It's true, he got enough money that time to buy all those chickens and the rooster, and now they had eggs every day, all the Roznovers. And if he had waited to gather together the *minyan*, the peddler would have been gone. But that wasn't the point. He was supposed to get everyone's opinion before doing something so important.

And he lied whenever it suited his own purposes; just last Tuesday, he told everyone he was going to Czernowitz to meet with her Uncle Jacob, and then he went instead to visit the matchmaker to find a husband for her older sister. Her family hadn't even known he was doing it and they were surprised when the husband Asher brought them paid a small dowry. Gitel liked the man, and, even more amazing, he liked her. Her parents were grateful, because they knew they would not have another chance

36

to marry her off; she was twenty-five now, and plain, and much too smart for a wife. What they hadn't known, which Sarah learned later, was that Asher had kept half the dowry for himself, paying the matchmaker only a small fee. He even used the rabbi to bring gain to himself, for it was the *rebbe* who had made the arrangement possible in the first place. It turned out well—he was lucky that way—but the arrogance!

And then, on *Shabbes*, he drank too much . . .

. . . she suddenly realized she had been so lost in her thoughts that she had passed the turn to the village. She went back to the fork and took the right path instead of the left. She would have to be more careful, stop living so much in her head, as she'd always been told.

The infant started to whimper and she realized that her breasts were swelling in pain. The turtle boulder she used to play on when she was as young as Avi, when all the village children were taken out berry-picking, was just around the bend. She would stop for a while, feed the baby and let Avi rest.

When she got to the boulder, she untied the shawl and gently held her little Dovidl in her arm. She pulled some cookies from her skirt pocket and, as she seated herself on the rock, she held onto the older child's arm so he wouldn't dart away.

"Avi," she said softly. "Here are some cookies I brought for you. Sit here next to me while I feed your brother and I'll tell you a story."

The child sat, took small bites from one cookie while holding the others on his knees. As the baby grabbed her breast hungrily, she sang, rather than spoke, the story of the comical *dybbuk*, a demon who tried to scare little children.

After a while, Avi lay across the rock, his head in his mother's lap, dozing a little in the sun. The infant's eyes were tightly shut, milk dribbling from his mouth. Sarah rocked him in her arm as she swayed back and forth and continued to sing softly to herself, enjoying her freedom and the sun on her back. She was a little sorry that she had left Label behind. But he was beginning some simple *cheder* exercises and needed to be with the other boys his age. When she was small, her mama had fought loud and hard for her daughters to learn with the boys. She had lost that battle, but Uncle Jacob had secretly come to the house evenings after that and himself had taught her sister. She didn't want to take Label away from his studies today, and she wouldn't like taking him away from his father eventually, but she planned to go back to Asher's village once she was settled at her parents' home, to get her other son—a child belonged with his mother, after all, even though Asher thought different—and that's when she would tell Asher she wanted him to divorce her.

The Amboy Duchess

She opened the knot of her shawl and pulled it off her flaming hair. Her hair was short, in the way a married woman's hair should be, but still full, a fiery bush her Uncle Jacob had always said, like the one Moses had struck into flame. She was glad Asher was proud of her hair and refused to let her shave her head, as some women did. She stroked Avi's blond hair as she daydreamed, her coarse hands gentle. She used to dream that her husband would stroke her hair the way she was now stroking Avi's. She thought that because she was beautiful, she would be admired by her man and even adored. But marriage wasn't like that, she thought, disappointed. At least not with Asher. Asher thought more of himself than he did of her.

After daydreaming awhile, she kissed the velvety head of the infant and lightly shook Avi's shoulder. "My Avi, we must hurry now. Soon the sun will start to go down behind that tree and it will be cold here. We must get to Zeyde and Bubbe Simkowitz's house before then. Come, my little one."

She stood and tied the swaddled infant around her chest again, fixing the shawl so it wouldn't cut into her sides as she walked and tying the other shawl over her hair once more. She took Avi's small hand, and they began to trudge, going more slowly this time.

No one was home when she arrived at her parents' house in the early afternoon. Her father, she knew, was still in *shul*. Her mother and her sister must be at the market. She unwrapped the baby and lay him on the bed in the corner. Then she took a cloth and washed Avi's face and hands and sent him outside to play.

"But don't go far," she cautioned. "I want to be able to look outside at any time and watch you."

She went to the shelf where her sister kept her books and she took one down and carried it to the table and started turning the pages. She could not read or speak seven languages as Gitel could. But she knew a little bit of Hebrew; Gitel had taught her. She liked to read the ancient stories, about Abraham and Sarah, about Deborah, about the young girl who followed her mother-in-law around like a calf in love. She would never follow her mother-in-law. The woman was a slave to her husband. She would never be like that! She felt pity for the woman, though. Her life had not been easy. While Sarah turned the pages, her mother and sister came in with Avi.

"Sarahle! What are you doing here? Are you all right? Where is my Label? Is anyone ill?"

"No, Mama, no one is ill. Label is learning today, so I didn't want to bring him with me."

"But how did you get here?"
"We walked."
"Such a long walk! Did you miss us so much?"

Her mother came and sat next to her younger daughter and hugged her. "We miss you, too, Sarah."

"We're coming to visit you in just a few weeks, you goose," Gitel said. "Poor little Avi." Gitel lifted the child who lay his head on her shoulder. "He must be so tired after such a long walk."

Sarah stood up and pulled her shoulders back, as if she were in the army. "I'm not visiting. I'm never going back there again."

The room was silent.

Her mother and her sister stared at her, as if they didn't understand what she had said.

Finally, Gitel spoke, her older sister, the smart one who was being married off in a few weeks to the egg-seller whom Asher had found for her. "What happened?" she asked softly.

"He's no husband!" Sarah said, her eyes flashing. "He's a dictator! He thinks he is law. He says he believes in God, but he is godless. He thinks God is only in him. He's not like Papa, kind and loving and teasing. He's cold and cruel and selfish." Her voice broke and lost its strength as she started to weep. She hadn't meant to say this, but how could she tell them about her fears? They didn't believe in her ability to discern things other people missed seeing; they would think her mad. They would think that anyway; what woman challenges her man?

"Shh, shh," her mother said. "Stop! Don't talk that way when your father gets home."

"You say what you want, why can't I?"

"No, Sarah. I never would say such things about my husband."

"I'm divorcing him. He's no husband."

"You can't divorce him. You know that. Only a man can divorce."

"I'll change that! I'll see the rabbi and tell him I want a get, a divorce decree, and he'll give it to me, I know, because I was always his favorite."

"Favorite has nothing to do with it. The law is law. Women can't divorce their husbands. Besides, he gave us gifts, the goat and the calf. And he would want them back if you were taken away from him. He needs you there . . ."

"Well, then we'll get him to divorce me. I won't go back . . ."

"You can stay for the night. But tomorrow, we'll give you food and you will go home to your husband."

"But, Mama . . ."

"I won't hear another word . . ."

Sarah's sister drew closer to her as their mother walked off to give Avi something to eat.

"What happened?" Gitel asked softly so their mother would not think she was siding with her younger sister. "Does he hit you?"

That's when they noticed Papa standing at the door. He'd been listening for some time.

"Sit! All of you!" he commanded.

"Papa!" Sarah yelled happily, and ran to hug him.

He put his arm out and held her off. "I told you to sit!" She stopped, surprised at his lack of warmth.

"Yes, Papa." She went back to the table and sat down next to her sister, so surprised to hear their father speak to them in this tone. Avi came and climbed into his Auntie Gitel's lap, and Sarah's mother stood nearby.

"What kind of talk am I hearing?" he asked, still standing in the doorway. "Divorce? I come home from synagogue and you talk about sacrilegious things. Women do not divorce their husbands. And even husbands, even they must have a very good reason to divorce their wives. Is there such a reason? Has either of you committed adultery? Killed anyone? Been convicted of a crime?" Sarah shook her head very slightly, and looked down into her lap. "No? I thought not. Then what are you speaking about? The gifts? The gifts, wife, are unimportant. The important thing is that this marriage, even though it was arranged, was not forced. Sarah, we did not force you into a marriage you did not want. We questioned you carefully. We know the family this man comes from, know his village well. Yet we wanted to be sure you wanted him. Many girls are not given that choice. But you were. You loved him, you said, after he came a few times and walked around with you and brought us some *Shabbes* wine. I didn't know how you could know that. I didn't know even what it meant. All we needed to know was if you liked the man enough, if he seemed like a good man. You were not unhappy, you said, to go off with him to another village. He's so handsome, you told us. Tall, eyes that sparkled like the lake water on a moonlit night. Such talk. But we were satisfied that you would not be unhappy, so we let you go. Now he is your husband. There will be no divorce."

He had been standing stiff, erect, his hands rolled into fists at his sides. Now he relaxed; now he looked more like their papa. He came to where they sat and put his hand on Sarah's shoulder. "You will get used to his ways, Sarah. Everyone is different. He will be well able, this man, to take good care of you and your family, your children; even your sister, he worries about. He is strong and resourceful. He will always know what to do in times of trouble."

"But, Papa . . ." She stopped herself. She was going to tell him about Gitel's dowry and how Asher had kept part of it for himself, but she didn't want to hurt her sister's feelings.

"That is enough!" her father said. "Let me enjoy my grandchildren!"

Sarah's fears were ignored, her voice stifled.

And it took nearly forty years before she understood the meaning of her vision.

The Amboy Duchess

Four

Asher
1911

"Asher!"

The tall, muscular farmer in the round-brimmed black fur hat turned, annoyed at the intrusion. As he stopped to wait under the old elderberry tree that marked the way to the dusty crossroad, he pulled on the watch-chain that was slung across his belly to check the time; he'd been wearing that watch and chain proudly since his papa had presented him with it as a wedding present. He was on his way to meet the re*bbe* from Czernovitz— the regional rabbi—coming to bless the boys who would be swimming today, and he didn't want to be late.

"What is it, Sender?" Reb Asher demanded.

His brother, Reb Sender, the candle-maker, came closer. "Asher, I'm worried. We have all the boys going at once today. What if something were to happen? It could be dangerous, all of them swimming to Darabani. Why don't we get all the Roznov rebs together and talk it over again . . ."

47

"There's nothing to talk about, Sender. We decided it already. They're all going. We need the money. Here we can't trade like we do at home."

The small hamlet of Roznov, located in Austria, had been attacked several weeks ago and everyone had run. Reb Asher, one of the most respected men in the tiny community, had been the last stubborn holdout. He had put his family through the terrible ordeal of waiting in terror while he kept saying, "They can't make me go; no hooligans can make this Jew leave his home." Then they had trekked the four days alone—he, his wife, their three sons and their daughter—until they had come to the small settlement just outside the Austrian city Czernowitz, where all the other Roznovites, all their *lantzmen*, all their countrymen, had created a temporary new home. When the men tried to return to their *shtetl* homes, the ones they had left in Roznov, the government declared them on illegal ground and ordered that they take the belongings from their houses and go back to their families at the settlement. So, angry and ashamed, they tried to make themselves at home in the strange region, trying to figure out how they would feed their families. Reb Asher had come up with the idea of smuggling his whiskey across the river to Romania to sell for the more valuable currency.

Everyone thought it was a good idea. All the boys in the village over the age of bar mitzvah would go, three or four at a time. Their fathers would strap flasks around their skinny waists and they would swim to make the sale.

Reb Asher's oldest boy had been among the first swimmers. They had set up a competition; whoever got the best price would get a commission. When the boys had returned, the village was richer—and so was Label, Reb Asher's eldest. Today, the elders had decided, all the boys would go.

"I don't like it," Sender wailed. "Sending all together is folly. We need at least some of the boys here to help us protect ourselves, in case another gang of *shtarkers* comes, those roughnecks, who'll decide they don't want us here, either."

Reb Asher stood there, one arm across his chest, his hand stroking his thick blond beard, his other hand tucked under his elbow. His shrewd blue eyes studied his brother before he spoke.

"You may be right, Sender, but we'll have to do all the protecting ourselves, you and me. They won't be gone long. It took only a few days last week. This time next week, we'll have a lot of money. We'll have a celebration."

Sender shook his head. His son, Ruben, just turned thirteen, would be going with the others today. While he was glad the boy would have so much company, he had hoped to hold off awhile and let the older ones go first. Maybe by the time it would be Ruben's turn, they would be able to return home to Roznov and continue their usual jobs—butcher, candle-maker, wine merchant, bookkeeper—serving customers in the area.

"I don't like it," he moaned. "I don't like it at all. It could be dangerous. They could drown. They could be attacked by highwaymen. Or by Russian soldiers. Or by village goyim, non-Jews. There are too many risks. There's too much at stake . . ."

Reb Asher kicked a pebble across the road and watched it bounce down the ravine on the other side. Then he put both his hands on the brim of his hat, pulled the brim resolutely so it sat more firmly on his head, and turned away from Sender.

"I don't have time today for your whining, Sender." he said, stepping over the puddle left from yesterday's rain, and continued on his way to the crossroad where he was meeting the *rebbe*, the regional *rabbi*. Reb Sender, a town elder, was left standing there by the tree, looking forlorn and worried.

* * * * *

"So, *Rebbe*. The town will be waiting by the river at noon, but my woman, my Sarahle, has a good lunch prepared for you first," Reb Asher said as the two men trudged back to the settlement.

The *rebbe* shrugged his shoulders, his head bouncing back and forth, somewhere between a yes and a no, as he hobbled along next to the taller man, struggling to keep up with his speedy pace. "We'll talk, Asher. We'll have a good talk over the meal. How is your beautiful Sarah today? Has she recovered from the childbed fever?"

"The woman is well. She's a Simkowitz. They're strong as bulls." Reb Asher didn't like talking about women's matters. He had more important things on his mind.

"And the child?"

"Gone."

"Ach, a shame. *Boruch ha-shem*. Lord bless him. May he rest in peace. He was your . . . how many do you have now Reb Asher?"

"Four living: the three boys, Label, Avi, and Dovid, and the youngest, a girl, Etke; five are dead. The strong ones, they survive. The weak ones are better off not living. Life would do them in, one way or another, anyway."

"A practical philosophy, Reb." The little man coughed, as though to put an end to such a conversation. Reb Asher was one of the village's most devout *shul*-goers. He showed up at the small enclosure that served as the community's synagogue for morning prayers, afternoon prayers, evening prayers, every day. He made the wine the village elders got drunk on every Friday night, donated money and more concrete things like clothing and household goods to the community's coffers, attended village meetings at the same enclosure that served as the synagogue, spoke up, had influence on the actions that were taken, often took the initiative in practical matters. The *rebbe* couldn't afford to argue with him. But his own view was that every soul, weak or strong, deserved a chance on this earth, it being the only chance it would get. It was up to the community, especially those who were stronger, to help the weaker ones. But these were hard times. Who knew where anyone would end up? Community life was threatened at every turn. They couldn't keep on being chased from village to village and hope to stay together. Each time there was an attack, or a decree to move, they lost a few. Some went to America, some to Palestine, some to other countries, France, England, who knew where? Eastern Europe was not a healthy place for Jews anymore. As if it ever had been. Yet communities used to stay together, he thought. "Ach," he sighed audibly, causing the Reb, the elder, to glance at him. Maybe, he thought, Reb Asher saw things which he, in his simpler way, did not.

"Here we are!" the larger man boomed. "Come in, come in. Sarah, make the r*ebbe* at home. Take his shoes, his prayer book. Make a place for him at table! My wife," he explained to the r*ebbe*, "is a true aristocrat in my poor kitchen. She can make you think you are dining with the Czar."

Sarah whisked a clean, starched tablecloth onto the battered table they had put together from logs and dragged into the hut they'd found. The *rebbe* looked surprised at the gleam of the linen.

"We managed to keep a few things of importance," Reb Asher shrugged.

Over lunch, the two men talked of the situation in Europe, how dangerous things were getting for Jews.

"It isn't safe for the boys to swim the river today," the r*ebbe* said, finally.

"Why?" Reb Asher wanted to know.

"We have news of a gang travelling around doing no good. A well-organized group, with not-so-secret orders, from the head of the police maybe, to stir things up. You should keep the boys at home today."

"Hmmmph. We need the money. We have nothing left to barter with. Only Romanian currency will they take. The people have to eat. What do we use to buy food with? The few rags the women are wearing? Their hair? Even that is going. The butcher Weidendorf's wife cut hers to the roots and sold it at market last week. Her *sheytl*, that wig she was married in, would be next if it were not so ugly. I refuse to let my Sarah do the same, though I found her with the shears in her hand the other day. I forbade her to cut that flaming bush of hers any shorter. But what are we to use for money? I ask you, r*ebbe*. Do you have any ideas?"

"Ay, *nein, nein*." He shook his head. He felt sorry for the Roznov townspeople, thrown out of their village, far from their livelihoods; they needed to be in their own homes, but those were probably being confiscated for official use as he and Reb Asher sat here and spoke. What were they to do, indeed? He had no answers.

"They go," Reb Asher declared. "The boys swim the river today and tomorrow they go to the Darabani market and get the Romanian money we need for the village. There is no better way."

* * * * *

At the river, the rebbe bowed and nodded his prayers as the villagers formed a silent circle around him, the swimmers among them, ready to plunge into the cold water.

"*Boruch ata adonuy, elohanu melach ha'olum, asher kid'shanu, b'mitsvosov . . .*" he sang. "Blessed art thou, O Lord, king of the universe . . ."

Sender held Ruben in front of him, his arms across the boy's chest as though he might not let go. The boy looked solemn, forlorn, a bit frightened. Reb Asher's boys were there, too, Label, just bar mitzvah, and Avi, eleven. Taller and broader than Ruben, they were more animated, as well, dancing around like prizefighters, punching one another, laughing. Asher's young Dovid, not even eight, tried to get his punches in, too. Mostly, the two older boys ignored him. He longed to go with them, but was denied the honor, as he was still too young. He stood with the group, hoping to sneak away with his brothers without being noticed by any of the adults.

In all, fifteen youngsters were intermingled in the throng, all in undergarments or ragged knickers their mothers had patched together for the occasion. Some, like Ruben, clearly dreaded the responsibility of swimming into what had become a foreign land and haggling with strangers. Others, more daring, like Asher's rowdier sons, were eager for the adventure. The adults, all the men from Roznov, stood sullen in their black garments, white fringes hanging from their shirts, thin-lipped and stiff-jawed, having made the decision to send the boys reluctantly. The women and younger children, those not of school age, were not at the water's edge today. Although some had wanted to stand nearby and listen as the *rebbe* blessed the occasion, the men had forbidden it. Some of the women had voiced their fears to their husbands, and those men had insisted at the last meeting that the women—and their sons, the swimmers—would be better off without the women's presence today.

"*Sh'ma Yisroel, Adonuy, Elohenu, Adonuy echod.*" the rebbe finished his prayer. "Hear O Israel, the Lord, God, the Lord is one."

"*Amen,*" the townsmen chanted, the high, clear voices of the boys rising above them. "*Amen.*"

The circle broke up into small groups, as fathers here and there tied flasks around the waists of their children. Others rubbed oil into the young men's skin to keep them warm in the early June water.

"Label, Avi, Dovid," Reb Asher called to his sons. Label turned, the heartiest of his sons, who, unlike some of Asher's others, had survived all manner of disasters, illnesses and accidents, pogroms and evacuations, and who took on responsibility with a capability that made Reb Asher depend on him more and more. The boy evoked an unbidden pride in the older man. Asher kept the feeling hidden most of the time, but the boy knew he was favored. Reb Asher indicated with his chin that he wanted them to come to him now. Label punched his brothers to get their attention and the three approached their father.

"Pa?"

"Label . . . ," he began. He turned his head to see who might be listening, and started to walk a little away from the crowd.

"Yes, Pa." The three boys straggled along with him until the four of them were standing near the copse of trees that stood between the river and their small huts.

"Listen, boy . . ." Again he turned to watch the goings-on at the river. He seemed to be pondering something. Then he took

Label's arm and spoke to him quickly and quietly. "Label, take your brothers there through the trees and go to your mother. She'll be needing your help this afternoon. I want you to stay inside with her and don't ask me any questions, just go."

"But Pa . . ."

"Now! *Mach schnell!*"

The Amboy Duchess

Five

Label
1914

Another hot July morning. It was Sunday, a new week, and the Roznover boys would swim to Darabani again. Label was in the small hut his family used as a barn, rubbing himself down with the oil all the swimmers used to protect against the cold water. He was skilled now at all the steps of the process.

By now, they were *shtarkers*, according to the pronouncements of Benjie's sister Donya, big shots who thought they were heroes, wise guys who would bully their little brothers—and their big sisters—with their new-found fame if the *rebbe* and the other men of the village didn't keep reminding them that they were *pisherkes* still, nobodies, boys who only yesterday, it seemed, had peed in their pants and needed diapers.

Donya was right, in a way. They had gotten tougher. By now, they had gone across the river to Romania so many times they'd had to learn how to fight.

The Amboy Duchess

The townspeople had many months ago forgiven Asher for his imperious selfishness that day of the Darabani skirmish, when he protected his own boys while advocating that all the others risk their lives. All the boys had returned, though two had been badly beaten, one of them Benjie, the only one who had still not forgiven Asher—or Label—for Asher's high-handedness. Well, there was nothing to be done about it, Label mused. Everyone else forgave them—and Benjie would forgive, after a while, as well—and they would all forgive this new transgression, swimming away with the town's money, he was sure. Especially when the boys would realize their dream of becoming rich and would send money for all their *lantzmen* to follow them to America.

At first, many of the Roznovites had thought, and some had said—not quietly, either—that Asher's behavior had been unforgivable. He should be brought to trial, they proclaimed, and handed a punishment, one that would bring him down from his high horse and maybe would remind him that others in the village had boys also in need of protection. Sender was one of the most vociferous of these. Label smiled at the thought of his uncle's ineffectual rantings. He knew his brother better than anyone, Sender had declared, and he hadn't been surprised, as others were, at what the man had done. Now they could all see, as he had always seen, how arrogant, how evil, his highly respected brother Asher was. Label shook his head at his uncle's innocence. Poor Uncle Sender would never survive this life. Didn't he see that the village couldn't afford to alienate the most decisive among them, the one who more than any other had an instinct for finding ways to feed them all? Even the fact that Asher had held onto his silver wine cups and the small, not-so-secret supply of gold bullion, instead of leaving them behind as everyone else had left their valuables, instead of turning the villagers against him, as Sender had thought it would, had only served to make him seem all the more powerful in their eyes, particularly as Asher insisted on sharing the gold. And, of course, he was the one who had started the negotiations they were now involved in to get back their land. Sender didn't understand—as Label did, even at the age of seventeen—that Asher was too valued a member of the community for them to nurse grudges against him for long.

Rubbing the oil into his thighs, his knees, his calves, his ankles, Label thought again about what Benjie's sister Donya had said about his own arrogance. Could she be right? She had a funny way of seeing to the center of things. He was arrogant, he knew. He hoped it didn't make him careless. On this day, more than all the others, he would remain alert, careful.

He knelt down and put the oil between his toes. Last time he'd gone, he'd realized halfway across that he'd forgotten to oil his feet altogether and he had suffered after the cold swim back and forth. He would be more careful about everything, he resolved. Never would he let himself be caught wanting for anything, or worse, suffering in any way, due to his own carelessness. He stood up, stretched his arms and legs, stamped his feet to get the circulation going.

He would miss his family, he knew, but he put the thought out of his mind. He jogged to the river at a brisk pace, the flasks secured firmly around his middle. The other three boys were there, Benjie and the Glazer brothers, all of them eager to get going.

The weekly swim had become routine. Hardly anyone ever came to see the boys off anymore. The first time the *rebbe* had failed to show up, he'd explained his failure defensively the next day. "Do I bless your walk to *shul* each day? *Nein.* Do you even think about the walk as you put one foot before the other? *Nein.* Is it an important journey? Who would deny it? Therefore, if I'm not called upon by *Hashem* to bless that sacred trip, then *al achas cammo v'cammo*, how much more, should I not be called on to bless this, so much less than sacred, one." After that, the parents felt easier about treating the journey as a regular assignment, like milking the village goat. Few now ever felt they had to stand at the riverside, shading their eyes until their sons disappeared over the horizon, and, *boruch Hashem*, none had felt so inclined today. Label scanned the area to be sure their voyage would be unremarked.

The Amboy Duchess

Pearl Riskoff, the matchmaker, was there, as usual. She regarded it as her duty to give them a blessing when they left, a kind of plea with Hashem to keep them safe, unlike the *rebbe's* blessing, which had been more of a celebration of Elohim. But whatever one called The Greatness of Being—in whatever tone of voice—it was always better to have more prayers than fewer. Madam Riskoff was always there when they returned, as well, which made Label think that either she never left the water's edge until she spied her potential clients swimming toward home, or else she nervously kept coming back to check for the sight of them. None of the boys paid her any mind. But today, he was uneasy about her presence.

He became especially wary when Ruben and Saul, his cousins, Uncle Sender's two older boys, suddenly ran up to him, each of them grabbing him roughly and giving him an awkward hug. Most of the boys were usually in *cheder*, school, when the swimmers left, studying in the small lean-to Asher had set up next to the *rebbe's* hut for the daily exercises. But today Ruben and Saul had no sooner disappeared into the copse of trees when his little brother, Dovid, arrived and refused to leave. Because he pleaded, Label let Dovid stay and hold the stick when he took off his clothes and tied them to the top. Then three more of the younger boys showed up, one shyly slipping a lucky rock into Label's fist, another lightly touching the arm of each swimmer and the third pulling Label's cap over his eyes as he did a small dance around the four swimmers. These were followed by two more boys, and they by still others, until the community's whole population of young boys had come and gone, giving today's swimmers hugs or slaps on the back, mumbling incomprehensible words that sounded a little like Madam Riskoff's prayer. Label and his friends had told no one else of their plan, yet all the younger boys somehow knew, and now Label hoped Madam Riskoff would not be suspicious of this unusual leave-taking.

"Let's get going," he said, gruffly.

The others nodded. "We've just been waiting for you," replied Benjie.

"You're okay?" Label asked them.

They shrugged. Benjie answered: "Are you?"

He shrugged also, but his shrug said: "Huh! I'm always okay," whereas theirs seemed a bit less certain. "Then let's go."

As they stepped into the knee-deep flow, Madam Riskoff approached them.

"Wait!" she commanded from the shore.

They obediently stopped and waited. Label impatiently moved his left foot back and forth, splashing them all, as she bowed her head, then lifted her arms, waving them in slow circles over the boys' heads as if she were *benching licht*, lighting candles, on Friday night to bless, and light, the Sabbath.

"Blessed art thou O Lord, King of the Universe, I beseech you to let these beautiful children go safely in your care and let them get their task done quickly and come back to us as soon as you can make it possible. Amen." She gave a curt nod. "*Schoin*, that's that," she pronounced, and before she could fold her hands over her ample stomach, the by-now-strong swimmers were well on their way.

* * * * *

They lay on the shore, drying in the afternoon sun, when they heard the clappety-clap of horses' hooves. Label was the first to leap to his feet and start grabbing for the flasks and their clothes, stretched out to dry alongside them, for the bundles they tied to their sticks didn't stay completely dry.

"Damn! Not today!" Label said between clenched teeth. "Come on, hurry up!" The others were slower to react. "Get the flasks, get the flasks!" They scrambled to tie the whiskey bottles around their naked bodies, then, with fumbling hands, covered them, and themselves, with still-damp shirts, underwear, knickers. As they did, they hopped toward the woods, avoiding the path, shoving aside vines and overgrown grasses, taking care not to trip over exposed tree roots or rocks.

"Where was that cave we hid in last time?"
"Just there, after that tree, go left!"

The cave was silent and dark, and, luckily, empty. They reached it as the four horses galloped past. Label shoved Benjie further in and whispered to him that he would put himself on watch.

"Can you see them?" Benjie hissed after a few moments, relieved that Label was the one near the mouth of the cave, but annoyed that his friend always seemed to take charge.

Label turned toward the others, hunched over as if his voice would be softer that way. "It's the four *paskudnyaks* from the inn, the no-goodniks we had so much trouble with on the trip before Pesach, before Passover."

"Where are they heading?" Benjie wondered.

"Looks like they're going to the village." This was Simon.

"Well, that's one village we stay away from," Label decided.

"Let's stay here and have a bite to eat," said Shmuel. "What did your mother give you this time? Ours made *m'lai*." The boys loved the corn bread with pot cheese and scallions Simon and Shmuel's mother baked for them.

Suddenly, the sound of galloping slowed down and a voice yelled, "Hey, the Jew-boys are here again."

"How do you know?" another shouted back.

"Look here, at the shore, footprints, dragging marks. They must have lay drying off here. They went into the woods."

The Amboy Duchess

The four Roznov youths backed into the darkness. The cave was larger than they'd realized; last time they had run here from the village and the gang that had followed them flew past the cave, missing it, unable to find them. Maybe they'd be lucky again. They kept moving backward, reaching behind them for the back wall. Finally, after it began to seem the cave must be endless, Label's fists grazed a rocky surface.

"Sh-h-h-h," he whispered.

"I didn't say anything," came back another whisper.

"I know, I know." He'd been cautioning himself for nearly shouting when he discovered that the cave was finite.

"Do you think they'll find us?" Simon and Shmuel said in a chorus of fear.

"Shhh." This time it was Benjie's harsh whispered hiss.

"How the hell should I know?" Label, uncertain of what to do, was annoyed with them for raising questions he didn't know the answers to. "Do you hear anything?"

"No, I think they're gone. They must have just gone past without stopping."

They stayed there awhile, not wanting to take any chances. But finally, Benjie said, "Hey, we're not getting anywhere like this. Let's get out of here."

"Just be careful," Label cautioned. "We don't want to move too quickly."

"Ahhh, we're okay," Benjie assured them.

Slowly they moved toward the front of the cave. Peering out, they saw nothing but trees. "I think it's safe," Benjie whispered.

"Why are you whispering, then?"

"I'm not!" Benjie declared. He stepped out of the cave, as if to show he was as brave as anyone, especially Label, and the two Glazer brothers followed him slowly. Label still stayed back a little, feeling uneasy. The three boys in front, Benjie and the Glazers, peered around, saw nothing. As Label was about to join them, a band of goyim, at least half a dozen of them, all older, maybe in their mid-twenties, charged out from behind the trees and attacked.

Label watched from inside the cave as his friends took a severe beating.

Finally, the hoodlums left. One of the Glazers lay on his back, swearing, his face bruised and swollen. His brother, nearby, was on his knees, struggling to get up. Benjie was curled up near the path, his knees pulled nearly to his chin, his face filthy from the mud and from the tears that had streamed down it. He had been running, and one of the hooligans had chased and tackled him, pulling him down and pummeling him until he couldn't take it anymore. Label approached him, knelt, and touched his buddy's shoulder.

"Benjie?" The boy was breathing, but he seemed to be unconscious. Label touched his forehead; it was burning, probably with the heat of shame. But Label, who thought his friend must have a fever, leaped up and raced to the nearby stream, pulled off his shirt and dipped it into the icy water. He wrung it out as he raced back to where Benjie lay, still, apparently knocked senseless. He gently placed the cold shirt on Benjie's forehead and took one of his hands and chafed it between his own. "Benjie! Come on, Ben, get up," he pleaded.

Meanwhile, the Glazer boys had joined him. "Is he dead?"

"No, fool," Label said. "Help me move him to the cave. In case they come back." He lifted Benjie by the shoulders and the Glazers took his legs.

"You think they'll come back?"

In the cave, Benjie came to. He grabbed the cold, wet shirt that still covered his forehead, pulled it off and flung it away. He tried to stand, but the others held him down. "Not yet, *kint*, child," Label said.

"I'm not your *kint*!" But he leaned back against the wall of the cave, too weak to stand. Then he glared at Label. "Where were you while we got beaten?"

"I . . ."

The Glazer boys, too, stared at him. "Yeah, what happened to you?"

"There was nothing I could do," Label said decisively, standing now, briskly rubbing his suddenly cold body. "There were too many of them."

Six

Etke
1916

Etke knelt on the hearth, stirring the soup. She and her mother were alone in the hut. Sarah sat at the table letting her daughter prepare their lunch for once. Etke stood, wiped her forehead, sweaty from the heat, with her forearm, then, still sweating, she lifted the corner of her apron and pressed it to her forehead and her cheeks, and under her eyes. Kneeling again, she ladled some soup into a bowl for Sarah and carried it to the table.

Before she had time to set the bowl down, they heard a commotion outside, someone yelling, "Watch out, you clumsy fool!" A voice they didn't recognize. Then the clip-clopping of horses! A scream, a child maybe, ten-year-old Malca from next door, Etke thought.

"What's going on?!" She started toward the door, still holding the steaming bowl, but before she got there, three ruffians barged their way in through the doorway.

Etke stopped where she was on her way to the door, backed up slowly to where she thought her mother was still

71

sitting at the table, thinking she would protect her. Sarah, meanwhile, had gotten up and was moving closer to where her daughter made too good a target. She calmly placed herself in front of the girl and demanded of the three housebreakers, "Who are you? What do you want?!"

She recognized one of them, the mayor's boy from the town just south of Roznov, *goyishe shtarkers* here to give the Roznovites more trouble, as if they hadn't had enough.

"Where are your men?!" the thugs demanded.

The men and boys of the village, Asher and Dovid with them, were in the meeting room today, learning a new skill, street fighting, so they could try to defend themselves against the increasing violence. Everyone knew the pogroms, well-planned, were the work of the government. The poor villagers could never be a match for such hired thugs. But it would be shameful not to try. Against the Russian and German armies, and the British, and now the American, as well, all waging the most brutal war ever known, they were helpless. But it helped them a little to at least create the illusion of strength.

Etke heard the horses shuffling and whinnying outside. The *shtarkers* often came on horseback when they could, as a show of power, though more often, the stories from other villages confirmed, they crept into the *shtetls* at twilight and set fire to people's homes while the families inside were eating their dinners. Then, when the villagers were forced out onto the rough cobble-stoned streets, the thugs would grab old men and young and knock them down, kicking them for good measure. They would taunt women for their close-cropped hair, pulling their dresses out at the necklines to see their breasts. "Are you a woman, after all, you ugly bitch?" they might shriek with laughter. Too often the shenanigans would become more violent, and recently more than one person had been trampled by a horse, killed in a brawl, or badly injured in some other way, one of many imaginative cruelties the gangs thought up.

"The men are not here," Sarah answered quietly, hoping her reply would send the three out to look for trouble in other places, maybe where all the men were. And maybe today the men would be strong and would beat them until they'd flee.

"Who is that behind you?!" one of the thugs yelled, grabbing Sarah's arm and yanking her aside.

Etke felt her already red cheeks heat up again when the hooligan moved closer, looking her up and down.

Sarah took the soup bowl from her daughter and tried to place herself between her and the three criminals nosing around her. She wanted to protect her daughter, but she was also frightened that the girl might suddenly become brave and provoke the three by tossing the hot soup at them.

But they didn't need provocation.

One of them knocked Sarah out of the way again and the three then circled Etke, walking around and appraising their lucky find. The first one touched Etke's dress where it tightened over her chest, just beginning to bud, lightly at first, then more firmly, cupping his hand over her tiny left breast. Another came from behind and lifted her dress and her petticoats to see her legs. The third one knelt down in front of her and poked his head up her skirt.

"She's just a baby . . . leave her alone . . . you don't want her!" Sarah didn't know how divert their attention from her daughter who was not even twelve. "Do you want lunch? Take the food, it's good. Nice hot soup."

She glanced toward the door, wished Asher and Dovid would get home, wondered if she should try to dash out and get them, realized she wouldn't have time, she and Etke were on their own.

But when she put her hands on Etke's shoulders and tried to ease her away from them, one of the thugs grabbed Sarah, shoved her toward the door, then threw her outside, kicking her as he knocked her to the ground. "You first!" he shouted to the other two. "When you're done I'll come back in."

"*NO-O-O-O-O-O!!!*" Sarah screamed, hoping Asher would hear and come running. But she understood the uselessness.

* * * * *

Asher, in an effort to keep one of his sons safe, had sent Avi to live for a while with a distant cousin in Vienna. He and

Dovid were the only Tannen men in the village when Etke was attacked. Dovid, nearly thirteen, was shy and soft-spoken, not one to threaten anyone, least of all the ruthless gangsters who raped his sister.

In any case, when they finally did come running, alerted by the tumult the rest of the gang was making throughout the village, it was already too late. Etke lay on the wooden planks covering the dirt floor of the house, sobbing, her dress and petticoats torn from her, blood streaming down her legs. The hoodlums, laughing, were just coming out of the hovel, the last one buckling his belt. Sarah had tried to rush in the minute the last one had let her go, but the others held her back until he was done, too. But now, when Asher and Dovid arrived, she was inside, kneeling next to her daughter, trying to control her own sobs as she tried to comfort the girl.

The rapists shoved Asher aside and knocked Dovid to the ground, retrieved their horses, leaped up onto them and clattered away.

Sarah shooed her stricken son and husband out of the house again while she helped Etke up and got her onto the bed. When she let the men back in, Etke had fallen into a sleep that was interrupted that whole night by her screams and cries as she relived the experience in her dreams.

Asher generally wrote to Avi every week, but he couldn't bring himself to tell his son what had happened to his sister. For one thing, Etke was a special favorite of Avi's and Asher didn't want to worry him more than was absolutely necessary. He and Sarah doctored Etke as well as they could and hoped she would recover from the violence, if not from the shame. In addition, he was sure Avi would want to come back, and Asher had no intention of bringing his son home yet.

Avi's stream of letters, arriving regularly twice a week, told Asher he had made a mistake sending the young man to the city. " . . . the cousins are so poor here I must steal rolls from the baker's to live." "People love my singing so much, they pay to hear me. I stand on street corners, my hat at my feet, and they throw money in . . ." "Everyone here is educated, Papa, why haven't you sent your children to schools in the city?"

Asher sighed with grief. But he would not send for Avi to come home where things were so much worse. And he wouldn't tell him about Etke's rape. He couldn't talk about it at all, to anyone. His shame was not only for what had happened to his only daughter, it was for himself, for having been unable to protect her. He told Avi only that things at home were bad.

Each day they got worse. Those who managed to hone their survival skills in the ersatz self-defense classes were quickly rounded up by government officials looking for cannon fodder for the Russian army. The army stories that trickled in were as bad, or maybe, in their way, worse than the news of pogroms that arrived each day with the wandering story-tellers from nearby villages. Boys drilled relentlessly by cruel officers in heat and cold died on their feet before reaching the front. Youngsters whipped for taking too long to eat a meager ration of black bread and a potato grew ill and died in their sleep.

Asher wrote Avi, pleading with him to be patient. "Things will get better here. Try to last until spring, at least. For now we barely have enough to eat and every day your brother and sister face dangers that you, at least, are safe from, for now."

The only bright news that winter came in Label's letters. *Boruch Hashem*, thank God, one of the Tannens was doing well. Label promised he would continue to work hard to bring his family to where they would have better lives.

Before Label's letters had reached them, Asher and the other villagers thought the boys had been killed by the Darabani gangs. Dovid, so young at the time, had known the truth, but having been sworn to secrecy by his oldest brother, he stayed silent. When the first letter arrived, finally, guilt-ridden, he told his father the terrible secret. This confession, though, created even more anxiety. How, Asher wondered, could four young boys, only a few years past bar mitzvah, survive in a foreign country where they knew nothing: not how to support themselves, not even how to speak the language. How, in fact, had they survived the journey, facing hooligans, *shtarkers*, real training armies? And then, if they *had* managed to get past those ever-lurking menaces, how did they trek more than five hundred miles of mountains and rivers, forests and towns, all replete with equivalent dangers, wild animals along with the human ones? And if they had managed *that*—though even holding Label's letters in his hand Asher had trouble believing such a *bubbe-mayse*, such a fairy tale—even if they had gotten as far as Germany, how did they know where to go or how to arrange for a boat to take them across the sea, such youngsters, barely out of diapers?

It was too much to swallow. When Asher showed the first letter to the other men of the village, they questioned him over and over, "How can you be sure it's really from Label? Maybe someone is trying to trick us."

Only after Asher pointed out—over and over, as well—that there couldn't be any reason for anyone to trick them this way, only then did they acknowledge that the boys must, indeed, have made such an unbelievable journey.

Yet, when they finished scratching their heads at the sheer mystery of such a feat, they wanted to know something else: *if* the boys had managed to do all that—*if they had!*, their fathers thundered—who could even think it?—these four village sons were thieves! They had taken the village's money and skipped off into the unknown, sentencing their families to even worse poverty than usual.

Nevertheless, they began to tell the story with a certain pride, at family gatherings, in *shul*, in the marketplace. And the more they told it, the more amazing it seemed. Four young Roznov boys, whose voices had barely grown deep, had not only overcome the cold waters of the river and managed to sell the contraband whiskey, they had also made their way, somehow, *Hashem* only knew how!, to a boat that took them across the Atlantic to New York City, America! And as the story spread among a wider and wider audience of elders and children in nearby towns, the legend became a mission to aspire to.

But the legend didn't solve the problem of how to cope with the violence right outside their doors. Their attackers seemed to attack with such rage, it was hard to understand. Maybe some of their anger was for their own helplessness in the face of their similarly impoverished lives. The Jews, they were being told, had more than they did; the Jews held the world in their hands, as one recent newspaper cartoon had famously depicted.

The irony of these rumors wasn't lost on the Roznovites. Mock tales of their own great wealth circulated throughout the village, along with the stories of violence from other towns, violence in the army's ranks, and the story that grew more fantastic with each telling: the story of Label's achievement.

But, despite the humor and the story-telling, in Asher and Sarah's house, things got worse.

After the rape, Etke became ill and medical care was scarcer than food. First she bled for weeks. She grew weaker and more pale, and lost her appetite, unable after a while to get out of bed. Sarah sat with her, tried unsuccessfully to make her eat, watched her become thinner and more anemic. Then Etke began to cough.

It was nearly spring when Avi got his father's letter, finally telling him what had happened to Etke. Etke, his favorite, his darling. He had to go home. Finally, Asher relented and sent him the money.

The sadness greeted him before he reached the small house. It was in the village air. Or maybe that was only his imagination, he would think looking back on it later. Maybe not in the actual air. But he did remember women standing in their doorways, nodding at him, unsmiling, as he strode along on the still snow-stained cobble-stones.

He knew it before he got there.

Etke was no more.

* * * * *

The Roznov boys got to American shores in time to join in the violence that was America, having been prepared for it by Russian, Polish, and Romanian thugs. Being poor couldn't beat them down; American poverty didn't hold a candle to the Eastern

European kind. If they felt like complaining as they adjusted to their new home, Etke's rape reminded them of the antiquated medical care they'd left, the pogroms, the intolerant military that conscripted and then tormented their friends; the wasteland where they'd seen no opportunity for adventure, no future for enterprise.

In New York things might get rough, but they knew how to fight. They might have to live in cramped rooms, rented from other poor immigrants, in overcrowded apartments, but they understood quickly how to use the opportunities that arose.

Instead of gold in the streets, they found work, errands that needed running, crates that needed strong backs for lifting, and they began collecting pennies and nickels, planning that when they had enough they would send for the rest of the clan— fathers and cousins and neighbors.

But Avi didn't wait to be sent for. Instead he and his gang of cronies showed up one day a few months after Etke's death, surprising Label. The two brothers couldn't stop bear-hugging, slapping each other on the back, their eyes, as blue as Sarah's, watering. Avi became the Roznovite raconteur. He held court among the *lantzmen* circling around him, telling them how he, too, "swam to America."

When Label stopped hugging Avi, he gripped the shoulders of his little brother—who was now almost as tall as he—and shook him, repeating over and over, "How did you do it?"

"We did the same thing you did! You think you're the only Roznover *shtarkers*?!"

Avi told him how after Label and his friends had disappeared, the villagers all thought they were dead. But when they learned from Label's letters that the boys had continued on to America after swimming to Darabani, they became famous, a kind of legend among Roznov families.

Younger brothers throughout the village vowed they, too, would undertake the journey. They helped each other plan the pilgrimage. But no one had the nerve to leave, mostly because their families needed them so badly. One or two did try, and drowned; one boy was beaten by the ever-growing number of gangs, but he made it safely back to his family, only to be permanently injured during a pogrom. The adventurous ones kept reading Label's letters and hoping for a time when they could carry out their plans. Meanwhile, everyone talked about the sanctified place now known to all the villagers New York City, Manhattan, and the name of another place that was appearing lately in Label's letters, as well, Flatbush, Brooklyn.

Label was glad to see the new arrivals, glad to be the one to teach them how to find work, how to cut corners and stash away the coins and bills that now, with more boys contributing, grew faster than he'd imagined they ever would.

But bringing the rest of the family to New York turned out to be a frustrating ordeal. In 1924, the American government set a quota on the procession of immigrants that could enter the United States. No matter how he tried, Label could not bribe any officials to get his parents into New York. So he made other arrangements. He managed to find sponsors in Montreal and he paid for a small house there.

In 1925, just eleven years after he had left the *shtetl*, Label's family finally joined him in North America, his mother, his father, his Aunt Gitel and her husband and their children, and the youngest Tannen brother, Dovid, now past twenty, whom Asher had persuaded not to swim the river as his brothers had, but to stay with his parents to help them, especially Sarah, make the difficult journey.

The Amboy Duchess

Seven

Asher
1925

Wind whipped the high grasses around their ankles as the two burly men high-stepped through the field, each preoccupied with his own thoughts even as they argued.

"America?! Asher, you think you'll find gold, but what is gold? Always you look at the wrong things. From a boy, you're like that. Your boys steal from you and they go away and now you follow them and you think they're leading you to the end of the rainbow. What will you find there? Two sons, grown-up men you don't know anymore, doing godless things in a world you're too old to fit yourself into."

Sender was working with a group that wanted to go east, not west. The area still known as Palestine lacked America's promise of gold, but it promised something else—a chance to develop a Jewish homeland.

"Ach! Sender! Always philosophizing. There's a time for philosophy. But now is not the time. Now is time for action. Open your eyes. Can't you see around you? The corruption, the

85

evil here. This is not a place for us anymore. Jews have to wander still. We aren't in the promised land yet."

"And America is the promised land? What does it promise? To make you rich? A homeland we need, not riches."

"Your Zionist organization is a dream, Sender. The Jews will never have Palestine."

"We'll build it, Asher. It's no dream. We'll build a land where we'll be strong. Maybe not rich, but we'll have all the riches we need, the family, the books, the *rebbe*. You should have sent your children to Vienna to school, you could still educate Dovid. That's what he needs better, an education, not to run after golden rainbows."

The two brothers stopped pleading with one another as the meadow gave way to a gentle rise. Asher strode up the embankment ahead of Sender and stopped at the top, his arms crossed over his wide, muscular chest. The strings of his *tsitsis*, the fringes of his prayer shawl, flapped against the hips of his loose black trousers. His blue eyes, the color of steel, glinted with mischief as he waited for his younger brother, puffing, to reach the top of the hill. He put his huge hand on Sender's shoulder, shaking his head.

"Sender, you must stop going so much to *shul* and start doing more work—milk the cow, deliver the milk. Look at you, a young man, and you can't keep up with your old brother."

"Forty-nine is not young, Asher. And fifty-five is old. You are too old to be going all the way around the world to a country where they won't even let you take a sip of schnapps on a *Shabbes nacht*."

"Ah, this law. They will overturn it soon. A woman's law! But you, Sender, why can't I make you see how much better life can be there? People are free to do any kind of business. Look at my Label, a restaurant he opens. Could he do that here? And Avi. Selling girdles and making a living at it and dressing like a prince, you saw the picture he sent. In America my Etke and all the other little ones wouldn't have died. There they have doctors and medicines and anyone can get them, Jewish, not Jewish, makes no difference."

"Doctors! They should be doctors! Like my boy, my Ruben. But send them to school, not you, Mr. Stingy-first-class."

"My sons learned to make their way on their own and they're stronger for it!"

"Hah!"

"And what can a doctor do who is also a Jew? A living he'll make here in the *shtetl*?"

"No, but he'll save people's lives and they'll take care of him. He'll bring them *naches*, good fortune, helping their children grow, and they'll help his children grow. The way it should be."

"Pah! A dreamer you are. He'll be poor as a little mouse in this field, poorer! A hovel he'll live in, like you. And you and he will be plagued by pogroms. *Zolst nit visn fun keyn shiekhts*, may you not know of such troubles."

Eight

Montreal
1925

Asher and Label sat together on a Tuesday evening at the long table in the dining room on De Boullion Street.

"I asked you here . . ." Asher began in a formal, ponderous manner, as if he were at the *bima*, the pulpit, in *shul*, reading on *Shabbes*, "because I had an idea . . ."

Sarah had made pot roast with boiled potatoes. She and Gitel walked back and forth from the kitchen to the table, serving the three men. Gitel and her husband, Nathan, had come for dinner. When the men finished eating the pot roast, the two women sat with them and they all had tea and dessert. When the meal was over, Nathan went home to sleep; he had to get up early tomorrow morning for work. The two sisters went back to the kitchen and left the two Tannen men to talk.

"So, what's your idea, Pa?"

"Listen. This law is an opportunity."

89

"What law? You mean Prohibition? An opportunity?" Label let out a guffaw. "I know a few people would agree with that, people Benjie hangs out with!"

The eighteenth amendment to the Constitution, which prohibited the manufacture, sale, or transportation of alcoholic beverages in the U.S. and which cut off the import and export of beer, wine, and hard liquor, had gone into effect in 1920 when the Volstead Act was passed, just two years after Label had opened Tannen's, the little deli on the east side of Manhattan that he'd scraped and borrowed and done some not-so-kosher things to finally establish. A dozen years of criminal mayhem and barbarous slaughter followed. Illegal trafficking of intoxicating liquors became one of the country's most lucrative businesses, operated by outlaws who murdered anyone who threatened their profits.

Asher didn't smile. His eyes, bland tonight, didn't twinkle as they always did when he was cooking up a joke or a complex argument. He just nodded, and raised an eyebrow.

"Tell me what you have on your mind, Pa."

"Here," he began. "I want to make some money. There's so much ways to do it, especially where you are in New York. You know. You always been where the action was." His voice grew soft and ominous.

"Yeah? So?" Label didn't like to challenge his father, but he wasn't sure he liked the way this conversation was going.

Crime had always been a rampant New York industry. Now opportunities were everywhere. Labor rackets flourished as workers fought to establish their combined power; numbers and other gambling schemes proliferated; "protection," petty pilfering, loan-sharking, dock rackets, garment district extortion were serious enterprises. Label had not only been where the action was, he'd taken chances, cut corners.

"I thought of a way . . ."

Label kept quiet; he knew enough to nod and wait for the idea to unfold. His father, like Avi, liked to stretch a story out for dramatic effect.

"I was sitting and thinking the other day, and having a *bissel* schnapps, just a little, with your Uncle Nathan, and we talked about how we could be arrested if we was in New York making our schnapps . . . And I said we could be arrested, but first we could make a lot of money. We could fill some glasses behind the counter . . ."

"What counter?"

"At Tannen's."

Label had set himself a goal soon after landing in New York. He wanted to be the proprietor of a legitimate business so he could send his family money and feel proud to show them the fruits of his work. He would open a shop, he had dreamed, that would attract a devoted clientele. People had to eat, he'd figured, and so a food store—a deli, he learned to call it—would be the perfect business. By 1918, Label had realized the first part of his dream; he had run enough errands, done enough favors, and completed enough jobs for well-connected Brooklynites and cronies from the old days that he had earned their respect. When he had approached them for a loan, he got it with no questions asked and little interest charged. He had opened the small deli and called it Tannen's.

The deli was located on the street level of a small, five-story tenement building on the east side of upper Manhattan, a building that boasted five apartments upstairs, one on each floor. Housing and rapid transit were being built all over the city during this period; the area, just burgeoning, was still inexpensive but with plenty of room left for expansion and growth. Label moved into the apartment directly over the deli; he used the space to stock such imperishables as coffee, tea, sugar, salt. Tannen's did well right away. The appetizings—herring and various kinds of smoked fish, cheeses, olives, rolls, and breads—were so popular that after a few years he was able to buy the building and earn additional income by renting out the other apartments.

Prohibition was well into its fifth year by the time the Tannen family arrived in Montreal in 1925, and Asher was eager to profit from it. As he saw it, Label would still sell the same foods he had become known for downstairs. But upstairs—rather than use it as an apartment, rather than keep it as a storage area—a new Tannen's would be established: Tannen's, the speakeasy.

Asher had given a good deal of thought to how he would make use of the new opportunities around him. He could spend his time daydreaming, all day in *shul*, drinking his own popular schnapps while arguing the fine points of the Talmud. Or he could make money. The new laws in both the U.S. and parts of Canada provided him with an opportunity he couldn't ignore. He was too used to drumming up ways to feed a whole village; he was too young to stop his mind from such computing. Whiskey—Canadian rye, in particular—had increased in value since the law had been passed. He was a skilled distiller; he had practiced this profession in Roznov and later in Czernowitz and he had kept the village alive with his talents. Now his son operated an establishment in New York with a clientele that purchased food. Why shouldn't they also purchase drink? He had two other sons who could bridge the distance for them and bring his excellent alcoholic beverages to the New York establishment. Coming to the obvious conclusion, Asher had called Label and asked him to come up for a visit.

Label didn't realize right away that his father had just exploded the bombshell, the idea he wanted Label to hear. When he understood, Label burst out laughing.

"Behind the counter! That's good! We'd do it once and land right in Sing-Sing."

"That was just a joke, me and Nathan told. We didn't mean it literal. Not really behind the counter. Somewhere else."

"I know that, Pa. I already sell Benjie's schnapps. Upstairs in the apartment. And once in a while, I bring up a woman, too . . ."

"Benjie. Benjie is a *dummkopf.* He doesn't have an idea of his own. One day he'll get in trouble . . ."

The Tannens and Benjie Kalmowitz had sold schnapps and other whiskies in Europe. That wasn't what Label was worried about and Asher knew it. In eastern Europe, where anti-Semitism kept Jews in segregated *shtetls* and outside of respectable professions, Label and Benjie had seen their fathers make ends meet in occupations that were on the fringes of respectability: lending money, making and selling whiskey, operating taverns. So they, too, Benjie and Label, were prepared to do whatever it took to survive. They were used to violence, as well—though never yet as perpetrators. When the violence became more than a threat, acted out as retaliation, they had no trouble joining in or looking the other way. Label mainly looked the other way.

Benjie, on the other hand, had tasted a new experience when he ran his first errands: for once, he found, he could be the feared rather than the fearful. He could not help admiring the older boys who bullied their customers. Label sneered at these hooligans behind their backs, boys who held court on street corners, in the backs of candy stores, showing off rolls of bills— sometimes with a thousand dollar bill rolled around a pile of ones—and boasting of the exploits that had earned them this bounty. But Benjie wanted to be like them.

While Label moved back to Manhattan to open a deli, Benjie stayed in Brooklyn. His favorite hangout in those days was the corner of Saratoga and Livonia. There he became part of a gang known at first as the Amboy Dukes.

On Saratoga and Livonia, Benjie knew boys like Pretty Levine and Dukey Maffeatore, who consorted with others who were making names for themselves: Costello, Luciano, Anastasia, Gambino. Benjie ran errands, did small jobs all over Brooklyn, and drove for other members of the Amboy Street gang, guys with colorful nicknames like Waxey Gordon, Kid Twist Reles, Bugsy Siegel.

"It's those others who Benjie gets his ideas from who are doing things that in the old country were just ways to get by.

Some of them are going to get in big trouble—and he with them.
But some of them are making more money than we ever thought
existed in Czernowitz. You know who I mean. Rothstein is one.
Bronfman another. They're getting their own schnapps, their
own whiskey, and bringing it in and selling it. That's how they're
getting rich. Not by selling a drink or two bought from some
goniff, some crook. My idea is . . . you could sell my schnapps . . .
and we'd make a bundle. Don't you see it?"

"And how would we get your schnapps to New York, Pa?"

"Dovid would drive it."

"Oh, no. I won't let my little brother take such a chance.
The border is guarded. They stop cars all the time."

"There are places they don't look. And Benjie could come
up and go with him once or twice."

"There's another problem, too, Pa. Benjie's boys, they
don't like anyone muscling in on them. They get mean with
people who do that."

"We can get mean, too."

"Pa . . ."

"Label, I learned a few things in my time. I didn't grow
up in a monastery. We fought plenty shtarkers . . ."

"They didn't have guns."

"So we'll get guns."

Label folded his arms across his chest. When his father
spoke with so much conviction, he knew nothing would change

his mind. It was impossible to argue with the old man—and it was equally impossible not to do what he wanted. But Label wasn't exactly an innocent; he'd listen to his father's idea with an open mind. Maybe it would work. Guns weren't things to play with, as he had once explained to Avi when Avi had foolishly brought one to his house and playfully twirled it around in front of one of the children. Label knew very well how dangerous this idea was. But he would use guns if he had to.

"Look. I'll show you," Asher said.

He got up and went to the sideboard and pulled out paper and pencil. Then the two sat together figuring out how much whiskey Asher would have to produce in a week to make it worthwhile to set up a new business, how much they would have to charge per glass, how much another car would cost, how much gas it would take to go back and forth from Canada to New York. Could they do it? What other expenses would they have? They calculated the costs of so much whiskey per glass, of transporting the whiskey—by car, driven by Dovid, maybe Avi, and even, they determined, Benjie, who had experience in such things—of serving food in the rooms upstairs from the deli, figured out how much they could charge if they called themselves a restaurant instead of a deli. They added the costs, determined the profit they'd like, figured the prices of this and that, the money that could be made if they also hired a couple of women to come in to entertain on a regular basis.

Together Label and Asher now worked out the details. When they filled several pages, worked out their ideas, and looked at the results, the old man and his son looked at one another in astonishment.

"We could be rich!" Label sang. "The Tannens could be a wealthy family!"

Asher raised his glass: "*L'chaim!*" he said quietly. "To life!" Life was finally opening up a portal to what he always knew it could: a path to comfort and security. He found himself wishing now that his brother Sender and his family, and the other Roznovites, were here to benefit from this new venture, as well.

They sipped their schnapps, father and son, set the glasses on the table, and called in Sarah and Gitel.

"We're going into business," Asher announced. "And we're including Dovid and Avi."

Sarah felt a familiar chill. She remembered this feeling.

Nine

Avi
1925

They were in the bleachers of the newly opened Yankee Stadium up in the rural area known as The Bronx, Avi and Label. Label couldn't understand how his little brother could become so engrossed in a game; grown men tossing around a ball, hitting it with a stick, running around in a circle. What was the point? But he sat and patiently explained again what he and Asher had in mind, and what they would like Avi to do.

"We'll be rich, Avi! All you'll have to do is drive the car once in a while with Dovid. We'll get Benjie to take over once in a while; you know Benjie; he'll do anything for the smell of *gelt*, money. What's wrong with you? Why won't you do it?"

"I have enough money," Avi said, not taking his eyes off the field. "Look, look!" He jumped up, pointing toward the field just as the ball flew up and nearly hit him in the eye. He jumped and tried to catch it, but it brushed his fingers and some kids a few rows behind them got it. It was becoming common practice for anyone who caught what they called a "fly ball" to keep it. Avi was excited. "They got it, those kids! Good for them!"

Label had turned around and watched as the boys danced around raising the ball in the air. Now he pulled on Avi's shirt. "Avi, we're talking about serious matters. How can you get so excited about such an unimportant thing?"

"This is fun, Label. I like having fun."

Label shook his head. "Fun. We can make so much money you'll never have to sell another girdle. Then you can have fun!"

"I like my life, Label. I even like selling girdles."

"Ach! How can you say that? You do it to get by. I know you'd like to be someone important, a lawyer maybe, a writer of stories, a teacher. I know how you like to read all those books you take from the library all the time. So you're a salesman. How can you tell me you like it?"

"What I like, Label, is that I take care of myself, no one bothers me, I go out with all the young ladies I want and I can take them to nice places. I put aside a few dollars, buy myself nice clothes. I'm happy this way. If I start running up to Canada all the time to drive a car filled with bootlegged whiskey, who knows, I'll worry about getting stopped, I won't be able to sleep so well. I'll have to quit my nice job where I get to talk to people, tell funny stories, shmooze, go out to lunch, meet buyers from all the big shops. What do I want that for? Leave me alone. Go do what you want and don't bother me no more."

Avi would have nothing to do with the old man's idea. He was living a life that pleased him, earning a living on his own, paying rent for a small apartment he had just rented in Brooklyn, taking women there, going to silent films and Yiddish theater and ball games, mostly in Brooklyn at Ebbets Field, but sometimes, like today, venturing out of the city and enjoying a game in the country, even putting a few dollars aside to buy a nice gift once in a while for that woman he especially liked, that American girl, Stella, who he hoped would one day agree to marry him. He didn't have the burning desire Label and his father did for wealth. He was happy; why should he mess around?

The Amboy Duchess

Ten

Avi
1931

When Avi and Stella were married, Avi was working for a small house in the garment district, a company that produced ladies "foundation" garments. But the Depression hit hard that year, and not long after the wedding the firm let him go.

Avi was furious. He might have understood if his former employers had been regretful, concerned, if they had promised to take him back when things got better. But the two partners, Mishkoff and Liebowitz, were unfeeling. They let him go without any severance pay in his envelope, and without a wedding gift.

He never told Stella he was jobless. He didn't tell his father or his brothers, either. The first few months of their married life, he got up early every morning and went out as usual, just as if he were going to work. But, in fact, he spent his days looking for work, trudging from corset house to corset house, up and down the stairs of the buildings that housed the wholesalers all along Seventh Avenue, in and out of all the retail establishments that carried ladies undergarments, without success. When he could no longer pay his bills, he still didn't tell

103

Stella or the Tannens, but rather he told Stella's father. Avi's father-in-law was the one who secretly supported the newlyweds for the next few months, until Avi found work with another house.

A few years later, Mishkoff and Liebowitz, grown large with twenty employees, looked Avi up and asked him to come back. He thanked them, and took up where he had left off. Or so it seemed.

But Avi had a plan.

Not long before, he had been to a meeting of the newly formed Ladies Under-Garment Workers, the LUGW. The men and women he met there intrigued him. He was attracted by their fierceness and their determination, and he decided to join the union and attend weekly leadership and organizing sessions.

His plan was simple: he would take the job and work hard for Mishkoff and Liebowitz. But evenings and weekends he would hold secret meetings, inviting groups of colleagues to his home to hear visiting LUGW speakers on the benefits of unity.

It took a year, but when the next Mishkoff and Liebowitz expansion took place and the staff of the manufacturing house more than doubled, Avi and his cohorts were ready. They quickly recruited the new workers, and within months the band of fifty, having had their demands for higher wages and shorter work hours turned down, called a strike. The organization they were now part of, the LUGW, backed them, and no worker in the industry would agree to scab. The picket line of hundreds paraded back and forth in front of the building, placards held high. Among them, the Mishkoff and Liebowitz workers, old men, young girls, pregnant women, felt protected.

Then things got nasty.

Mishkoff and Liebowitz threatened to bring in union busters. The threat was clear; things would become violent if the workers did not back down and return to their sewing machines.

Benjie Kalmowitz approached Avi on the sly. He offered to speak to the two cigar-chomping bosses and make a deal.

"What kind of deal?" Avi demanded.

"You know, Avi. I know people."

"What's that supposed to mean?"

"I can set it up for you. We'll let them know it's in their interest to negotiate."

Avi didn't like Benjie's deals, but he knew that what Benjie was telling him was he'd better be ready to settle—or else. Lepke and Gurrah, the Gold Dust Twins, were behind Benjie— the five-foot-seven Lepke Buchalter, with his cow-brown eyes, and his loud, burly, strong-arm Russian sidekick, Gurrah Shapiro. The labor wars had stirred up mob ambition, and these two were cashing in on the most lucrative of all the rackets besides Prohibition—labor and management disputes. Benjie Kalmowitz was their messenger.

Even though Avi's impulse was to fight it out, he knew he'd better do something to keep the violence to a minimum. But when he went to the union to propose a settlement, he was sickened to learn they had already hired a crew to fight off the strikers, and one that wasn't afraid of violence. What he didn't know was that it was the same crew. Benjie had been to both the bosses and the union and had talked "sense" into both—collecting hefty fees from each, both for the Gold Dust Twins and for himself.

Still, the upshot was that the firm of Mishkoff and Liebowitz became a union shop, paying for protection, but also paying its employees slightly higher wages for a slightly shorter work week.

Avi had had his revenge and now he took home more money each week. But now he was indebted to Benjie.

Eleven

Label
1932

Label stood on the front lawn of his new home in Scarsdale, his hands in the pockets of his white slacks. His great dream had been realized. His family was in America, even if some were in Canada. He had also succeeded in transporting much of Roznov here, though many still remained in the Bucovina.

He kicked a weed, trying to dislodge it with his toe, failed and strolled away; the gardener will get it tomorrow, he thought. He took great pleasure in walking around the property, "embracing it with his eyes," a new expression he had picked up from the movies. Inside, his wife, Donya, Benjie's sister, and their two small daughters played in the room Donya called the library. He breathed deeply; he loved the spring here in Westchester County, not like the old country, but beautiful, and he was wealthy beyond his most ambitious dreams.

The Amboy Duchess

He wasn't a man to look back, but now and then he reminded himself of what he'd accomplished, of what it had taken: he was the first of the Tannen family to come to New York, and he and his friends the first ones from Roznov. That meant that no one but his comrades and his brother had seen him scared, running through the chaotic streets to find work, picking up an errand here, a favor there, wrapping fruit for pushcart vendors, finding women for some of the hotshot shtarkers, the street hoods he couldn't help running into all the time, *tuchas-leching*, ass-licking, the ones who had the biggest rolls of dollar bills, even though that's all they were most of the time, just dollar-bills, not tens, or fives, or twenties.

The family back home and all his *lantzmen* didn't see, either, how he slept in cellars at first, on steps of dirty tenements, in a crowded room he rented with his friends, then in the beds of whores, before he got the few extra dollars he needed to stay in a room where he could be by himself and count what he was saving, both the money and the favors that he figured out were owed him.

They didn't see. And he didn't tell.

He wrote to them before they came to America. But he didn't tell them about the bread he stole or the favors he did the *shtarkers* or the threats they sometimes carried out against the factory foremen. He didn't tell because who knew what they might think, what they might say, his father and the *rebbe* and his uncle, Sender, the pious candle maker. They might have thought that he, too, was a hood, a *shtarker*, he got so good at talking his way into and out of all kinds of trouble with those free-wheeling no-goodniks who held money out to greenhorns in hands that only asked favors in return.

And, in a way, he *was* like them. In a way, he *was* one of them. Like the others in his gang, he started dressing in white trousers and in shoes with fancy white leather on the sides, and combing his hair slicked back with Vaseline. Like them, he got good at taking his cut when they ran a delivery from the docks, and he got especially good at never asking where, or who, it came from.

Maybe he never hit anyone in the knees with an iron pipe like Benjie learned to do. And maybe he wasn't one of the ones who broke the store windows when a shopkeeper couldn't pay them for an order. But he was there when Solly the butcher got his nuts cut off for bragging about how he gave it to Meyer's woman on the roof. Maybe he didn't hold the knife, and maybe Solly deserved it. But such distinctions, he knew, would be ignored if the *rebbe* could see how his favorite yeshiva *buche*, his favorite schoolboy, was making it good in the new country called America.

He'd kept quiet, too, about what he'd done to buy the deli he finally got the chance to open—not with the money he'd saved, because that was to bring the family here. The deli he bought with the loan from the *shtarkers*, a loan he got for favors they still owed him, and he used the money to buy counters and a cash register and even an ice-box in the back. The rest, the inventory, he bought with money from the Hester Street loan boss, paid back in increments plus interest as his profits multiplied. Meanwhile, he outfitted the upstairs apartment with furniture supplied by one of the downtown foremen he still serviced for the same Hester Street boss and, at first, he lived there alone, and then with Donya and their children.

The small deli was uptown in a neighborhood as different from the downtown community as it was from Roznov. This area was filled with new five-story tenements equipped with large air shafts overlooking alleyways, wrought iron fire escapes and rope-pulleyed dumb-waiters that would take your garbage to the cellar or carry up your groceries. The elevated train, just a few blocks away on Third Avenue, took some of the wealthier Jews who had moved to The Bronx back and forth from their jobs or their businesses downtown, and made it possible for them to also stop off at Label Tannen's for a fancy tray of cold cuts or hors d'oeuvres for company, or with a holiday order. Or they would come downtown with their wives on a Sunday to buy their weekly bialys and appetizings.

He kept quiet about what he'd done to get the deli, but when he opened it, he told them what a success he was. He wasn't afraid of working like some of the *shtarkers* who did what they did from laziness. He enjoyed the labor of getting up at four in the morning and going to the markets near the docks and haggling for the schmaltz herring the ladies would examine with critical eyes, and noses. He liked the ladies, and he enjoyed carrying the heavy boxes for them filled with their weekly supplies of salt and bread and pot cheese; liked feeling his back muscles pull and grow, feeling himself turning into someone even he didn't recognize anymore as the *boychik* from Roznov.

He worked and grew to a man, and eventually married, and all the time he and his *shtarker* pals kept in touch, he and Benjie still did business here and there. Lately, Benjie wasn't too happy with him, he knew, because he'd seen him downtown with that Helen, dressed to the nines, her thick hair brushed clean off her beautiful face and knotted in back like he liked it. Benjie knew that Label was carrying on a little behind Donya's back. But so what? Benjie never had a woman aside from his wife Ruthie? Who didn't fool around a little? What did it mean? He still honored his family. Only when it's your sister, maybe you saw it different. He also knew that Benjie had carried

111

around a grudge against him for years, since before they had even gotten to New York. But he wasn't worried about Benjie; Benjie owed him big for what he had done introducing him to Abe Reles. Benjie was the Kid's favorite driver now, and Reles was grooming Benjie for other things, too, bigger things, though Benjie never said what they were. That Reles was into stuff Label didn't want to know too much about, not just running numbers, not just getting booze into all the speakeasies. He had connections, Reles, out of Brooklyn with the Broadway boys, and not just with Luciano and Costello, but all the way up, were the rumors, with that mysterious Rothstein, Mr. Moneybags, was how Label thought of Arnold Rothstein. Reles and his crew of killers did jobs for those boys, and Benjie, who was in with all of them, owed his place there to Label. And Label knew some things about Benjie, no one else knew, things Benjie wouldn't want him telling, about how he played one against another. Loyalty wasn't Benjie's strong suit, and he, Label, knew all about his *lantzman's* dealings. No, Label didn't worry about Benjie.

His family didn't know that either, about Label's women, except for Avi who would probably do the same if he could, if he weren't so madly in love with that new wife of his, Stella, the American girl.

Label liked his life. He liked being the one who drove in his new Ford to the Canadian border to help his father and mother and his Auntie Gitel and her husband, none of whom could speak a word of English, or French, neither, liked helping them find places they could live in, paid for by him.

And now, now when it was Prohibition, he could hardly believe it was his pa who did this, gave them the push that really helped the Tannens make it big. The deli stayed the same downstairs, but upstairs it became a different kind of establishment, with dark shades that pulled down in the daytime and stayed down until it was time to signal the boys who delivered their supplies. He stopped buying from Benjie, and the "supplies" he got came from Canada, in fact from his own father's cellar. He bought whiskey and wine for Tannen's, the deli turned speakeasy, from Asher at cut-rate prices, and sold it for even more than ten times the price of wholesale, the amount they made from other speakeasies that they also sold to. For in addition to the wine Asher made for *Shabbes*, like he used to do in Czernowitz, now the old man made also a kind of slivovitz that burned all the way down, so you knew you weren't being cheated, it was the real stuff. And instead of selling it watered down before *Shabbes* only to the greenhorns and the goyim on De Bouillon Street, the old man got Dovid, and Benjie with him sometimes for the little extra money he wanted, to drive the illegal schnapps and other whiskies across the border to where the family could make that ten-times amount, selling to suppliers of other establishments, even horning in on some of Benjie's other business once in a while.

Only Avi refused to come in on the arrangement, preferring instead to sell girdles and do a small job or two for Benjie when it didn't involve anything too low or too dangerous.

Now Label strolled around to the backyard, where he recently had a crew of workers build a gazebo that he furnished with a small round table and some ice cream chairs. He climbed the two steps and straightened the chairs.

In a few days, he and Donya and their children would drive to Montreal, Avi and his Stella would take the train, and they would all celebrate Pesach in their mother's house.

Satisfied, he came down the two steps of the gazebo, brushed off his hands, and strolled around again to the front of the house.

Twelve

Winnie
1974

"Are you sorry you joined us for the volleyball game?" Stu asked later that afternoon as we strolled toward my lawn. He insisted on walking me home, though I lived right across the street.

"No. It was fun."

"Maybe you'll join Marilyn's book discussion group tomorrow night, too."

"Don't push your luck."

He laughed. "Listen, I really do want to ask you to join something I think you might enjoy—and even profit from."

I had to make a half turn to look at him, because he was walking a few inches behind me to the left. "What's that?"

He was silent a few moments. Then he said, "I don't know how to describe it. What I'm looking for is . . . sort of like a . . . let's see, now, how can I say it? I need . . . someone to talk to.

115

The Amboy Duchess

And I thought . . . I don't want to see a therapist, so I thought . . . I might be able to get someone else who could use an ear . . . to form a kind of . . . encounter group . . . with me. A two-person encounter group."

I stopped dead and stared at him. Was he serious? Was this a pass? It was certainly original, but did he really think such a disingenuous move would work? His eyes grabbed onto mine and he waited for my answer without a glimmer of a smile. He was serious.

I couldn't decide what to make of this idea. Certainly it was exceptional. How many men would have thought of it? Could he be so simple-minded that he would think I would buy such an obvious come-on? Was the man such a sleaze? Like father, like son, I was thinking.

Or was he even more hypocritical, not even realizing himself how it must look? Did he plan to tell Marilyn about this? Or about the things he imagined we would discuss? Could he seriously be considering carrying on such an intimate activity with a total stranger? Or, maybe weirder yet, with a neighbor who was probably destined to become a friend? Would he really confide—things—to me, things about Marilyn, maybe? About their marriage and their divorce? And did he expect me to confide in him?

The idea was strangely tantalizing.

But I couldn't figure out how to respond. "What do you mean?" was the best I could do.

"Nothing bad. I'm not . . . that is, I don't mean to scare you. I mean it exactly as I said it. I need to talk to someone. I think you do, too. I thought we might be able to help each other."

"What have you got against therapists?"

"Nothing. I just don't think they can help me."

"But you think I *can*?"

He nodded.

I laughed, shaking my head in disbelief. "You're an original," I said. "I don't know. I don't know what to say. I'll think about it." It came out sounding like a promise; I could tell by the way his face brightened. Damn, I didn't want to encourage him. "It's probably too crazy an idea for me, though," I added, lamely. "Anyway, so long! I had a good time."

I turned and ran up the walk to the front door. I wanted to get into the house to feed Annie—that's what I'd named the kitten. The children had left without giving her a name. Now she and I, two orphans, would keep each other company. She'd been alone all afternoon and I wanted to hold her.

But there he stood in the middle of the lawn, watching me, knowing just what to say to mesmerize me. "Good," he said, nodding. He started to turn away when I turned the knob and pushed the door open, but then he stopped and turned back.

"Also," he said, waiting for me to stop on my way in. Then he continued quickly, "I think I may have an opening for you at the bank."

I whirled around. "What?!"

"Don't get excited. I wasn't sure I should say anything yet because I'm not sure. But you seemed so dejected today, I thought it might cheer you up a little to know there's at least the possibility of a job. We may have an opening, but don't count on it yet. I'll have to let you know. I have an idea I want to explore with our board of directors. Depending on what they say, I may be able to hire someone; I'll let you know as soon as I know. So long."

He turned suddenly, and he was gone, across the lawn and into his house, Marilyn's house, before I could speak.

* * * * *

Two weeks later, after the July 4th weekend, I trudged up the stairs of the Sixth Avenue subway, emerged on 48th Street and walked up the block to the Allerton Bank. From Blue Wood, by bus and two trains, the trip took an hour and a half. It was my first day as what Stu called a New Business Developer. A fancy name for "saleswoman," I sneered when he first told me the title. But he'd assured me it would be more interesting than that.

The Amboy Duchess

I needed the job; nothing else I'd interviewed for was even a remote possibility. Yet I'd resisted his offer. Did I want *this* job? Did I want to work for *Stu*? Should I work for Allerton Bank? I remembered that I'd read some articles about the bank in the *Village Voice*. Jack Newfield implied, though he couldn't prove, that members of the board of directors were mixed up in some kind of racketeering. What was I getting myself into?

I had a trip planned for the fall, I told Stu, to visit my aunt and uncle in Montreal. That's fine, he said. We'll arrange it. I didn't know anything about selling, I told him, and I knew even less about banking. I'll teach you, he replied. And I bet you'll like it, he insisted.

Yeah, I bet. The thought depressed me when he told me about it, and it continued to depress me when I finally took the job. But I had no other offers. My August mortgage payment would be due soon, not to mention all the other bills that were sitting, unpaid, on my desk upstairs. What else could I do? I needed a job. I supposed I should be grateful to Stu Lewen. I wasn't, though.

Not just because it was hard to feel grateful to Moe Lewenthal's son. It was more because Stu seemed to *expect* me to feel grateful. He was so smug about what he seemed to take for granted was his own altruism. It was his wanting so much to be seen as a good guy that kept me from feeling a "proper" amount of gratitude. Why did he need to be thought of as good? Why did he have to go out of his way to prove what a good soul he was? And why did he want *my* gratitude? Did doing me a favor give him some kind of power over me? I wouldn't go out with my boss, never mind my neighbor's former husband. I don't care if he won the Nobel Peace Prize.

Ah! I couldn't afford to be so analytic.

He *was* doing me a favor. And I would thank him by doing the best job I could. Still, I was nervous about taking on work that I had no aptitude for. I knew almost as little about selling as I did about balancing my checking account. What kind of banker could I be? I didn't tell Stu, of course, but I still planned to look for another job, something more suitable. Gratitude notwithstanding!

I got to the bank early. An elderly man in his late sixties was just opening the doors. "Good morning! I'm Winnie Charles. I'm starting a new job here today . . ."

"Oh, yeah!" The man's voice was soft and gravely, like the voice of a thug in the movies. But he shoved out his right hand and grabbed mine, shaking it vigorously, his oversized arm muscles rippling with each shake. "I know all about you! You're the girl he hired to bring in new accounts. I'm Gus. I'm the security guard. Glad to meetcha! C'mon in!"

"What time does everyone get here?" The clock on the far wall said eight fifteen. Stu had told me to be here at eight thirty.

The Amboy Duchess

"Soon, soon. Mostly around eight-thirty or so. But that's all right. That's all right. Come on in. Come on in. I open up every day. But they all have to be in early to get their cash drawers set up. They'll be here soon. At least all the tellers will. And the auditors come in early, too. Mr. Lewen usually does, also. So, just go down and help yourself . . . what am I saying? There's no coffee, yet. Sit down. Sit down. Take a chair, any chair. They'll be here soon. Someone will make coffee and show you where to sit."

He shuffled off and disappeared, leaving me in the middle of a great amphitheater. I wandered around the circumference of the open expanse, my footsteps echoing on the marble floor; a new experience, being in an empty bank. To my right was the vault, safe deposit boxes stacked up on either side of it, guarded by a steel and brass gate, so shiny it looked like the prop for a movie about an old Roman bathhouse. Ahead to my left were the tellers' cages and behind me, near the front door, near where I had come in, were the desks where the officers sat.

I wandered to the rear, past the tellers' cages. There to my left was another desk and behind it an office, which I figured must be Stu's. Behind the rear wall to the right, a staircase rose to the second floor, and a few paces beyond was another staircase going down.

Just as I was trying to decide whether to investigate further or go out to try and find a cup of coffee, two women strolled in, laughing together.

". . . and so he says to me, he says, honey, your hips look good enough to my tired eyes . . ."

"That ol' lech!"

I stopped wandering and waited for them to see me.

"Oh! You must be the new woman Mr. Lewen hired!" said the tall black woman with the round hips who had been telling the story. "I'm Melba Jefferson and this here is Roberta Brooks, otherwise known as Bobbie."

"Hi! I'm Winnie Charles."

"Winnie," the shorter woman said, nodding and putting out her hand for me to shake. "Welcome to Allerton." With her severe haircut, her dark, tailored suit, and her unsmiling manner, the woman was a little intimidating.

The taller one, Melba, seemed friendlier. When she started walking toward the staircases, she called me.

"Come on downstairs," she said. "That's where I'm stationed. I'm one of the auditors and we got banished to the cellar when we arrived. Bobbie can be more uppity. Mr. Lewen just promoted her to vice president. The only woman VP in the bank. She stays upstairs in the tower with the bank's comptroller and the switchboard operator. We can't tell you where you'll be sitting. You'll have to wait until Mr. Lewen comes in later or 'til Margaret, his secretary, gets here. But you can have some coffee with us. Before we start our day, we get together for some breakfast. So c'mon down and we'll get the coffee going."

Downstairs one of the two offices on the left was Melba's. We entered the small kitchen to the right, complete with refrigerator, sink and three tables. Straight ahead, at the end of the long corridor, a store room was lit by a bare bulb hanging from the ceiling. Gus, the security guard, was just coming out of there, dressed in his uniform: dark blue slacks, light blue shirt, and gun, holstered at his hip.

"Melba, Bobbie," he nodded as he passed. "I see you've met our new young lady. Take good care of her, now, you hear?"

He clumped upstairs as Bobbie made the coffee. Melba went into her office and slung her briefcase onto the desk. I wandered in behind her; both of the old wooden desks were starkly empty, except for a few file folders stuffed with ledger sheets.

"Does every bank have its own auditors?"

Melba, engrossed in a pink phone slip she'd picked up from her desk, looked up, surprised. "No, of course not. Auditors check on the books from outside. We were appointed."

I wondered if I was overstepping my bounds by asking, but I figured I might as well start my banking education. "By an accounting firm?"

"Sometimes auditors are from accounting firms. They come in to give an organization's records their seal of approval. If they warrant it. But not us. We were hired by the State Banking Commission. And Allerton's records don't warrant anyone's seal of approval."

Suddenly I realized what she was talking about.

"Oh! Of course. Those *Voice* articles. There's some kind of investigation going on. The commission suspects that Allerton is involved in . . . in what? Something . . . to do with . . . rackets? Are you involved with that?"

Melba smiled. "That's my job. To investigate." She seemed to be testing the phrase. She picked up a pencil, scribbled on a piece of paper, then came out from behind her desk. "But it's only a suspicion," she warned. "Okay," she said, steering me back into the corridor. "That's enough work for the moment. Let's have our coffee."

A tight knot of anxiety established itself in my stomach, but I decided to ignore it. I couldn't afford to start having any more doubts than I already had about this job. I followed Melba to the kitchen, but then lingered outside wondering if it was appropriate to be having coffee down here on my first day when I

124

probably ought to be upstairs waiting for Stu to arrive. I didn't want to be rude, though, so I followed Melba to the kitchen and stood near the doorway, ready to make my getaway.

"So, I hear you're going to sell for us," Bobbie said, her eyes on the coffeemaker as she measured the coffee.

A little embarrassed, I wasn't sure how to reply. Probably the right response would have been something like: oh, yes, I've had such-and-such experience and I expect to do so-and-so and so-and-so here. But in light of my total lack of either banking or sales experience, I could think of nothing that would satisfy anyone's curiosity about why I, of all people, had been hired for this job. I couldn't even tell them how I had turned down Stu's offer at first and had only agreed to take the job when Stu had promised—taken an oath!—to train me and had patiently explained that he would have had to train anyone, not just me, because "every operation is different." Somehow, Melba's being with the banking commission and in the midst of conducting an investigation also intimidated me.

I just nodded, dumbly, and said, "Right."

"Mmm-Hmmm." Bobbie filled the pot with water, watching the lines to be sure she had exactly the right number of cups for the right amount of coffee—still not looking up. "Well, we sure can use a good sales person around here."

"Yes. I've heard."

125

Bobbie exchanged a quick glance with Melba, who was standing behind me. I realized my remark might have sounded rude, even inappropriately critical, if not ominous, in light of the recent bad publicity in the *Voice* and the current investigation.

"I mean, that is, I know *any* bank these days can use some aggressive marketing." I hoped that sounded more professional than I felt, but maybe it would satisfy them. How did *I* know what banks these days needed? What did *I* know of marketing? Not a thing. I wasn't even sure if marketing and selling were the same thing. Or, for that matter, if "New Business Development" referred, strictly speaking, to either.

I hadn't even been shown to a desk yet, and already I felt like a fraud.

When Bobbie got the coffee going, she set the table. "Let's see," she said. "You'll need a cup; you'll probably want to bring in one of your own tomorrow. But for now you can use Harry's." She reached into the cabinet, pulled out a mug with the word "Kingfisher" printed across its side, and handed it to me. "He won't need it until lunchtime."

"Oh, I don't know if I should take the time to have coffee with you right now," I said, not taking the cup. "I mean, it's very nice of you to offer, but I think I'd better go upstairs and see if Stu, I mean Mr. Lewen, is in yet."

More glances back and forth between the two women. God! Now what were they thinking? Was calling him "Stu" too familiar?

"You'll have to fill out some forms before you do anything else, and I'm the one who has to give them to you," Bobbie said. "So just sit tight and relax for now. And don't expect to see Stu this morning. He may not be in 'til eleven or so. He's gone to Brooklyn."

Over coffee, Melba and Bobbie asked about my background.

"To tell the truth," I finally said, "I've been teaching until now. I teach French at Hunter College. I've never worked in a bank before."

"Is that right?" Bobbie said. "How did Stu happen to hire you, then?"

"Well, his ex-wife and I are neighbors." I stopped. I knew it wasn't smart to be too candid with these women. But I didn't know what else to say. The truth was I had no banking experience and no sales experience. But why should I feel guilty? The president of the bank had seen fit to hire me. If anyone should feel guilty, he should, not me. I hadn't misrepresented myself to him and I didn't mean to do so to anyone else, either. I would do my best to learn the job and do it well. That was all I could manage. I couldn't also lie.

The Amboy Duchess

After coffee, Bobbie and I went upstairs to "the tower," our heels clacking on the staircase, leaving Melba to her auditing. Bobbie gave me the forms and I spent the next half hour filling them out.

When I was done, Bobbie accompanied me back to the main floor and settled me at an empty desk that stood facing the vault. "I don't really know where Stu had in mind to put you," she told me, "but for now this will do." She handed me a pile of papers. "You can read all about Allerton in these old employee newsletters, so you can become more familiar with us."

I wondered if these publications would offer any clues to whatever it was that Melba and her assistant were investigating for the State Banking Commission. I arranged the newsletters in a pile by date and began reading. I was disappointed. The newsletters were nothing more than hype, filled with short articles about the accomplishments of employees. "John O'Connor brought in a new retail account this week . . ." "Peter Hanlon was promoted to executive vice president . . ." I learned nothing about Allerton and I realized how naïve it was to think the bank would advertise its own offences. Suspected offences, I reminded myself.

At lunchtime, Bobbie and Melba invited me to join them. "We play bridge every day," Melba said.

I begged off. "No, thanks, I'm not a bridge player. And, anyway, I have some errands to run."

I explored the neighborhood for restaurants, women's clothing shops, window-shopped, grabbed a frank and a soda on a street corner, and bought myself a coffee mug in a shop that sold cigarettes, newspapers and candy bars. When I got back to the bank, at one on the dot, a young woman who sat near the front desks—the platform—stood when I walked by.

"You're Winnie Charles, right?" the woman asked.

"Yes, that's right."

"I'm Alison Goodman, Pete Hanlon's secretary. And yours, too. That is, I really work for everyone on the platform. I'm the one who wrote those newsletters you've been reading."

"Ah! I'm glad to meet you!"

"I'm supposed to tell you that Margaret, Mr. Lewen's secretary, would like to see you. She can't leave her desk right now because there's no one else to answer Stu's . . . that is, Mr. Lewen's phone, so she'd like you to go there, if you wouldn't mind."

I introduced myself to Margaret.

The woman stood and put out her hand. "Margaret Billings. Stu called and asked me to let you know he won't be in until later. Meanwhile, he wants me to have your phone hooked up. He said the desk where Bobbie put you is fine, so I've got someone coming to get you set up there. Is there anything else you'll need for now?"

"Um, some paper and pens, I guess. And I guess I'll need a calendar, paper clips, a Rolodex . . ."

When I got back to my desk, a wiry, high-energy man with molasses-colored skin and gleaming black eyes bustled over carrying a cardboard box filled with supplies.

"Harry Prince," he announced, his face lit by a grin as he took my hand in his and patted it with his other hand. "I'm in charge of the supply room. Anything you need, you just give me a holler."

"Well, that was fast!"

"We aim to please!" he said, sauntering away with a wave. Then, before trotting back down the stairs, he turned back to me. "Tomorrow you have to have lunch with us. We need a fourth for bridge."

I laughed. "I haven't played bridge in years!"

"We'll bring you up to speed!"

Forty-five minutes later Stu strode across the floor, waving at me as he passed. Half an hour later, my phone rang. My first call.

"Allerton Bank. This is Winnie Charles," I said, trying to sound official.

The Amboy Duchess

"Winnie, this is Margaret. I'm calling for two reasons. First, I wanted to test your phone. And second, Mr. Lewen wants you to be ready to go out in the field in ten minutes."

"This guy's an old client," Stu told me in the car. "Someone I've been doing business with for years. And I've gotten lots of referrals from him. That's how you do this. Pick a group, a certain kind of business, and offer them service. Show them you're interested, really get to know their business, drop by every once in a while. Then things will happen. The first one will recommend someone to you, then that one will send you someone else. And so on. After a while, you'll have the whole industry all sewn up."

We entered a vestibule where a glass-encased receptionist gave Stu a big smile, then pressed a button opening a door with the name "Jerry Buchalter, President" printed in gold letters.

"Stu!" Jerry stood up and came out from behind his desk when we entered his office.

"Jerry." Stu and Jerry shook hands and Jerry clapped Stu on the shoulder. "This is my new assistant, Winnie Charles. She may service some of your accounts or handle loan applications from time to time. I'm not going anywhere. Your accounts are still mine. But I'm breaking her in, teaching her the business. You won't mind helping her out once in a while with something or other, will you?"

Jerry leaned back as if to scrutinize me, but his smile told me that he was ready to accommodate Stu in any request he might have. He put his hand on my shoulder, then stood there for a few moments with a hand on each of our shoulders, mine and Stu's. "Welcome to the world of the jukebox, Miss Charles. Would you like to see our operation?"

"Sure."

In the vast, cement-floored storage area, lined up along the walls and on either side of several aisles, were rows and rows of gleaming jukeboxes. We strolled along one of the aisles.

"Four companies manufacture these babies," Jerry explained. "We're faithful to the biggest one. Each of our operators buys a couple, maybe three, hundred from us for his area, maybe the Bronx, maybe some part of Brooklyn or New Jersey. It works like an auto dealership. We supply records and repairs for a cut of the take. Our operators are the best, the ones who know how to wrap up an area, make it their own. They go in and convince the owner of a bar, say, that we're the best in the business, we're the ones they should deal with. We got a very good rep.

"Lotta guys'll get a rundown route and beef it up for us with fresh outlets. We help 'em out sometimes, help finance 'em when they're in trouble." He grinned, again patting Stu on the shoulder as they strolled along. "Or else we'll send 'em to Mr. L. here."

At the end of the aisle, we made a right turn, rounded the corner and came back along another, identical aisle. Back in the office, Jerry again agreed to help me out any way he could, again clapping Stu on the back as he saw us out the door.

In the car, Stu answered my unasked questions.

"I know what you're thinking. Aren't they all crooks or associated in some way with the so-called mob?" He shook his head, watching the road on our way back to New Jersey. "That's what people think. But it's not like that anymore. Used to be they were known for, let's say, some questionable ways of getting customers—intimidation, threats, sometimes worse. There were stories of people ending up dead in some alley when they refused to take in a machine. Who knows if they were true? Just the story could be enough to convince some people, I guess. Sometimes, I've heard, the operators used to band together and pretend they were a bona fide union and they'd picket any holdouts. But no one does anything like that anymore. Some pretty flamboyant types used to run the distributorships, Lucky Luciano's pals, Meyer Lansky. But no more. They're all gone. Now they all regard themselves as legitimate."

He maneuvered the car through the Lincoln Tunnel and up the Turnpike, keeping quiet while he drove, letting me digest everything I'd learned today. He certainly wasn't aware that I'd started out with more information from the *Voice* articles than I was letting on. And, he didn't know what I'd learned from Melba about Allerton being under investigation by the State Banking Commission. I would have loved to know what Allerton was being investigated for, and what part Stu played—was he, too, being investigated? Or was he working with Melba? My curiosity by now overrode any reservations I had about working for the bank.

I was also aware that the questionable tactics of the vending machine business were by no means as out of style as he claimed. My cousin Josh, who took over Tannen's Restaurant when Uncle Label died, had just recently had a run-in with the jukebox industry. When he decided to redecorate, to turn it into a more upscale place, a restaurant or a pub, instead of a neighborhood hangout joint, he'd had a lot of trouble getting rid of both the jukebox and the two pinball machines. I wasn't sure how he had finally managed to get what he wanted. But he'd complained about those *goniffs*, those crooks, and how they controlled everything.

I listened to Stu's explanation, though, and made no comment.

"So, what do you think?" he asked, finally, as we drove through the streets of Blue Wood. "Think you'll be able to handle it?"

"Handle it?"

"Find some group other banks are not nice to and go after them. Beef up our business, Allerton Bank's clientele."

The words "some group other banks are not nice to" suddenly resonated. But what I thought of was not vending machines or juke boxes. I thought of a minority of some kind, people who had trouble getting loans for their businesses because of discrimination, Blacks, Dominicans, Puerto Ricans. Or . . . suddenly I realized who my group was. But I decided not to say anything to Stu until I could do some research.

Suddenly I felt excited. I was still planning to job-hunt on the side. But going out to sell could be a challenge.

And, I realized, I had enjoyed the day, my first day at Allerton.

I shrugged. "Sure," I said. "I can handle it."

I figured I could handle anything, if I had to. Learn how to read profit and loss statements, learn to go after new business for the bank. Sell up a storm. Even prove other people's checking account statements. That didn't mean I'd *like* any of it. But I supposed I could *do* it. After all, I was Avi Tannen's daughter.

When we got to my house, Stu leaned across to open the door on the passenger side, keeping his hand on the handle and looking into my face a little disconcertingly. I felt he'd deliberately trapped me. I wanted to shove his arm away, but he was my employer now; that seemed like a wrong move.

"Ye-es?" I said, playfully, getting a knot of anxiety or guilt in my chest. Why was I humoring him? Why didn't I just knock his hand out of the way and get out of the damn car?

"Pick you up in the morning?" he asked.

"What?"

"That's a big trip you've got by public transportation. And I'll be going in early tomorrow."

I knew it would be better to remain independent. Still, going in by car could save a good forty minutes, even during rush hour. I wondered if this was another of Stu's altruistic offers, or if he meant it as an assignment, part of my new job. Ride with the boss; keep him company on his way to work.

No. I was just being silly.

"Sure," I said, shrugging again. "Why not?"

* * * * *

His red Jag pulled into the driveway at seven thirty. I took my last sip of coffee and dashed out.

"'Morning," I said through the open window.

Apparently he was one of those people who takes some time to wake up because he didn't answer; but he reached across the car to open the door for me.

"Thanks," I said, getting in. He zoomed backward out of the driveway.

"How are you today?" I chirped, sounding, I realized, like Marilyn; maybe he was the cause of the woman's personality, I thought.

"Mmph." He nodded. I supposed that meant "okay." Or maybe it meant "don't talk to me at this hour." I decided to shut up and enjoy the ride.

He drove through Blue Wood and into Cliffside Park, then took a route I wasn't familiar with. "Are we taking the Lincoln Tunnel?" He nodded.

"Mmph," I said, mimicking him. He didn't notice the sarcasm, though. I kept quiet.

We were going in the right general direction, but wending our way through streets I'd never been on, through a neighborhood of Tudor houses, then a row of shops, a cleaner's, a stationery store, a small market, a post office. After that, we came to an area with relatively little development, no houses, no stores, and then to a park of some sort. He turned into a park road and stopped under some trees.

"What's the matter?" Were we having "car trouble"?

"I, um . . ." He put his hand on my shoulder. I leaned back and looked down at the hand, not shoving it off, but making it clear by my expression that he was out of line.

He had the good sense to remove it.

"What's going on?" I demanded.

"I don't know. I thought . . ."

"What?"

"I thought . . . I detected . . . some, uh . . . some attraction . . . between us."

I pressed myself back, as close against the door as possible, and stared at him. Had I done anything to make him think that? I tried to remember. I didn't think so.

I shook my head, feeling more and more uncomfortable as he stared at me with an odd intensity, waiting for my reply. Attraction. I knew I hadn't given out such a message. But, for some reason, I couldn't bring myself to deny it.

"Come on, Stu," I said, avoiding the question. "We'll be late for work."

Now I was as angry with myself as I was with him. Why didn't I just say, "No, Stu. No attraction between us"? I couldn't. Denying that his perception was accurate would make him feel foolish and I didn't want to make him feel like a fool. Nor did I want to hurt his feelings by telling him I wasn't attracted to him. Besides, I wasn't sure that would be true.

"Am I wrong?" he persisted.

"Stu. This isn't the time to have such a conversation."

"Am I wrong?!" Louder.

Was the man a masochist?

"Yes. Yes, you're wrong."

Was I imagining it or had he turned pale?

"And, anyway," I tried to soften it, "I work for you now. It would be terribly inappropriate."

The Amboy Duchess

Thirteen

When we got to the bank, I felt awkward. Stu and I had made small talk in the car and eased the tension a bit. But walking past the platform, I was certain everyone must see more going on between the boss and the new employee than should— or than actually was. I put on my best poker face and went to my desk. Despite the anxiety, I was actually looking forward to working. I had an idea and I wanted to do some research to see if it would work.

Last night, re-reading the *Village Voice* articles about Allerton, I had come across a display ad promoting another newspaper called *Majority Report*, a small paper for women in their own businesses. The Vietnam War had contributed to the proliferation of alternative presses, and so had the women's movement. And now the women's movement seemed to be entering a new phase. The previous phase had been one of guerilla action and foundational theorizing. Women picketed places like McSorley's Bar for not letting in women customers and the Miss America contest just for existing; they wrote articles like Carol Hanisch's "The Personal is Political" and "Program for

Feminist Consciousness-Raising," by Kathie Sarachild. Now they were building on these ideas to penetrate mainstream culture, clamoring for equal pay and equal opportunities. The ad I saw said that *Majority Report* "served the needs of New York's women business owners." When Stu had said "find a group other banks don't treat well," that's who I thought of, women, and today I wanted to call the paper and go downtown for a visit.

At my desk, I pulled out the *Voice* and looked for the ad. I dialled the number of the paper. *"Majority Report,"* a woman's voice answered.

Introducing myself, I explained that I was a representative of Allerton Bank. "We'd like to do business with women business owners, and I saw your ad in the *Voice*. Could we meet? Today, maybe?"

"You're from a *bank*? And you're asking to meet with *us*?" The woman sounded amazed.

I was downtown in less than half an hour. *Majority Report* was on Grove Street in the Village. The newsroom and offices were on the second floor of a corner office building. The antiquated staircase creaked as I made my way upstairs. The many layers of now-dirty white paint on the old half-wood, half-glass door prevented it from closing all the way. I held onto the knob and shoved my way into a corner room with open ceiling-to-floor windows. I was greeted by a refreshing cross breeze.

"Hello!?"

A woman in a T-shirt, khaki shorts, and hiking boots wandered in from another room and stuck her hand out. "I'm Leslie. Are you Winnie? I can't believe you're actually interested in women's businesses. My partner said that once banks see how many women are going into their own businesses they won't be able to ignore them anymore, but I still had my doubts."

"What made you start a paper for women business owners?"

"We think it's going to be a good market pretty soon. The number of women-owned businesses is rising rapidly, there are thousands now, whereas just five years ago there were hardly any. We publish lists in the paper of the names and addresses of women-owned businesses—and the lists are growing longer each week. What we're trying to do is encourage women to buy from each other."

"Lists of names are just what I'm looking for." I told Leslie about Stu's advice of the day before. "He said I should find a group that other banks aren't nice to."

"Well, you certainly picked the right group! 'Not nice' is an understatement. A woman with a flourishing business can go into a bank to apply for a loan with equipment as collateral, or for a line of credit to help her cash flow, and even if she's got the greatest profit-and-loss statements, the best balance sheet, even if what she wants is to expand because her business is so good, the banker can say no without giving her any explanation at all. All he has to do is say 'because you're a woman,' and she hasn't a leg to stand on. And that applies to any kind of credit, not only business loans. If you want a credit card, no one has to give you one—if you're a woman. All they have to do is say 'no,' no reason offered. Washington is working on the Equal Credit Opportunity Act, but it hasn't been passed yet.

"When that passes—which we're pretty sure it will soon—bankers and department stores will at least have to have a good reason to turn down a woman who applies for credit. If she's creditworthy, they'll have to grant her request—just like they do with men. White men, that is. Minorities are starting to have an easier time, though, too."

As we talked, Leslie took me through the office to a room in the back. Several old typewriters were on two scratched school desks and an old Linotype machine was in the corner. In another corner was an artist's drawing table.

"This is where we get the paper out. That's"—she pointed toward the typewriters—"the newsroom, and that over there is where we set type, and that's composing. Not fancy, but it does the job. We run the paper by consensus. No hierarchy. Everyone has a say. You know, teamwork. We find it works better than handing down orders. Women operate that way naturally. Men are always having to outdo one another, grab their place in the pecking order. Women listen; men bark. We have articles on this new style of management in back issues." She went to a file cabinet, flipped through some folders, and handed me several back issues of *Majority Report.*

When I left, the first thing I did was turn to the lists of names.

Great! I thought. *I'll get in touch with every one of them.*

* * * * *

That whole day turned out to be a success. When I began to make the calls from the *Majority Report* lists, I got several appointments right away: a mail order artist, a film producer, and a number of people who called themselves "financial counsellors."

The filmmaker would come to the bank the next day. She wanted to talk about funding for a film. An experienced producer of five successful documentaries, she now had contracts to produce two more for the federal Department of Environmental Protection totalling $100,000. But the money wasn't due until October, and she was itching to get started. What she wanted from Allerton was a loan against the contracts so she could start at least one of the films, which was to be about the logging industry.

Another appointment was for the following week with a woman who wanted to expand her shop on the Upper West Side of Manhattan. She sold jewelry, sculpture, and fabric from Guatemala. The financial counsellor and the lawyer wanted to have breakfast with me later in the week.

I had found the "group" I wanted to pursue.

Late in the afternoon, Stu came out of his office and headed for my desk. When he got to me, he put his hand up and beckoned me with his finger, then went back to his office. I wanted to type up some notes while everything was still fresh in my mind, but I followed him.

"What's up?"

"I've got a client for you."

"Great!"

"I want you to take a ride out to Allerton's Brooklyn branch tomorrow morning. He'll meet you there. He's got a small printing company and wants to expand. He'll give you all the information you need. Just bring everything back and we'll go over it here. I'll explain the whole thing to you tomorrow."

"Terrific! I've got an appointment with someone else in Brooklyn tomorrow, too."

"Who's that?"

The Amboy Duchess

I told him about the ad in *Majority Report* and the lists of women-owned businesses, and explained how his telling me to "find a group other banks aren't nice to" led to my idea. "I've already got a number of appointments. What do you think?"

"Sounds okay. Maybe we'll be able to play it up with press coverage if you can get some business. You know? 'Bank goes after women's market'?"

I understood that he wanted to deflect the press from the coverage the bank was already getting, but that seemed to be in my favor. "Maybe so," I said.

"Well, keep me posted on whatever you get." He handed me a piece of paper with the new client's name on it and, relieved he was being so quick, I turned to leave.

"Wait a minute!"

I turned back. "What?"

He came out from behind his desk. As he approached me, he reached out and put a hand on each of my shoulders. For a moment, I thought he was going to praise me for my good idea; then I panicked. Was he going to kiss me? He slid his hands down my arms, then put his arms around me and tried to pull me to him.

I shoved him away. "What are you doing?!"

"Don't push me away," he pleaded.

I turned and fled.

The Amboy Duchess

As I hurried back to my desk, I forced myself to put Stu out of my mind and focus on my successes. I'd never expected "new business" to get moving so fast. I rolled a sheet of paper into my old manual typewriter, the one that had been sitting in the storeroom for who knew how long, according to Harry Prince. The typing went slowly. First, I typed the names and addresses of each of the businesses I had contacted, including the time we had talked, and a few brief notes of the discussions we'd had so I'd be able to refresh my memory whenever I needed to look at the list. Then I added the appointments I had made. By the time I'd finished, I realized the bank was nearly empty.

The tellers had done their tallying after three o'clock, when the doors closed to the public, and they'd all packed up now and gone home. The switchboard operator and Gus, the security guard, had left at around the same time. One person from upstairs, the comptroller, was on vacation.

Harry, Melba and Bobbie were just wandering past my desk together, waving on their way out. I waved back.

All the men from the platform were gone. I had been introduced to them the other day when Stu and I had arrived together. But I had trouble remembering their names. They were the three loan officers, two white men with Irish-sounding names and a black man. Two other men sat opposite Alison Goodman, the woman who produced Allerton's newsletters; they were Pete

Hanlon and Sam Bitterman. Pete, Allerton's executive vice president, supervised the loan officers; Sam, who had the same title, was in charge of personnel. Although Alison worked for everyone on the platform, her deference to Pete made it clear whom she regarded as her boss.

Stu's secretary, Margaret, was closing up her desk, locking the top drawer. I could just see her if I leaned back against my typewriter table. Once Margaret had gone home, the only two people who would still be left in the bank with me were Stu and Benjamin Kalmowitz. Why did that name sound familiar? When Margaret told me the two men were in a meeting together, I got a nagging in the back of my mind. Stu had mentioned this morning that he had an important meeting with the man who was his boss. Could that be it? It seemed like something more, a name I should know. But I couldn't place it.

I decided I'd better wrap things up now, too. I wanted to get out of there before Stu wandered out of his office and offered me a lift home.

* * * * *

The next day, I trudged up the subway stairs at Montague and Court, passed the pizza place, the stationery store and the five-and-ten, crossed Remsen Street, and began to look for a porn shop called The Head Man. At the end of the block, I spotted the dildoes and other paraphernalia in the window that

Anne DeMarco had told me was located under the second-floor office of Liberation Limited. Entering the door to the right of the establishment, I tottered up a narrow, rickety staircase to the small mail-order factory that rented the second-story warehouse and office space.

"Hi!" I called, opening the creaking wooden door and peering in.

Liberation Limited occupied about twelve hundred square feet of rectangular space which the two women artists who ran the enterprise had filled with several drafting boards, two old school desks, a row of file cabinets, and a near-forest of thriving semi-tropical plants. Streams of sunlight spilled in through the wall-to-wall window at the far end. In front of the window was a long table that held a coffeemaker and an array of teas.

A tall woman, maybe in her mid-thirties, her dark hair pinned up somewhat messily, jumped up from one of the drafting boards and hurried to greet me. "Oh, you must be Winnie Charles!" Her strong voice cracked a little. She wore faded jeans and a T-shirt with the words 'Liberation Limited' arcing across her chest in rainbow lettering. She grabbed my hand in both of hers.

"I'm Anne DeMarco." She squeezed my hand and pumped it up and down with both of hers. "C'mon in. We've been looking forward to your visit. Josie!" She leaned backward, still gripping my hand, sending her voice in the general direction of a half-open door to what seemed to be a large closet. "The woman from the bank is here!"

A smaller woman, whose Liberation Limited uniform was covered by a long white photographer's apron, came out.

"Hi!" She wiped her hands on her apron and stuck one out to me. "Sorry. I was just finishing up in the darkroom. We do our own marketing, and I've been developing some photos we want to send out with our next mailing. I'm Josie Marks."

"Would you like some coffee?" Anne asked. "We can sit over here near the window."

Anne and Josie had been freelance artists before they got the entrepreneurial bug. Having designed stationery, brochures and all manner of marketing publications for large corporations, they had decided four years ago to put their skills to work for themselves. They started by buying mailing lists from every women's organization they could find all over the country, and sending out direct mail pieces to each name on every list, offering such items as T-shirts, coffeepots, stationery—all with graphics depicting women's lives silk-screened on them.

They showed me some of their inventory. Several cartons lined up along one wall held boxes filled with fancy paper napkins decorated with scenes from the 1890s of women in different work situations: one using a quill pen to write on a long ledger pad, wearing a green visor-cap; another tapping out messages on an old-style Teletype. A row of coffeepots and other electrical appliances on an overhead shelf depicted famous women: Sojourner Truth, Elizabeth Cady Stanton, Susan B. Anthony. A few displayed faces from current newspapers, rather than history books: Bella Abzug, Gloria Steinem, Shirley Chisholm.

Some T-shirts lying across one of the desks were decorated with feminist humor: "A Woman's Place Is in the House . . . And the Senate," "God Hates War; She's Really Pissed."

They told me the response was overwhelming, far beyond their wildest expectations. The first year, they had sold out their meager stock and each had pocketed $15,000. The business had also showed a profit—unheard of for a first year, let alone an enterprise run by women, and artists, at that. The next two years, they had charted their growth with sharply rising lines which they drew on a piece of oaktag that hung, framed, over Anne's drawing board.

Now, in their fourth year, the two artists expected sales to soar to an unprecedented $250,000. They wanted to expand—stock up on inventory and also open a retail shop next door to a women's bookstore in the Village. To do that, they needed $75,000, a loan they would take against inventory.

"Where do you keep your business accounts?" I asked, as Stu had counselled.

When they told me, I replied: "Well, if you'll switch to Allerton, we may be able to consider your loan application."

By the end of our meeting, I had my first bona fide client.

When I left, I realized I would have to become far more educated in financial matters before I could do a proper job of selling banking services. I'd have to really work at absorbing everything in the Dun and Bradstreet home studies course I'd signed up for. I needed to know more about profit-and-loss statements and balance sheets, how to determine what ratio of revenue could be used for debt, how much should go to partnership insurance, how to reduce corporate taxes and much, much more.

I went next to the man Stu had told me about, got all the papers I needed and brought them back to the bank. Later in the day, while typing my notes, I noticed a small man with oiled gray hair and a pencil black mustache in a flashy, but expensive, gray silk suit hurrying by and heading into Stu's office. That had to be Benjamin Kalmowitz, the chairman of the board of directors who Stu shared his office with. I knew Stu was expecting him again today for an important meeting.

* * * * *

At seven thirty the next morning, when I arrived at the outdoor coffee shop facing Rockefeller Plaza, Barbara Woolfson and Sarah Priest were already there, waiting for me. They were sitting at the table closest to the fountain, as we'd all agreed.

"Well, this is efficient," I said, after we placed our orders. "Do you do this often?"

"I do," Sarah said. "I get out early. This is a great place to meet clients."

"What exactly does a financial counsellor do?" I asked. I wasn't being facetious; I really had no idea.

But Sarah scowled, nodding, as though she'd heard that question before, apparently not for a moment considering that a banker might really be ignorant. "I know. I know. It seems like a made-up kind of thing. But believe me, you'd be surprised at how precious little people know about how to manage their money. And small business owners know even less about how to run their businesses. Everyone just gets by on the fly and tries to make the world think they know what they're doing."

"But *you* really *do* know!" Barbara laughed.

Now Sarah looked a little put out. "Well, I don't mean to imply that no one knows the intricacies of their own *professions*." She emphasized the word "professions." "Money management is *my* profession. I educate people about how to

154

spend, how to save, how to make money grow. We go over their incomes and their fixed expenses and I prepare budgets for them. Then we talk about finances. Insurance, investments, tax shelters. When they're in debt, I work out payment plans that make sense. We discuss long-range planning, annuities . . ."

"Ah. And the small business part? What do you do for businesses?" I asked.

"That's the meaty part. You know, partnership agreements, key man insurance, the best way to structure a corporation . . ."

I was realizing more and more how much I was in over my head. At that moment I felt furious with Stu for dragging me into an environment where I was so out of place.

"But, you know," Sarah was confiding now, "I've been consciously gearing my business toward women lately. Partly because I feel it's a market I can relate to, partly because women have been so neglected in this area. But, God! Have we got a long way to go, baby! My sisters know nothing about business. They've got imagination; some of the people I've met have put together the most unusual arrangements, like the woman in the Bronx who's selling silk-screen-decorated vibrators, with orchids and roses and things all over them. They're selling like crazy! And some sure have got guts! Like the woman I met last week who designs her own clothes and hustles around from department store to department store promoting a line she calls Allure. But most of the women I meet haven't got a clue about good *money* sense. Of course, most of them haven't got any money . . ."

"You'd better believe it!" Barbara broke in. "That's the big problem. Though you're right that there's some basic thing, some competitive self-preservation that seems to be missing, too. Something little boys are brought up with from the moment they shove their way out screaming. Maybe they pull little girls out more gently, or something, with someone saying to them first thing, now smile pretty, honey."

"You're . . . what kind of lawyer?" I asked.

"I've got my own practice. I used to work for the State Insurance Department, but I decided I could do as well income-wise on my own and enjoy the freedom of not having to punch a clock. Or twist myself into a Play-Doh puppet to follow all their rules and regulations. So, I do all sorts of law, divorce, accident suits, labor fights. I've had some really interesting cases since I've been on my own. Now I'm trying to establish myself as a small business expert. That's why I advertised in *Majority Report*. I've been doing a lot of work with women, also. For the same reasons as Sarah. In fact, we've been going around together giving talks to women's groups to drum up business and to corporations to

156

give out the message that there's a women's market out there and
we know how to tap it."

"We'd like to develop a consulting firm, marketing to
women," Sarah added.

I felt a glow of satisfaction. This was going to be a good
connection, I thought, pleased with myself for such an easy
success. Maybe I would end up liking sales, after all.

"Sarah is right, though . . ." Barbara continued. "Most
women who own their own businesses know even less than Sarah
thinks they do about how to run them. That's why so few make it.
And the ones that do are still pretty small potatoes. Also, of
course, there's not much opportunity for them to get their hands
on the kind of money that would help to make up for their lack of
savvy. As there is for men in the same boat."

"Why not?"

"Even for a small business owner, there's the old boy's
thing. Bankers, investment brokers, other financial types—they
all go out of their way for their buddies from the fraternity or the
guys from the old neighborhood or the ball field or the Friday
night card game . . ."

"Oh." That was disappointing, I thought. Maybe going
after women business owners wasn't going to be the grand
financial success I'd hoped it would be. But I had a sudden

thought. If I can help them get the money they need, maybe they'll do better. We can *create* an old girl's network! "Well, that's what I'm here for," I said, with more confidence than I felt. "Opportunity knocking on their doors."

Sarah and Barbara exchanged looks.

"Well," Barbara said. "Let's hope so . . ."

When Abbie Lord, the film producer, arrived at the bank later, I led her to Stu's office after we introduced ourselves.

"That may or may not be a good piece of business," Stu had said when I told him she was coming. "By the way, I honked outside your door this morning. I thought you'd like another lift in . . ."

"I had a breakfast meeting." I left it at that. I wasn't ready to tell him about my new contacts, not until they yielded some success. And I didn't want to get in the habit of reporting all my activities to him, especially not the ones at six o'clock in the morning. I thought that was a good way to avoid telling him I wouldn't be travelling to work with him anymore. I didn't want to have to tell my boss that I was unhappy with his behavior.

Now I stood with Stu and Abbie Lord at the round glass-topped table that marked the midway point between the two halves of the office, Stu's half and Kalmowitz's half. Kalmowitz, chairman of the board. The name still nagged me. Stu and I both held yellow legal pads; Abbie Lord lugged a heavy black briefcase which she set down next to one of the chairs. She was a severe-looking woman, attractive, but leanly so, her face bare of makeup and her chestnut-colored hair pulled back, every strand of it, into a tight knot at the nape of her neck. She wore a dark gray suit, well-fitting, with a black turtleneck and no jewelry, sheer black hose with thick, low-heeled black pumps.

She nodded, without smiling, when I introduced her to Stu. He held his hand out toward the table, fingers facing up, not to shake hands, but indicating that she should sit. She pulled out one of the chairs and slid into it.

Stu did the same, laying the legal pad in front of him. I was left standing and realized they were way ahead of me, not just by being seated, either. I was afraid I was going to have trouble following their conversation.

"Mr. Lewen," Abbie began, forgoing amenities. "I want $100,000 against a government contract to begin work on a film."

Stu nodded. "So I hear."

The filmmaker leaned down and opened her briefcase, pulling out a manila file folder jammed with papers, a clipboard that held a white legal pad, and a Mark Cross pen which she unscrewed. She lay it all on the table in front of her.

"What do you need?" she asked.

"How long have you been in business?" he asked, conversationally, sketching Donald Duck in the margin of the pad.

"Ten years."

He looked up, surprised. "Your own business? For ten years?"

For the first time, Abbie Lord showed emotion; she blushed. "Well, no. I've been a producer for ten years."

"I meant, how long have you been operating a business of your own?"

"For two years," she mumbled.

"I see." He jotted that down. "And how many films have you completed?"

"One."

He jotted down the numeral one, a quick, straight, vertical jot, on his pad, and looked up. "So why should we give you $100,000?" he asked, smiling, his eyes meeting hers. He slumped down in his chair, his hands on top of the glass, playing with his pen.

She matched his eye contact, leaning forward just a bit, as if getting closer would get her message to him faster; she did not match his smile. Her voice was firm as she answered. "Because I've got a contract from the government. A good receivable."

"Good?" Stu laughed. "You have that much faith in your government?"

"Mr. Lewen . . ." Abbie Lord said, emphasizing the "Mr." "I only need your money short-term. Three months. I believe this contract is good. But if you require further collateral, I also have a house . . ."

He snapped back to attention, his pen already on the pad. "Ah. Now you're talking my language. Where is the house?"

When Abbie Lord left, her forms all filled out, Stu instructed me to get a credit report going on her. He would have her corporation and her real estate checked out. He had told the woman they would have an answer for her by the following week. I was sure he'd set the deadline so far ahead, at least in part, to maintain control of the situation. He probably could have let her know if she qualified for the loan much sooner.

I also wondered if he would have required the house as collateral if Abbie Lord had been a man. I asked him as much.

"I always require a house as collateral. If the client owns one. And if the client defaults, I foreclose. That's why I've been a successful loan man." He turned sharply, strode to his desk and got busy, indicating that I was dismissed.

Back at my desk, I called in the request to TRW, the credit bureau that would send us her credit history. It was nearly noon when I began typing up the information on my morning's meetings.

Fourteen

A little farther uptown, on the East Side of Manhattan, another woman, far more sophisticated in the realm of high finance than I, sat in her penthouse study at an elegant replica of a Louis Quatorze desk, filling out application forms for the Small Business Administration. I'd never seen her apartment. At least not yet. Not then. But now, so much later, after the whole thing has passed, I can picture her sitting there. I know just what she would have been doing.

Pam Freeman wanted approval to start the first federally licensed investment corporation in the United States to be headed by a woman. She wanted to call it the Women's First Investment Corporation.

Her plan was to use the investment company as a vehicle to fund minority businesses, particularly those run by women. One of the benefits offered to small minority businesses by the not-even-twenty-year-old SBA was a program that allowed groups of private investors who could manage to pool $500,000 or more to apply for loans. If they qualified, they could get up to four dollars of federal money for every dollar they put up themselves. Pam figured if her businesses could somehow manage to put up one million dollars, she would haul in a small fortune.

Her mini-conglomerate consisted of four businesses, all in women's names, all backed by Pam. She, herself, had three corporate identities: the "Woman Executive" newsletter, which aimed at getting out an issue at least twice a year; Woman Executives Inc., a firm that would hold events, such as dinners, conferences and the like, when the right opportunities arose; and Sandpower, a company that planned to operate oil wells, fund archeological digs, and otherwise get involved in outdoor ventures.

In answer to one of the questions on the SBA form, Pam wrote: "New companies create jobs for Americans, as well as happiness . . ." As she speculated about the best way to fill out the rest of the ponderous questionnaire that lay on the desk in front of her, the phone rang.

"This is Pam Freeman. What can I do for you?"
"Hi, I'm Winnie Charles . . ."

I was calling everyone on the list I'd found in Majority Report and I'd gotten up to "Woman Executives Inc," the name she used to represent all her businesses. At least, for now.

"I represent an effort by Allerton Bank to reach out to small businesses . . . and I'm calling on businesses owned by women . . ."

I hadn't perfected my spiel yet; I knew I still sounded a little stiff and formal.

"O-oh. Is that right?"

"Yes. I understand you operate an organization called Woman Executive."

"That's right."

"Uh-huh. Well, uh, what is that exactly?"

"We run events. For corporate women. And we put out a newsletter."

"Oh, I see . . . I think it would be a really good idea for you and me to meet. I'm trying to spotlight women-owned businesses . . . "

"Is that right? I'm just this very minute filling out an application form asking the SBA for permission to do exactly the same thing."

"What for?"

"For investment purposes."

"Well, we really *should* meet!"

"Why don't we meet for lunch? I'll come to your area. In fact, I could come right to the bank and we could go from there. Where are you located?"

I could just picture her: hanging up, putting down the pen after jotting down my address, leaning back and stretching, a long, slow stretch, her manicured fingers laced far up over her head, standing up and skipping around the room, her bare feet hardly touching the tight weave of her Arabian carpet.

"Hah!" she might have yelled. "What do you know? Right in my lap!"

When Pam Freeman walked through the glass doors of the bank, it was twelve fifteen; she was fifteen minutes early. I didn't notice the platinum blonde in the mink coat approaching my desk until she was right next to me. She startled me when she held out her leather-gloved hand and introduced herself in a voice just a bit louder than the one used by Marilyn Monroe.

I looked up.

The mink had slid back so the shoulders of Pam's red silk dress were exposed; she seemed to be carrying the coat on her forearms.

I stood, slowly.

"Hi," I said. "I, uh, I'm not quite ready for you yet. You wouldn't mind waiting just a few moments?" I pointed toward the couches lining the window that looked out on the street.

Pam looked surprised, but smiled. She turned, took in the couches, and said, "No. Not at all. Take your time."

I realized that what I had done must have looked to this woman like a stall. A busy bank executive making herself important. But I hadn't meant it that way. I needed a few minutes to recover from the shock of the woman's appearance. This wasn't the sort of business look I had expected from the head of Woman Executives Inc.

Also, I wanted to go to the bathroom to comb my hair and put on a little lipstick. I hadn't looked in a mirror since I'd left the house in the morning.

I wasn't intentionally keeping Pam waiting; but, I realized on my way downstairs, doing so with this particular client was probably good for my image. Maybe being a saleswoman wasn't so far beyond my instincts and my abilities, after all, I congratulated myself.

We took a cab to 42nd Street. Pam had made reservations at the Oyster Bar. The maitre d' ushered us to a table as soon as we walked in. "Miss Freeman," he acknowledged, nodding.

Pam swept through the crowd as if she were Moses parting the Red Sea. Because she expected people to move and make room for her, they did; she never even had to say "excuse me."

I followed behind and felt the crush. For some reason, the Red Sea went immediately back to high tide for me.

"I'll have the scallops," Pam told the waiter, waving away the menu he handed her. "I recommend them," she told me. "They're really special here."

"Why not?" I laughed.

"Very good." The waiter nodded. "Anything to drink?"

Pam ordered a vodka gimlet.

"Diet coke," I said.

"So, you're going after the women's market," Pam pronounced. "I think that's smart. Good timing. How did you manage to talk Allerton's higher-ups into it?"

I tried to read the expression on Pam's face to figure out just what she meant.

"I tried—unsuccessfully—to sell the idea to other banks," she explained candidly, as if reading my mind.

Should I try to keep up the false impression that I was as savvy as Pam seemed to be, and had managed to pull off a neat trick? Or should I be honest and admit that I had just fallen into a lucky situation? If, in fact, that's what it would turn out to be.

I shrugged. "Just lucky, I guess." That, I thought, should cover me; let Pam interpret my answer any way she liked.

"What's your background?" Pam asked. She nodded as the waiter placed our drinks in front of us.

"Not banking," I said, hoping to avoid having to explain my situation.

"No? Marketing?"

I shook my head. "No, I come from the academic world."

"Really?" Pam smiled broadly. "Did you teach?"

"Yes. French. At Hunter College."

"I taught chemistry. At a high school upstate. I got tired of being paid like a serf, so I decided to become an entrepreneur."

"And you started Woman Executive? Is that a lucrative business?"

"I have a few other things going on, too," she said, sipping her gimlet.

"Oh? Like what?"

"A few other businesses. I head an investment firm. We underwrite start-up ventures."

Before I could ask how Pam's investment firm got the money to underwrite other businesses, our salads arrived. I decided to approach the question from another angle.

"Tell me about Woman Executive. Who's your audience?"

"Corporate women. Or entrepreneurs. But women business owners haven't got the money for a subscription."

I was a little confused. "Isn't Woman Executive the name of your investment firm?"

"Oh, no. That's another company. Woman Executive is a corporate entity under which I run events. And sell a newsletter. I've tried it as a membership deal. But that didn't work. So I'm in the process of reconfiguring it."

"Does Woman Executive provide funds for your investment firm?"

Pam looked at me as if I was from outer space. "Are you kidding?! No way! I get investors to put up the money. You know, venture capital." Pam leaned forward, as if she wanted to tell me a secret. "I'd like to meet Allerton's president."

"Is that right? Why?"

"I have an idea for him. I want to propose that he let me run seminars for women business owners. Tap into the women's market by giving them something they need."

I recalled the things I'd heard yesterday morning during my breakfast with the lawyer and the financial consultant.

"Yes," I said, as if I'd given this years, or anyway months, of thought. "I know, women entrepreneurs do have a lot to learn about management."

"That's for sure!" Pam snorted.

"So, you'd like to run seminars for them on business management?"

Pam nodded. "Business management. Personal money management. Whatever."

I nodded, as if I could see just what Pam had in mind.

"Will you talk to him for me?" Pam asked.

"Sure," I promised. "Why not?"

* * * * *

I advertised the classes in *Majority Report*, a small display ad on page thirty four to appear for ten days, and psyched myself up to wait for the calls. I felt only a little guilty for the promise I'd made to Pam Freeman. After all, Pam's only qualifications to run seminars on business management were— like mine—her teaching credentials. Pam, too, would have had to find financial people to talk about accounting, law and so on. Why shouldn't I do the planning myself?

When I spoke to Stu about it, he gave me permission to use the boardroom downstairs after the bank was closed, on my own time. His attitude said this had nothing to do with bank business anyway, and probably no one would even be interested in attending.

At nine o'clock on Monday morning, the first day of the ad's appearance, the calls started. They continued, nearly non-stop, for the entire week. By Friday, I'd scheduled months ahead, setting up six different four-week sessions, thirty women in each, and started a waiting list that now had three hundred names.

In addition, I had been called by a *Daily News* reporter, who wanted to do a center page spread on me, the bank and the seminars. Other reporters also called, from the *Village Voice,*

Glamour magazine, WNBC-TV for News Center Four asking me
come to the studio one day next week for its early morning talk
show, and several cable stations wanting to interview me here or
at their studios.

The subject of women and money, it seemed, was hot.

* * * * *

It was six p.m. Allerton's main entrance on East 48th
Street had a festive look, unlike the darkened innocuous exterior
it usually presented to the street at that hour. A chartreuse
banner—Stu's idea—had been hung in the window next to the
double-glass doors saying, "Welcome New York Business
Women." One of the doors was wide open, and a table was set up
just inside with Sarah Priest sitting at it, ready to check the
names and addresses of participants and their businesses and to
give them their name tags.

A camera crew from CBS was toting cameras, lights and
a heavy mass of tangled wiring into the bank from the white van
parked outside, the one decorated with the station's eye. I was
busy directing the CBS crew to the same room—when I wasn't
pacing from my desk to the table to the rear of the bank, where
caterers had set up the trays they were now carrying downstairs
to the boardroom. My four speakers, women from the world of
finance, were all down there, waiting to direct the caterers and
the camera crew to set up their paraphernalia in the agreed-upon
places, and checking their notes one last time.

172

The Amboy Duchess

Everyone who normally worked for the bank—Stu; Harry; Melba; Gus; Gladys; the phone operator; and all the platform staff—had gone home an hour ago, leaving me in charge. A thrill of anxiety kept sending an acidic shiver upward from my stomach through my ribcage to my esophagus. I kept checking my watch. The classes were scheduled to begin at seven. None of the women, not even the *Daily News* reporter to whom I'd given permission to sit in on the first class of this first series of seminars, was expected for at least another half hour.

I went back to my desk again and picked up the yellow pad on which I had made the final, consolidated list of lists. Everything was crossed off, but I went down it anyway, one item at a time: "food, coffee, pencils, pads . . ." I had taken care of it all.

I wanted to check my hair in the mirror again, but I couldn't leave the bank floor unattended. After everyone arrived and got settled downstairs, I would lock the front doors. But meanwhile, I had to play hostess—and security guard.

Why hadn't Stu hired Gus to stay on after hours tonight? I hadn't thought of that before now. Wouldn't this be a perfect time for someone to decide to rob the vault? I glanced toward the huge, gold gate that protected the heavy locked doors to the vault room. No one could get into it. And even if they did, an alarm would immediately alert the police.

"Miss Charles?"

173

I turned toward the voice. It was someone from the CBS crew, one of the cameramen.

"We set up a camera over there . . ." He pointed toward the rear of the main floor. A woman sat in one of two chairs that were set up facing the camera and two standing lights. ". . . for your interview."

"Oh!" I'd forgotten I'd agreed to let them interview me. "Now?"

I followed him and sat where he indicated, facing the reporter.

"This won't take very long," the woman assured me. "We just want you to set the scene for us. You can relax. We're going to shoot a lot of footage, and then cut most of it."

"Okay." My hands, cold and damp, were twisted together in my lap.

"Ready? We're going to start shooting now."

"I guess so." I forced myself to untwist my hands and made them lie, neat and calm, one on top of the other, on my thigh. I glanced toward the camera as I heard a click and then a soft hum.

"How does it feel to be a feminist banker?"

Startled by the question, I jerked my head toward the interviewer. "What?"

"That's all right. Don't worry. You can answer now. I told you, we'll cut most of the tape, anyhow. I'll ask you again. How does it feel to be a feminist banker?"

I made an effort to slow my pounding heart. It wasn't the word "feminist" that had startled me; it was "banker." Was I a "banker"? Is that how people would see me? Is that how I wanted them to see me? I didn't have a chance to mull this; I had to answer.

Ignoring the woman's question, I began my prepared remarks, as Stu had coached me to do. "Women all over the city are entering the work force in unprecedented numbers, starting and buying their own businesses . . . Allerton Bank wants to help them . . ."

When it was all over, my hands were wringing wet, and so was my dress, under the arms and at the collar. I stood up, thanked the woman woodenly, stepped over the wires, and walked toward the front door where the first women were coming in.

I held my hand out to them as they turned away from the table, their shoulders labelled with their names.

"Hello," I said, smiling automatically. "I'm Winnie Charles . . ."

The Amboy Duchess

Fifteen

After a couple of weeks of the most hectic work schedule I could ever remember, I decided to treat myself. A neighbor had invited me to a party, and I decided to go. She had said there would be single people there and maybe I would meet someone. Not that I looked forward to meeting anyone! I wasn't ready to date. But I was missing the children—all I had was Annie, my little orphan kitty!—and I figured a party might cheer me up.

The night of the party I stood in front of my closet deciding whether to wear a dress or pants, dress up or down. I finally decided on a long peasant skirt and a black pullover top, with my most exotic dangling earrings.

I took the car even though it was only blocks away in the only apartment development in town.

The door flew open when I got there, as if of its own volition; no one greeted me. I peered in at swarms of people circling one another in the small foyer and in the living room beyond, clouds of smoke circling with them, and I nearly left. It was a long time since I'd been to a party like this. But I had promised myself an evening out; now that I was working, I wanted to give myself some fun. If I took off, I'd have to go somewhere else, but I had no idea where. It was here or home, so I walked in and shut the door.

I made my way through the foyer, stepping over three people sitting on the floor, knees up, backs against the wall, sharing a joint. One of them, the man, wore a green velvet suit. I'd never seen a man in a green velvet suit before, or any color velvet, for that matter. He looked up at me, and I realized I was staring at him. His hair, bleached flaxen from summers outdoors, I guessed, fell limply into his eyes. He brushed it back and flashed a smile at me. Confused, I smiled back, but then turned away, embarrassed, and kept going.

At the edge of the living room, intimidated by the crowd, I stopped. None of the faces looked familiar. Didn't I know anyone here? Where was the hostess?

"Hi!"

I turned.

A tall brunette woman held her hand out. I took it, a little puzzled.

"Winnie! How are you?! How's your new job? The last time I saw you was weeks ago, at the Lewen's volleyball game! "

"Oh, Janet! I didn't recognize you. You look beautiful!" She wore a Chinese silk smock over black silk pants and black-

and-red beaded earrings that hung to her shoulders. She carried a long cigarette holder, for effect, I guessed; it held no cigarette.

"Thanks, you too. How do you know the Twomblys?"

"Oh, Bryna teaches where I . . . used to . . . teach."

My eyes casually brushed the crowd and spotted a face on the other side of the room aimed in my direction, the eyes sending lasers across at me; it was the man in the green velvet suit. I forced myself to look back at Janet, then I glanced up again, sure the staring face, especially those eyes, must have been my imagination. Yes, they were gone. "What? I'm sorry . . ."

"I said I haven't seen you at any of our games lately."

"Oh. I don't really play. I just went that one time . . ." I looked across the room again. No face. Yes, I'd been mistaken. But then I saw it again, gliding around the crowd to my right, stopping, the eyes still boring through me. There were too many people. I couldn't really tell who it was, just got a flash of the blond hair.

"That's a shame," Janet was saying. "We're starting to get really good. We play every Sunday now. You really should join us again."

"Well, maybe one Sunday . . ." I wasn't concentrating on the conversation. The face with the blond hair was distracting me. Where was it now, that face? There it was, to my left. It had circled around to the other side of the room, but the eyes were still on me, I was sure. I could see it more clearly as it moved a little closer. It was a man. It was definitely a man and he was clearly staring at me. Who was he?

"Yes, do come. We have a great time. People have started bringing snacks and we picnic on the lawn after the game."

"Sounds like a lot of fun." But I was still having trouble paying attention. I was trying to catch a glimpse of the man, the blond man who kept staring at me from all sides of the room. He was on the move again. Where was he? There. He had his back to me now; he was leaving the living room. His green velvet jacket glowed under the glare of the lamp as he passed it. It was the man who had been sitting on the floor just moments before. How could he have moved so fast? I turned and looked at the people on the floor behind me. There were only two of them. He was gone. I looked back to where he'd been a second ago. Gone. I searched the crowd for his face. Nowhere in sight. I felt let down.

"Well, it's really nice seeing you again," said Janet. "Listen, I'm going to the back room. Some of the party is moving there. Come with me!" She grabbed my hand and pulled me down a hallway to a closed door.

"What's there?" I asked.

"Shhh. Bryna doesn't want people—you know, smoking— so near the door. She told them to go in here." Janet flung the door open and pushed her way in, still pulling me with her. The smoke in the tiny, jammed room was choking-thick. At first, my

180

eyes felt as though they would not be able to take the heat; I shut them for a moment. When I opened them, he was there in front of me on the couch, a joint held to his lips with three fingers. I'd have fled, but Janet was still gripping my hand.

He looked up, saw me and smiled, his eyes gleaming black, his teeth even and white.

"Here," he said. "Have some." He thrust the joint in my direction.

Janet grabbed it and took a long toke, then passed it to me.

I took it between my thumb and forefinger, put it to my lips and sucked in. I nodded, as if to indicate that I knew good stuff when I tasted it, and passed it back to him. "Thanks," I said. As he passed it to the woman sitting next to him, I whispered to Janet: "Who is he?"

"Oh, that's Jim Battle. You know? From Channel Nine news? The anchor?"

"Oh, yeah." I'd heard of him, seen him a couple of times, but hadn't recognized him. He had a reputation as a rebel. He often ignored the script and reported the news his own way. He looked like an anchor, though, I thought. A little too good-looking.

He stood up. He had an athletic body under the green velvet jacket, and he was tall, maybe half a head or so taller than

181

me. His black eyes burned out at me under half-closed lids as the smoke from the joint wafted upward. "I'm Jim," he said in a soft, half-whispering voice that matched his suit. Somehow, my hand was in his; Janet had disappeared.

Afraid my voice would be gone, I didn't try to answer him, just stood there, feeling obliterated by his glow.

"What's *your* name?"

"What?"

"Your name?"

"Oh." My throat felt numb, but I managed to get it out. "Winnie."

"Winnie," he repeated in the velvet-fog voice.

I felt him pressing my hand between both of his and wrenched it away, shoved my arm behind me so he wouldn't grab it again. "Do you, uh, live in Blue Wood?" I asked, finally recovering some composure.

"On the hill," he replied.

"Is that right? Where?"

"By the nature center. I just had the house built. Just moved in, maybe four, five weeks ago. Where do you live?"

"On this side of town. Near the brook."

"Oh, yeah. The brook. I pass it on my way to the market."

I could hardly picture it, him going to the market. "You shop?" I asked, stupidly.

"Do I shop? Sure. I shop. I eat. I blow my nose."

I giggled. He laughed, too. I took a deep breath and looked at him again. He had a mole over his left eyebrow. "Really? I thought you must have come down from the beanstalk. I didn't think those people blew their noses."

"That was Jack. I'm Jim."

"Oh, I got you mixed up."

"What are you doing later?"

"Later?"

"After the party."

"What do you mean? After the party I'm going home."

He grinned. "How would you like to go somewhere else?"

I stared at him. This party definitely wasn't going the way I'd expected it to. I wrinkled my nose and turned away from him. "No, thanks," I threw back over my shoulder as I went to get my jacket.

We met again outside.

"Over here," that already familiar voice called softly when I got to my car. I turned toward it. He was standing, his arms resting on top of the open door of the black BMW I'd noticed when I'd arrived.

I walked slowly toward him. "Hi," I said, uncertainly, wondering if he had been waiting for me.

"I thought you'd never come out."

"I never did."

"What?"

"I don't know. I'm just being stupid. Listen, I never said I'd meet you here. I told you I have to get home."

"I know. But I can hope, can't I?"

"Sure, go ahead and hope." I turned and started walking back to my own car.

"Ah, come on, wait a minute."

I turned halfway back, tilted my head and waited.

"Let's just go for a drink. Just a drink."

"Another time. I have a very busy day tomorrow. Really," I promised. "Call me."

"How can I call you? I don't know your last name."

"Charles."

"Winnie Charles. Why don't you just give me your number?"

* * * * *

The day after Labor Day was very busy. A man had come in for a loan for some equipment, and because everyone else was occupied Alison Goodman, Pete Hanlon's secretary, had sent him to me. His request was simple; all I had to do was write it up and give it to Stu to present to the loan committee.

I opened the third drawer of my desk and flipped through the pendaflex folders looking for the one marked "Forms" and then went through that one to find the manila folder labeled "Unsecured Loans." Empty. Damn! I'd have to go downstairs for more of the forms. I wanted to get the application done and into Stu's office before the committee meeting tomorrow morning, so in case I'd forgotten anything and they had to turn it down, Stu could still complete it and get the loan approved by the end of the week. I jumped up and headed for the stairs.

No one was in the supply room when I got there.

Surveying the shelves quickly, I didn't see the forms I needed. I stood on my toes and backed up so I could read the labels at the top, bumping into the file cabinet and knocking off a folder with some papers. As I knelt to pick them up—pages from some kind of ledger—my eye caught some of the names. Harry's name was there and so was Bobbie's, as well as some of the loan officers from the platform and a couple of the women who worked the teller windows. Next to each name were columns of figures. These must be the payroll lists, I realized. What were they doing here? I started to put them back, not wanting to invade anyone's privacy, but then I noticed the name DiNatale. *Vince* DiNatale? The *politician*? I couldn't help taking another look to see if his name was on an Allerton payroll list. DiNatale was on the list several times, with a number of different first names. No Vince, though. Well, that didn't mean anything. DiNatale could be a common enough name in some New York neighborhoods.

But as I looked, I noticed that some of the other names were also familiar. D'Angelo and Infantale were repeated a number of times, as well, the names of two other public officials who frequently made the newspapers, along with DiNatale. I looked on the top line of the sheet to see the date. Last month. I didn't think anyone by those names worked for Allerton. No one did at our small branch. I'd have to check to be sure about Brooklyn, but if I was right, it was strange. Both Stu and the personnel director had boasted that the bank's staff was very stable. "We have a small staff, but no one has left us in nearly two years." Were those empty boasts? Why were those names on the list?

I looked behind me to be sure no one was nearby and quickly shoved the sheets back into the folder. What was it doing out in the open this way? Didn't whoever had left it there care if such proprietary information was seen? I couldn't believe anyone would be so casual about leaving payroll sheets around. Standing, I returned the folder, against my better judgment, to the top of the file cabinet and continued to search for the forms I needed. Finally, I found them on the top shelf, took a handful and covered the box they came from. Now I'd better get back upstairs to my desk.

But my curiosity was too great. I would never read payroll sheets just to find out what anyone's salary was. Well, almost never. But I wanted to know more about those mysterious names. Were they on all the sheets? How far back did they go?

What were they doing there? Who were those people? *Did* they work for Allerton?

I reached for the folder again, stood in the middle of the supply room, clutching it and listening for footfalls. No one was coming. But now what? I could hardly stand here and read all of them. Someone would show up soon. What should I do? I hated to just put them back. I could copy them and peruse the lists more carefully at home. That would be awful. Still, I remembered seeing those same names in the *Voice* articles I'd read about the mess Allerton Bank was in with the State Banking Commission. The *Voice* said Allerton had "mob connections." I had to know more.

I headed for the copy machine in the lunchroom, folder in hand. When I got there, I put the folder on top of the machine, reached in and pulled out one of the sheets. Careful to keep the rest of them out of sight, I lifted the machine's cover and placed the first one on the glass. I pressed the button, grabbed the copy as it came out and placed it under the folder so it wouldn't be seen if anyone walked in.

I was nearly done, a neat pile of copied payroll sheets growing under the file folder, when I heard someone coming down the stairs.

One of the last sheets was lying on the glass ready to be copied. Whoever was approaching had reached the bottom of the steps and was heading toward the lunchroom. I closed the cover of the machine slowly, but did not press the button. I turned toward the doorway just as Harry appeared.

"Hello! What are you doing down here?"

"I came down to get some unsecured loan forms from the storeroom," I said, stalling for time so I could think of a reason to be using this out-of-the-way copy machine. "And I had a lot to copy, so I decided to do it here so I wouldn't hog the machine upstairs."

Pretty good, I thought. I hoped he'd buy it.

"Good idea . . ."

I let out a breath, realizing I'd been holding it.

". . . Did you find the forms you wanted?"

I nodded, pointing to them.

"Okay, you've got things under control, I see. You going to join us for bridge today?"

"Sure," I said. I didn't want to play, but I didn't want him to stick around trying to persuade me. The surprised look on his face told me I'd used the wrong approach.

"No kidding! You're going to grace us with your presence?"

"You know, Harry, the only reason I'm reluctant to play is I'm not very good."

"Don't worry. We'll bring you up to speed. You can be Melba's partner."

"Oh, you don't want me?"

188

"Not me! This is my big chance to beat Melba."

"Maybe I'll have beginner's luck."

"May-be, may-be. Well, I'll look forward to it. See you later, then."

He walked out, turned in the direction of the supply room and headed for his office in the corner. I finished copying the lists, but I wouldn't be able to return the file folder until later.

* * * * *

I kept my eye on the stairs all morning, but Harry never came up. The file folder, along with the copies I'd made, were in my briefcase under my desk. Every time someone approached, I jumped, startled.

At one point, I went downstairs to the bathroom. I worried about the briefcase the whole time and raced up the stairs to get back as fast as I could. Back at my desk, I plunked myself into my chair, out of breath. I bent down. At first, I didn't see the briefcase. My head started pounding. Then I spotted it; somehow it had fallen, but it was there. How had it fallen? Had someone tried to take it? I opened it and peered inside. The file folder and all the copies were still there. I knew I was being paranoid, but I sighed with relief, placed the case back on the floor and held it between my feet for the rest of the morning.

At lunchtime, I was reluctant to leave it again, this time for a whole hour, but I had no choice. I couldn't very well carry it with me to the bridge game.

All through the game, I worried about it. And I couldn't help wondering who had left the folder on top of the cabinet. Bobbie? Wasn't she the one who was in charge of payroll? How could she be so careless? And why would she have the folder down in the basement, anyway? I couldn't think of a single reason she would have for bringing such a folder down here. If she needed to copy something, she had her own copier upstairs. Only she and the comptroller shared it and he was out.

Melba? What would Melba be doing with payroll sheets? One of the officers, one of the executive officers? One of the secretaries? Ditto for all of them. No one would have any reason for bringing them to the basement. And the carelessness was nearly as hard to account for.

Everyone was quiet, looking at me. It was my turn to bid again.

"Four hearts."

"You're bidding *four* hearts?" Melba asked. Melba's last bid was three.

I nodded, recounting my points. My mind wasn't on the game, but I could always claim ignorance. Still, I thought I had enough. "Yes," I said, looking up from my hand and across the table to my partner, wishing for some kind of sign from her that it was all right. Though Melba and I were winning, I had screwed up the last hand and didn't want to do it again.

"Ho! I knew it was a good idea, inviting you to play with us!" Harry said.

"All right," Melba said. "Five hearts."

My heart was pounding as I started to lay out my cards.

"You'd better give me something to play with," Melba said, shaking her head as I laid out the five hearts I had to the jack. When the rest of the cards were on the table—six spades, including the queen and the king; two diamonds, the king and the ace; and a void in clubs—Melba nodded. "Okay, not too bad."

"Not too bad! Woman, you've got a slam hand there," Harry chided.

"This one has to be the last hand," said Bobbie, Harry's partner. "I've got to get back. I left everything sitting on my desk that I'm getting ready for tomorrow's committee meeting. I'll never get to the payroll today. It will just have to wait until tomorrow afternoon. I'll have to call Kalmowitz's accountant later and put him off. Good thing, too. I searched my office, but I couldn't find the manila folder Kalmowitz was supposed to leave. I'm sure I saw it earlier this morning. I don't know what I did with it. It better not be lost or I'm in big trouble."

So it was Bobbie who left the sheets downstairs. I could hardly look at her now. But then I wondered why she had taken them to the basement if they were so important. She had her own copy machine upstairs. I was glad she wanted to end the game. I had wanted each hand to be the last.

"Oh, right, when we're winning, you want to stop," Melba teased Bobbie. "Just lead now and be quiet."

Bobbie led with a four of spades. Melba covered it with a five, Harry with a jack, and Melba pulled the queen from the board.

"I thought you had spades!" Bobbie complained.

Harry glared at her. "I keep explaining what that bid means, but you keep forgetting."

"Just play," Melba said.

"It's your turn."

"I know. I played the king."

Harry took the trick with his ace. Then Melba laid her cards on the table. "The rest are mine," she announced, grinning. "Good game!" she said, congratulating me.

"Beginner's luck, huh?" Harry said. "You've gotta play with us again tomorrow. Give me and Bobbie a chance to beat you back."

* * * * *

After lunch, I again watched the stairs, but Harry didn't come up. The afternoon went by slowly. I read the third chapter in the Dun and Bradstreet home study course that Stu had signed me up for, glancing up every few seconds to be sure I wouldn't miss Harry in case he came up. Several customers sat down next to my desk to ask for information or to open accounts. I took care of them, the briefcase locked between my legs, the corner of my eye on the basement staircase. No Harry.

Finally, at four thirty, just as I was wondering if I would have to stay late, waiting for everyone to leave the bank in order to put the folder back on top of the file cabinet downstairs, he appeared. I watched him as he walked around to the staircase that led to the second floor, then I reached down and grabbed the handles of the briefcase, hefted it up and went quickly to the basement.

In the supply room, I pulled the folder out of the case and returned it to the top of the file cabinet. No one came, and I got back to my desk without any problem, waving at Melba as I passed her office again. I breathed deeply, and suddenly felt a thrill of excitement. I could hardly wait to get home and study the lists.

* * * * *

Copies of payroll sheets for the last year lay all over my coffee table. There was little doubt that's what they were. Yet all had names of people I believed were not Allerton employees. I had to find out for sure.

My feet on the coffee table, I leaned my head back on the couch and closed my eyes. It seemed they were padding the payroll. But I could hardly believe that evidence like this—if that was, indeed, what it was—would be lying around where anyone, even a new employee, could find it.

Did Stu know about this? I wondered if I would have taken the job if I'd known this before. Probably, I admitted to myself. I'd read the *Voice* articles, hadn't I? They hadn't stopped me. I couldn't afford to be choosy right then. But what bothered me most was the nagging thought that Stu might be involved in what surely looked like fraud.

I got up, shut the light and went upstairs to bed. Tomorrow, I would figure out a way to find out more about Stu's part in whatever it was that was going on. I hated to admit it to myself, but if Stu was involved, I had found my chance at revenge. I was sure his father, the cop, Moe Lewenthal, had been involved in my father's death. It was too coincidental that he would have found Avi's body just moments after he had also been on the scene when Reles "fell" out that window. I would probably never get the chance to prove his involvement. But I *could* get even. Here, perhaps, was my opportunity.

In the morning, I left the house before six to avoid any chance of running into Stu. The copies of the mysterious papers were tucked away in my clothing closet.

* * * * *

The group of thirty women was straggling out of the boardroom in twos and threes. Some were lagging behind to ask questions of the speakers, others questioned the camera crew as they rewound the wires, closed their standing lamps and began to carry their equipment back up the stairs. A few women were having one last cup of coffee and another bun, as if reluctant to leave.

It was nine thirty p.m., the day after I'd found the payroll sheets. The classes were successful beyond anyone's expectations. The women who attended asked lots of questions, got involved in discussions about the complications of sole proprietorship, partnership, incorporating, what key man insurance would do for them, how to get lines of credit, lease equipment, use receivables as collateral. They were always enthusiastic, always said they looked forward to the next week's session. Each time they returned, they were eager to get more information.

Tonight had been the same. Now I piled the extra packets of class materials on my arm and carried them to the supply room. This morning, I noticed that the folder of the original payroll sheets that I had returned to the top of the cabinet was gone; I wondered who had taken it and what was going on. But I'd been too busy getting ready for the seminar to look for evidence that those people were not and hadn't ever been Allerton employees. I had promised myself earlier that I would start my search tonight, when things quieted down and everyone left.

When I got back to the boardroom, it was emptying out. The news people were gone, as were most of the women. The speakers stayed behind to help me clean up.

The Amboy Duchess

"Come with us, Winnie," Sarah Priest pleaded when we were done. "You shouldn't be here all by yourself so late at night."

"I'll be okay. I've got work to catch up on. These seminars aren't my real job, even if they do take most of my time. They're an extra thing Stu is *letting* me do. I never got to my *real* work at all this week."

I wasn't actually lying, but I had no intention of doing work. I was anxious to look in the files now that I had the bank all to myself. I locked the two front glass doors after seeing everyone out, then went to my desk and got out the flashlight I'd brought from home. I didn't want to turn on any more lights downstairs than I had to; someone, a cop or some conscientious passerby, might see it.

I tiptoed back downstairs—as if someone might hear me—and headed through the small basement corridor for the storeroom. It was creepy down there at this hour. As I passed the now locked-up boardroom to my right and the empty office opposite it, then the lunchroom and opposite that, to my left, Melba's locked office, I thought I heard a noise upstairs. I stopped and listened. Nothing. It must have been my imagination.

In the storeroom, I went right for the file cabinet. The top drawer was jammed with file folders labelled with the names of companies. Some I recognized as customers; they either had

196

accounts with Allerton or their names appeared on the outstanding loan lists that came around every week. What should I do, go through them? I knew what I was looking for. But I had no idea where to look. I opened one folder, carefully, with my two index fingers. What was I afraid of, leaving fingerprints? I smiled at my caution, then pulled the folder out halfway and peered inside. Letters. Old loan applications. Nothing that seemed suspicious. Not that I would know what would be suspicious.

I looked through a few more, then decided I would have to have some kind of plan. This could take all night and I didn't have a clue what to search for. I would go through the files without opening them unless a strange name, like the ones on the payroll list, jumped out at me. What I really hoped to find was a list of the actual employees at each branch. I was nearly through the folders in this drawer when I heard something upstairs again. This time I was sure it wasn't my imagination. It sounded as if something were being rolled or pulled across the marble floor, screeching softly every once in a while like chalk on a blackboard.

Someone was in the bank.

I didn't know if I should feel scared or guilty. Was it someone breaking in? Was it someone I should hide from?

Then I realized I'd better hide whether someone was breaking in or not. Because if it was someone from the bank, I'd have a hard time explaining what I was doing. But where? I clicked off the flashlight and tiptoed to Harry's office; I tried the door. It was open. I went inside and looked around. The only place to hide was under the desk. I felt ridiculous getting down on my knees and crawling in there. I told myself I'd seen too many cop shows on TV.

But then I heard the footsteps.

They were coming down the stairs. I knelt down and crawled in. I found that if I pressed my face to the floor I could look under the desk's front panel to get a view of the storeroom floor and, beyond it, the floor of the corridor. A man in black wingtip shoes and gray slacks with a neatly pressed sharp crease was coming toward the storeroom. My chest felt as if the drumbeat of my heart would pound it open. I was afraid to let out a breath. He stopped at the file cabinet and I could hear him opening one of the drawers.

My neck was getting cramped from peering under the desk panel, but I was afraid to move, afraid any motion would alert him to my presence. I could hear him rifling through the folders. What was he looking for? It obviously wasn't a crook; there wasn't any money down here. I wished I could see who it was. And which drawer he'd opened.

Finally, he closed the drawer and headed back toward the staircase.

I waited. Sounds still echoed through the bank from upstairs. I was afraid to come out. What if he came downstairs again? He might want to return whatever it was he'd taken.

After a while, I couldn't tell how long, I heard the scratching, rolling noise again. Then I heard footsteps echoing across the bank's marble floor. Then a noise that must have been the front door being opened, possibly the click of a key, unless I was imagining it, then the door squeaking closed.

What should I do?

I stayed where I was.

It was quiet for a long time. It was too dark under here, and I was in too twisted a position, to look at my watch. At last, convinced he'd gone, I crawled out.

I was too shaken to look through the files again. But I had found out something. Those files were important enough for someone to come for late at night when everyone else was gone. And when I stood up and brushed off my skirt, I noticed that one of the drawers was not completely shut. That must have been the drawer he was searching through. I would come down here next time and try again, starting with that drawer.

When I looked at my watch, I was surprised at the time. Eleven thirty. I'd been down here for nearly an hour. I needed to get out of there and head home.

I climbed the stairs slowly. When I was nearly to the top, I peered out across the bank floor cautiously. I could see the secretary's empty desk in front of Stu's office, the starkness of the vacant platform, the double-glass doors, closed and still, and the dark, silent street. All clear.

Relieved, I walked across the marble floor, my own tapping footsteps echoing now. I would get my briefcase and get home as fast as I could.

"Who's there?!!"

I stopped, afraid for a moment to move. Then I turned slowly.

He was coming out of Stu's office.

Kalmowitz!

I sucked in my breath, my mind blanked out by terror.

He marched across the floor, his scowl turning his face a dangerous red. I noticed his shoes. Black. Wing-tipped.

"Who are you?! What are you doing here?!"

"Mr. Kalmowitz. Uh, hi. I'm Winnie. Remember me? Winnie Charles? You met me in Stu's office a few weeks ago? And you pass my desk every day? I'm new here. Remember? We were holding one of our seminars tonight . . ."

"One of your what?"

"Seminars? Didn't Stu tell you about them? For women?"

"Women?" He said it as if he wasn't quite sure what they were.

"Women business owners. We're running classes for them. It's a promotional thing. We'd like their business. It was my idea. I started them."

He peered at me, still not trusting me.

"Well, where are they?"

"What?"

"The women. Your class. Where are they?"

"Oh." I sighed in relief. Maybe he was starting to believe me. "They went home. I, uh, was just cleaning up."

"Where? Where were you cleaning? I was just downstairs. Isn't that where you're coming from? The stairs?"

"Uh, yes. I, uh, was in the, uh, boardroom. I never heard you. The, uh, the door was closed."

He narrowed his eyes, studied me for a few moments, then, finally, seemed to decide I was harmless.

"Well, are you finished?"

"Finished?"

"Cleaning up." His high-pitched, slightly grainy tenor voice was edged with exasperation.

"Oh. Yes. Yes, I'm done. I was just going to get my briefcase from under my . . ." I pointed toward my desk; his eyes followed my hand as if he'd never seen me before.

"Well, get it and get out," he said.

I hurried to the desk, pulled my briefcase from underneath it and raced to the double-glass doors. As I knelt down to unlock the doors, he called out, menacingly:

"This is no time for you to be in the bank alone."

* * * * *

Benjamin Kalmowitz. I knew him! But how? The confusion lasted a few moments before I finally realized the connection. Then I knew. Benjie.

Uncle Label's *lantzman*, his buddy from the old country.

My Uncle Benjie! Not really my uncle, but that's what I'd always called him.

Uncle Benjie? How could I *not* know him? He was in my house often enough when I was a kid. But that was in my old life. Before Avi's death. In fact, I realized, he was there the night my father died. He'd picked Avi up in the car.

I guess his name *should* sound familiar! Had I known his last name? I must have. But it was so long since I'd heard it—and then it was in another context.

But what was he doing here?

Even if I had recognized his name right away, I'd have been surprised. What was Uncle Benjie doing in Stu's bank? What a coincidence, I might've thought. Imagine me getting a job at the bank that's run by my Uncle Label's buddy from the old country.

But now it seemed even weirder. What *was* he doing working with Stu?! How did they know each other?

Uncle Benjie and the cop's son? Kalmowitz and Moe Lewenthal?

Why not?

Why shouldn't they know each other?

Of course, I finally decided, it made sense. We all came from the same Brooklyn neighborhood, in fact the very neighborhood where Allerton's branches were now. Stu and Benjie. Really, not such a surprising connection, after all. Why wouldn't they know each other?

But now, his sinister tone of voice, the implied threat, jarred me and I suddenly saw the man who used to visit my father and my uncles when I was growing up in a new light. This was no coincidence; it was *bashert*, as Bubbe Sarah would say, ordained by fate.

The story of my father's family was always told by men. My uncles were the ones who roared with laughter at family gatherings, their gruff, schnapps-coated voices devising the mythologies of their forebears, generations of men, to hear them tell it, tales that went back as far as memory could stretch to the days when stories were the only entertainment. Zeyde Moshe Yussel, Zeyde Asher, Uncle Yaakov, Uncle Naftulim. These were the names I heard, immortalized in gravelly baritones and throaty tenors that still rang in my head. The men shaped the family history, passing down legends about the only heroes and buffoons worth memorializing, themselves. They were the chroniclers and the chronicled.

I never questioned it. The views of my father, my uncles and my grandfather—and, as if by decree, my male cousins and, now, even my own sons—were thought to be universal laws. Recalling those tales through the prism of my female experience gives me vertigo, as if I were Alice, falling down the rabbit hole. Nothing seems true; everything is distorted. But whose distortion, mine or theirs, I can't tell.

They were there when "rackets" became big business. The era of Prohibition, violent labor wars. Murder and other mayhem. Jews, known more for trying to avoid violence than for adding to it, nevertheless had some training in the European skirmishes my uncles fled, and they did better than just survive in New York's street wars. They fared better than their cousins did in Europe. Some even excelled at the art of carnage: Meyer Lansky, Bugsy Siegel, Lepke Buchalter made their mark on twentieth century America. Dutch Schultz, Longie Zwillman, Abe Reles, Mendy Weiss, Allie Tannenbaum made the annals of criminal history. Others, as well, Gurrah Shapiro. Joey Amberg. Gangy Cohen, who even had a Christian-sounding alias: Jack Gordon. Their names ring death knells in stories about Brooklyn's gangs and incorporated murder.

You won't read about Label Tannen, or Asher, or Dovid in those annals. Violence wasn't their forte. They were less flamboyant, less daring, less connected than the smallest cogs in the evolving machinery of syndicated American crime.

But surviving in early New York took moxie; enduring the struggle required payoffs and appeasements. They were right in the fray, the Tannens, and they knew some of the leading combatants.

My father's death proves it.

I know what I know now from eavesdropping, asking questions where I wasn't welcome, remembering things I was meant to forget. First-hand memories, fifth-hand stories.

You'll just have to take it on faith.

The Amboy Duchess

Sixteen

Benjie
1941

Ruth Kalmowitz stirred more sugar into the glass of tea she had been nursing for the past hour. She glanced up at the kitchen clock. Four a.m. The pot roast she had prepared hours ago for Benjie's dinner, for their anniversary dinner, was cold, the dishes long ago put away. It was November 13th, their tenth anniversary. Prohibition had still been in full swing when they had eloped. Benjie had been flush then. Her engagement ring was a two-karat diamond in a white gold setting. She held her hand out now, having saved the ring through the bad times, too. The night they'd eloped, she'd worn her mink stole over that light blue suit she loved. She smiled at the memory as she got up and put the glass in the sink. She wished Benjie hadn't stayed out late tonight, of all nights.

Things had changed for the Kalmowitzes since their elopement. When she had first met him in the late '20s, Benjie had been a big spender. Benjie and his cohorts were in on some of New York's hottest activities; that's when gangs were forming relationships with government officials; the docks were perpetual sites of violence and sinister intrigue; unsolved murders, prostitution, and child abuse were rampant. Amidst all this mayhem, Ruthie had found Benjie exciting. The danger, the menace, somehow, had thrilled her.

When Benjie and Label and their young Roznover cronies had first landed in this hubbub, immigrants with gut-clenching ambition and few legitimate options struggled to survive, they could hardly avoid becoming part of it all; they learned to take advantage of whatever opportunities presented themselves. Many boys who spoke no English, burning for adventure and success, began by running errands on the Lower East Side of Manhattan, errands that often included delivery of numbers receipts, cash payoffs, even guns. Pretty soon, they made enough money to get a cheap apartment in Brownsville where they found other opportunities. Benjie liked the street life. On the corner of Lavonia and Saratoga, he met kids who taught him things Label mostly stayed away from, like how to use the guns they sometimes delivered.

These Brownsville boys soon became the arm of a large conglomerate that would eventually span the country and even, much later, the world. The Amboy Dukes, as they first called themselves, were the killer arm, which came to be known as

Murder Incorporated; the conglomerate it merged with was sometimes called the Mafia.

Salvatore Luciana, aka Charles "Lucky" Luciano, was chief overlord. Based in New York at the Waldorf Astoria as a year-round resident, Luciano lived under the name Charles Rose. His clout was unchallenged; he commanded protection from Tammany Hall, wielded influence in Albany, was owed the allegiance of judges he'd hand-picked in backroom meetings. His was the first organized racketeering combine to control criminal enterprises all over the country. Originally a thief and narcotics runner on the Lower East Side of New York, as well as a messenger and solicitor for brothels, Luciano now controlled every crooked enterprise in the United States.

With the merger of the Mafia and Murder Incorporated—made up largely of Brownsville Jews and Italians—Luciano got rid of costly and complicated inter-mob warfare. Now crime machines could work together on a national scale. The members of Murder Inc, the mob's official executioners, were put on retainer to kill only those who threatened this empire. The leader of the Brownsville gang was a young man named Abe "Kid Twist" Reles. Benjie was his frequent driver.

Albert Anastasia, the main executioner, supervised Reles and his killers. Louis "Lepke" Buchalter commanded the group. Gang murder became an organized assembly-line, a hierarchy operating like modern big business. Hired killers from the killing arm of the Mafia went all over the country, their hits sustaining the rackets in all of the nation's industrialized cities. Within a decade, Murder Inc committed some one thousand contract killings. Benjie was an integral part of this organization.

But Benjie, always a big spender when things were good, had not put aside enough for bad times. When Repeal of Prohibition came in the midst of the country's worst depression, the Kalmowitzes weren't prepared. Jobs dried up for freelancers like Benjie. The couple managed for a while by cutting expenses. They moved from the spacious apartment on Ocean Avenue to the small, dark walk-up they still lived in on Avenue P. Then Tom Dewey began his investigations and Lepke went into hiding. That meant everyone had to lie low. Benjie took a job in the garment industry as a messenger.

But he still did a few jobs once in a while. Lepke in hiding was crazy, scared that every goon would turn on him. Bodies were turning up everywhere, in vacant lots on every block, the trunks of abandoned cars, ditches. Benjie got work this way, getting rid of the people who made Lepke nervous. He was trying, Lepke, to get rid of anyone who might be a witness, but all the killing was scaring everyone. People who might not have informed were turning themselves in just to steer clear of his killing squad. And the cops still searched everywhere for Lepke.

Benjie and Ruth thought things couldn't get worse, but then Abe Reles turned himself in and started talking. Everyone ran or hid out. The Kalmowitzes' social life dried up. They used to go out to restaurants every Saturday night with four other couples. Even when things got bad, they still used to get together at least once a week, maybe at a local deli or a club or at someone's house. But lately no one was around. The boys were gone, if not in hiding, then probably dead; the girls hocked their furs and their diamonds. Ruthie still managed to save a few things, but she missed the old days.

Now she worried about Benjie. Had someone—one of the boys, a cop—picked him up? Was he on a job? She was good about his work; she generally understood she had to keep quiet and sit tight. But now she wished he could at least make a phone call and let her know what was happening.

She washed out the glass, dried it, put it away, and made up her mind to stop worrying. Things were getting to her, too; she had to get hold of herself. She decided to go to bed. They would celebrate their anniversary when she awoke—she hoped.

When she woke up at ten o'clock, Benjie still hadn't come home. She dressed, had her coffee and went downstairs for a newspaper. The headlines were shocking. "Abe Reles Killed Trying to Escape." "Song Bird Can't Fly." She bought all the local papers and hurried home.

After reading every version of how and why Reles might have fallen or jumped or been shoved from the sixth-floor window of the Half Moon Hotel in Coney Island, Ruth understood it would probably be some time before she would see

The Amboy Duchess

Benjie again. She didn't know if Benjie had played any part in Reles's death, but she knew the cops would step up their efforts to haul in anyone remotely connected with Reles. Even if he hadn't been anywhere near Reles, he would get out of town.

She was right.

Benjie was gone more than a year.

* * * * *

The sirens screamed through the Brooklyn streets that morning, as I slept in our Flatbush apartment. The spine-chilling shrieks startled me awake.

That night my dreams had been of birthday parties. My best friend would be celebrating her ninth birthday after school and Aunt Golde and Uncle Dovid were there to take me to the party. They were visiting from Montreal because Avi, my dad, would be working for someone for a few nights—no one ever said what *kind* of work—and he'd asked them to stay with me. I went off to school in my plaid cotton dress, my handkerchief pinned to my shoulder, unaware of just how sinister those sirens actually were. I'd enjoyed the party over and over in my dreams, changing the dress I would wear, redoing my hair, with and without barrettes, in a ponytail, in braids. Which was lucky, because in real life, there was no party for me that day.

When I charged into the house after school, expecting my crisply ironed dress, my lacey socks, and my Mary Janes to be laid out on the bed, all I found were my somber-looking aunt and uncle, Dovid in my father's big chair, Golde on the couch, alert and watchful.

I stopped in the doorway, suddenly understanding that the sirens had been for us. I whirled around and fled. Whatever had happened to exchange the grim faces of my relatives for the raucous ones of my friends, I didn't want to hear about it.

I stayed away until dark.

I only went to sit on Mrs. DiGennaro's fire escape. She fed me supper, spaghetti and meatballs, and convinced me to go home finally, long after her first pleas that my aunt and uncle would be worried.

Poor Aunt Golde and Uncle Dovid greeted me with tears and hugs when I slunk back through the door, the last time I would enter that door, it turned out. After that, my home was with them, in an alternate universe, a different time. I was transplanted to an alien Eastern European 1900's-style *shtetl*, a twentieth century Catholic city in North America: Montreal. There, a teeming immigrant world did its best to imitate what it had known, its refugees holding onto all their baggage—their language, their religion, their fears—as the city battered them with its culture, though less brutally than the culture surrounding the *shtetl* had done.

I went to a new school, a religious school, though not my religion, a school more strange to me even than this new neighborhood, and I grew as some kind of weird hybrid: a New York Jewish street kid—who had been barely aware of my

213

Jewishness—transformed into a Canadian *Yid,* doomed forever to outsider status. Too often, the teacher caught me staring into space or looking out the window, daydreaming. My dreams were always the same: I imagined myself finding the *shtarker*, the *bulvon,* who killed my father.

What Ruth Kalmowitz didn't know was that Benjie was also in Canada. Like others, Benjie had worked his way up in the rackets. He had gone from breaking strikes to late night meetings in smoke-filled back rooms. He was a small part of the organization, but visible enough to be scared. Montreal was the town a lot of the boys hid out in. Benjie had connections there that some of the others didn't have; he had the Tannens. He hid out until his money was gone. Then he showed up at Dovid's house. He told him he was in trouble, though he couldn't say what, and needed help badly.

Dovid agreed to help him, though reluctantly. An avid fisherman, Dovid took Benjie to the backwoods cabin in northern Ontario that no one would be using in the cold months.

They rented a car, filled it with food and other supplies, and drove north. Every few weeks, Dovid went—ostensibly to fish, but really to see if Benjie had everything he needed. When the weather got warmer, he took Benjie out for a little recreation, teaching him the pleasures of fishing.

Seventeen

Winnie
1974

It was a couple of weeks since I'd met Jim Battle at Bryna Twombly's party and I'd given up expecting to hear from him. When he finally called, it took me a minute to remember who he was.

"Oh, the one who was stoned."

The silence lasted only a moment. "Yeah, that's right. And you're the one who knows all the fairy tales."

"Just one. Jack and the Beanstalk."

"Right. What are you doing?"

"When?"

"Now."

"Now I'm going upstairs and I'm going to take a bath."

"Come out and play instead."

"Look, Jim. Or whatever your name is. If you'll conform a little more to convention, maybe I'll . . ."

"Convention! I knew it! The woman follows the rules. That's why we're having such a hard time."

I held the phone away from my ear, looking at it, trying to decide if I should just hang up on him. "Look, what do you want?"

"I want to get together with you."

"Are you stoned again?"

"No."

"Then ask me for a date. A normal date."

Silence. Then, "I swear to god I don't know how."

"Oh, come on. A man like you . . ."

"I've been married for twenty years."

"You're married?!"

"No. I mean, I was. Not anymore. We just . . .You're the first woman I've tried to ask out."

"You know something? I don't believe you."

"It's true. People have asked *me* out. Women. And I've gone. But I don't know how to do this right. It's humiliating."

I pulled the phone over to the stairs and sat down.

"You there?" he asked.

I nodded. "Mmm-hmm."

"Why don't you believe me?"

"Why?! Because you're too arrogant. You know exactly what you're doing."

"Yeah, I look that way. But it's all a front. You know why it took me so long to call you? I thought you'd say no again."

"Again? What do you mean again?"

"Like you did in the parking lot."

"I gave you my phone number, didn't I?"

"Look, have pity. Tell me what to do and I'll do it."

"Ask me if I'd like to go out with you."

"Would you like to go out with me?"

"Sure."

"When?"

"How about Thursday evening?"

"Thursday? Thursday's so far away."

"It's not a couple of weeks."

"Touché. Thursday, then. Where will we go?"

"You'll take me out to dinner. To the nicest restaurant you know."

"You got it. Where do we meet?"

"Are you from Mars or something? Didn't you date your wife? You'll pick me up. Here."

"Okay. Where's 'here'?"

* * * * *

This time he was in jeans and a white T-shirt.

I stood in the open doorway, my black silk suit suddenly clinging inappropriately. I crossed my arms, and deliberately didn't ask him in.

"You coming?"

"You're impossible. Where do you plan to take me, a fast-food burger joint?"

"Don't you believe in women's lib?"

I cringed. I hated people calling the women's movement "women's lib." "What does that have to do with anything?"

"Men don't take women out anymore. They go somewhere that they both decide on and they both pay."

"I'm not going anywhere with you. I don't even like you. You're arrogant and crude and inconsiderate. And you're probably stoned again."

I shut the door on him and went back inside. A few minutes later I heard his car pulling out of the driveway. I'd never met anyone like him.

* * * * *

I was dreaming about crowds of women, pressing in on me, clamoring for something . . . The phone woke me. Annie was curled on the pillow next to me, a furry little ball, sound asleep, her tail circling up between her hind legs, her front paws tucked under her head. I glanced at the clock. Two a.m.

"Hello?"

"Hi."

"Who is this?"

"It's me. Jim.

"Oh, come on. What's going on? It's two o'clock."

"I know. I'm sorry. Really. I'm not as crude as you think."

"Then call me at a more reasonable time."

"I will. I just . . ."

"What?"

"I apologize. For this evening."

"Okay."

"Does that mean, okay, you accept my apology? Or okay, you don't?"

"Why does it matter?"

"I don't know. I can't get you out of my head."

"Oh, bull."

"Can we start again?"

"How?"

"Let's meet somewhere. Tomorrow. After work."

The nerve!

"What do you say?"

I coughed. "Okay . . . Where?"

* * * * *

Looking down the block from Rockefeller Plaza at 52nd Street to the bank on 48th, you couldn't miss being hit in the eye by the large chartreuse poster in Allerton's front window. It was a little different from the sign we had up the night of the first seminar. This one, much bigger, said in huge black capital letters, "WINNIE CHARLES IS HERE." Under that, in only slightly smaller letters, it said: "WE ARE THE BANK THAT CATERS TO WOMEN'S FINANCIAL AND BUSINESS NEEDS" Both signs had been Stu's idea. The seminars—and I—were getting so much public acclaim, he'd decided to capitalize on them, use them as an antidote to the notoriety the bank had earned before my arrival.

It hit me as I walked toward it after lunch, that I could hardly be more visible.

How was I going to hide out?

The women's business management classes were a stupendous hit, as if New York had been waiting for this phase of the women's movement to get going. Besides being called every day by newspaper, radio and TV reporters, I was speaking at conferences, colleges, community centers. A book was being dedicated to me by one of the seminar participants who ran a business called Super Girls. McGraw Hill was about to publish a book about successful career women that included a section about me. Suddenly I was *the* authority on women and money. I was even offered—and accepted—an invitation by Pam Freeman to speak after my vacation at one of the Woman Executive dinners. Other companies called, as well, investment firms, insurance companies. Their perception, from all the newspaper and magazine articles—appearing almost daily, it seemed—was that I knew how to sell financial products to women. And they all suddenly wanted to use my knowledge to sell *their* products. Overnight, women had gone from being creatures who needed husbands to protect them from the complications of finance to being the latest hot market in financial services. With all those women starting their own businesses, and with the divorce rate soaring through the roof, must have come the insight that women could handle their own insurance policies and investment portfolios. There was also a rumor that a bank for women would be opening soon. Would they turn *men* away, I wondered. "No, we can't lend to you because you're a man"?

My days were now filled, too, with calls from more and more women who wanted to attend the seminars, and I was busy making plans for classes that were scheduled for the following year. Women in New York who owned their own businesses came to Allerton to open accounts or apply for loans before they tried anywhere else. They refused to see any of the bank's loan officers, who were all men. They would talk only to me. If I couldn't see them, they would leave. So Stu promoted me. Not with any raise in pay, just in status. I would now be an officer of the bank, assistant treasurer. I had finished the Dun and Bradstreet course and was a bona fide loan officer, only I was making five thousand a year less than any of the other loan officers, all men.

I was looking forward to visiting Aunt Golde and Uncle Dovid in Montreal for my vacation; it was coming up soon. No one would know where I'd be. That way, if I found anything proving shady activities, or if Benjie were to suddenly realize who I was, I'd be safe.

This morning I'd been too busy to look in the files. Every time I'd hung up from a call, someone else had stopped by, or it was time for my eleven a.m. appointment, or I had papers to fill out. At lunchtime, I had to rush over to tape a radio show.

Now I made up my mind I would head down to the storeroom at the end of the day. I was meeting Jim at eight and would have lots of time after everyone left the bank to do some investigating. Maybe I was getting involved in things I'd better stay away from. But I was fast becoming *the* spokesperson for Allerton, its most public representative. I had to know what kind of bank this really was.

The afternoon was just as hectic as the morning had been. By five o'clock I was itching to start my search of the files. This time, at least, I knew which file cabinet to look through, the one Kalmowitz had been so anxious to check out. I was willing to bet that was where I'd find what I was looking for. The last *Voice* articles had said that so far the State Banking Commission's investigation of Allerton had yielded no evidence of wrong doing. But how could the commissioners have missed those payroll sheets? Could someone be paying them off? Was Melba being paid off? Was Stu? Were they all in it together? Whatever *it* was?

Stu was the last to leave. He stopped at my desk on his way out and asked what I was still doing in the bank at five thirty p.m.

"I have some work to catch up on," I replied. "I've been so busy, my paper-work has piled up."

"I'll wait for you. Give you a lift home," he offered.

"Thanks, but no." I shook my head for emphasis. "I have a date later, here in the city."

His frown told me to expect some kind of reprisal. I was beginning to learn his pattern when he didn't get his way. One day, a reporter from the *Post* called and asked to interview him. He'd seen her all right. He thought she wanted to interview him as the president who was going to clean up Allerton. But all she wanted to talk about was those women's seminars his bank was sponsoring. Going against his own inclinations to cash in on them, he told her the seminars were a dismal failure, not bringing any business to the bank, and that women were poor credit risks anyway. And that was what the paper printed. Another time—right after I refused to stay in the city after work and have dinner with him—he threatened to send me to one of the bank's Brooklyn branches—permanently. I would have to suspend the seminars if he sent me there; most of the women were from Manhattan, The Bronx, Westchester, Connecticut or Jersey. None of them would travel to Brooklyn. He also turned down my request for a pay increase. That was after I told him I wasn't interested in having an affair with him. My work, he said, was not bringing the bank any money and, therefore, it couldn't afford to pay me any more. When I reminded him of how much it would have cost Allerton to pay for the publicity and the new image my work was giving the bank, he was adamant. "I did you a favor hiring you," he'd said. "You should be more grateful." I didn't remind him that the other loan officers were making more than I was.

Now he had another concern. "I don't like you staying here alone and locking up by yourself. This is a bank, not an office."

"I close up myself every time we hold a seminar. And it's much later then."

"I know. And I'm not sure I like that either."

"Don't worry. I'll be all right."

After he left, the bank was quiet, spooky even, and I wondered if I had made the right decision to stay. After all, something *could* happen, someone could break in, for example, though I knew by now that the vault was empty. The money was brought in each morning by Brinks and picked up again in the late afternoon. Robbing a bank would not be what it was when Bonnie and Clyde were doing it. Only the safe deposit boxes would yield any rewards.

I put my purse in the bottom drawer of my desk and locked the desk. No point in tempting anyone who might look in the window. People tended to peer in more often these days with the chartreuse sign plastered up there, even pressing their noses against the glass and shading their eyes to see more clearly.

Downstairs I headed straight for the file cabinet Kalmowitz had searched, and pulled open the drawer I thought he had gone through. It was jammed with folders. "Internal

Correspondence" and "External Correspondence" for each of the
ten board members, each of the bank's executive officers: Stu,
Bobbie, John O'Connor, Pete Hanlon, and for each of the other
three loan officers. So far, no one had had a chance to add a
folder with my name on it. For now I kept my own rapidly
expanding files in the small cabinet next to my desk. I went
through the contents of each folder slowly, carefully, examining
each memo, each letter, for any bit of information that might
enlighten me.

Most of the correspondence I found was routine bank
business. Thank-you letters to customers, memos informing the
board of directors of new loan applications. Many of these had
the same last name as one I had seen on the payroll sheets,
DiNatale, but with different first names. That was interesting,
but not proof of anything. Still, I pulled out a bunch of them. In
Stu's folders I found two interesting pieces of correspondence.
One was a memo to Stu from Melba urging him to keep
Kalmowitz from "throwing more good loan money after bad to
those hoods in Brooklyn." The other was a letter from Stu to
Vincent DiNatale, Manhattan's Republican County leader,
thanking him for "the windfall." I pulled these, as well.

It was getting late, close to seven o'clock, and I would
have to get going soon. I had gone through only half the drawer. I
decided to copy everything that was left, along with the few
pieces I'd pulled, and take the photostats home to look them over

more carefully. Making all the copies and replacing the originals took until seven thirty.

I met Jim at Arlette's. He was at the bar, waiting, when I got there.

"So, I see you *can* be more conventional when you want to be. This is a nice place."

Beyond the bar, round tables, mostly small and intimate, were covered with gracefully draped to-the-floor white tablecloths and lit by candlelight. A crystal chandelier shone dimly in the center of the domed ceiling. On each table was a single flower, a freshly cut yellow rose. A pianist in the corner between the bar and the dining room played soft, mellow jazz.

"You look beautiful," he replied.

I grinned. I was wearing the same black silk suit I had had on when he came to the house, the kind sales ladies tell you can be "dressed up or down," depending on the occasion. Today I had dressed it down for work with a pair of low-heeled black pumps I'd left in my desk drawer and a pair of pearl earring studs. I was more dressed up this evening with black sling-backed high heels and dangling crystal earrings, to match the chandelier, I thought, touching one earring. I tilted my head to one side and my eyes met his. God, it's been a long time since I'd flirted with anyone, I thought. Was I doing it right? When he grinned back, I decided I was.

226

"What would you like to drink while we're waiting for our table?" he asked.

"Bloody Mary."

Only two other people were at the bar, an older man, in his sixties maybe, probably waiting for someone, and a twenty-something man with longish hair who was flirting with the good-looking bartender. Actors, I decided. Jim managed to get the bartender's attention and he ordered my drink.

"I understand you're a newsman?"

"You *understand*? Don't you watch TV?"

"Sure, sometimes. I guess I may have seen you."

He was leaning one elbow on the bar, his foot on the rung of the nearest stool, and was playing with a napkin, twisting it and tying it into a knot. Had I said the wrong thing? Should I have pretended I knew exactly who he was, watched him every night, was a big fan? He didn't say anything for a moment as he studied me with those intense black eyes.

He shook his head as if he wasn't sure if he should be insulted that I *wasn't* a fan; then he grinned. "I've seen *you*," he said. "All over the place lately."

I felt my face flush as I nodded. "Mmm," was all I could say.

"I'm curious. How did you come up with the idea to run a women's program at a bank?"

"Run a women's program?"

"Isn't that what you're doing?"

"I didn't think of it that way, but yes, I guess that's what I'm doing."

He narrowed his eyes and scrutinized me again. "It's interesting. How long have you been a feminist banker?"

There it was again. Feminist banker. I was liking the sound of that less and less, but I didn't know why. My drink came and I picked it up, glad to have something to do with my hands. "Is this an interview?" I asked.

Now he grinned. "I don't know. My producer did want me to find out what you're doing. It wasn't my idea. My idea was—very different."

"Is that right? What was your idea?"

He flushed. "I'm sorry. I'm being stupid again. I feel all tongue-tied with you, I don't know why."

Now I was the one to do the scrutinizing as I sipped. Somehow we were both out of our element. What was *my* element? The classroom? The bank? The kitchen? Surely not a bar with a sophisticated and good-looking man? Why was *he* having trouble? I had no idea.

At that moment, the maitre d' approached and told Jim our table was ready.

Jim put his hand on my back, lightly, and steered me toward the dining room. "I'm starved," he said. "I hope you brought your appetite with you."

The maitre d' led us to a table in the corner, where the light was even dimmer than in the rest of the room. I wondered if this notorious iconoclast was actually wooing me.

We were handed huge menus, but he took mine from me, gently. "Would you mind very much if I order for both of us? I know the chef and he'll give me things that aren't on the menu." It must have been the stricken look on my face that made him add: "I promise not to ask for anything you don't like."

I grinned again. "Sure, okay." Why spoil his fun? I didn't like grinning so much, though. It reminded me of when I was a little girl and my uncles used to order me to "smile pretty" for them. But smiling seemed to be the only response to this suddenly chivalrous behavior of his, so different from the way he'd behaved the other two times I'd seen him. Or was it? He still seemed too sure of himself. And controlling.

"I really do want to hear about the work you're doing," he said after ordering with my approval. "For myself, because I'm interested. And, partly, I'll admit, to satisfy the curiosity of my producer. Have you been a banker very long?"

I shook my head and laughed. "No. Only a few months. I'm a graduate school dropout."

"Come on. What do you mean?"

"I needed a job and Allerton's president offered me one."

"This is getting intriguing."

"You want the story of my life."

"Okay. That sounds good. Tell me the story of your life. First, you're divorced, I take it."

"Oh." The sudden switch to my marital status flustered me. "Right."

"Recently?"

I nodded, looking down at my fork. I guessed dating was going to be like this; you have to tell your "story" to everyone you go out with. "Richie left nearly a year ago." I looked up at him. "We haven't gotten along for a while. He was itching to get away, be free, and, I guess I was, too, in a way. Anyway, we wanted different lives. He's a psychiatrist, he works for a research center that was moving its offices to the Florida Keys. That just up his alley, he didn't even pause to ask if we'd like to go there, too. He took the opportunity to end the marriage. He lives on his boat, sees patients there when he's not at the research center. My kids are going there—to live with him on the boat—when camp ends. That's our deal; he gets six months with them and I get the other six months."

"Didn't you want to move to Florida?"

"He never asked. But no, I wouldn't have gone, really. We just don't get along. I need to live my own life. Here."

"What are your plans?"

Our salads and the bread arrived. I plunged my fork into the lettuce, though my appetite had disappeared.

"Oh, I don't know. I was so wrapped up in the anxiety after he left of how I would support the three of us, me and my two kids, I never even thought about . . . I don't know . . . what I *want*. I mean, I want to make a living, pay my bills. I want to survive."

"That can't be all you want. We're beyond the basic subsistence level."

"Well, you are, maybe. I don't know about myself."

There was that eye-narrowing scrutiny again. What did he see?

"What were you doing in graduate school?"

"I was studying Romance Languages, teaching French at Hunter College."

"Why couldn't you keep on doing that?"

"I was an instructor. I made a pittance. They exploit people like me, the school, and the regular faculty. Instructors, adjuncts, part-timers, non-tenured faculty. We're given the worst courses, low pay, no benefits, no job security of any kind. I could get four or five courses one semester, then one the next, or none. You can't support a family that way. As a second income it was fine—until I'd get my doctorate and a full-time job. But those are getting scarcer and scarcer, full-time jobs, in liberal arts. In a few years part-timers may be the only faculty there are. The schools are realizing they've got a good source of cheap labor. I can see them just getting rid of all the regular faculty by attrition. In the public colleges, anyway."

"So, here you are, a banker. Sounds like a far cry from teaching French."

"Stu, my neighbor—his ex-wife lives across the street from me—offered me this job, he said he'd train me to sell the bank's services."

"Where did the women's thing come from?"

"That was my idea. It just . . . took on."

He laughed. "Just took on! I'll say. Pretty good idea. Do you always hit on just the thing that will 'take on'?"

"Always? No, of course not. This was a fluke. It just happened."

"Nothing 'just happens.' I think you have some kind of knack you aren't aware of yet."

I didn't tell him about Pam, how I'd stolen the idea from her.

"I'd like to do a story about the bank."

"Oh, sure. Jump on the bandwagon. Women bankers are hot . . ."

He didn't let me finish. Laughing, he cut me off. "No, I've got a different story in mind."

"What story?" Now that I was starting to like him, a small voice inside nagged at me: was he only interested in me for my story?

"There's something strange, don't you think, about a bank with that board of directors letting you run a women's program? You know, 'the Mafia and the feminist.' That kind of thing."

I didn't know how to answer him. That's just what I'd been thinking. But that wasn't the kind of story I wanted anyone to do about my seminars. Still, if what I'd stumbled on in that file was what I thought it was, maybe my clients needed to know about it. I'd have to give his suggestion some thought.

"I'll talk to Stu," I hedged. "I'll see what he thinks about your doing a story. What about you?" I changed the subject. "When did you get divorced?"

"Well, I'm not exactly divorced . . ."

"What?! You said you were . . ."

"No, I never said that . . ."

"Oh, come on."

"Actually, I don't recall saying much. This is my situation: I'm separated. Officially. We've been apart for more than a year. We'll have the divorce in a few months. We're still arguing things out. Honest!"

"Where is she?"

"In Blue Wood."

"In town? You lived there and I didn't know you?"

"Do you know everyone in town?"

"Where did you, does she, live?"

"On the hill."

"You said that's where *you* live."

"I do. There's more than one house up there."

"The hill" was the most exclusive section of Blue Wood. The homes were mainly large estates. I really *was* out of my element. Suddenly I felt uneasy. Did my hair look all right? Had I worn the right earrings? I touched my crystal earring again. Then I felt annoyed with myself. Why should I care? I tossed my hair back—though I have the kind of hair that never moves when I do that, like Bette Midler; it's a gesture I picked up from the movies. I wasn't going to let myself be intimidated, not by him, especially not by the thought of his success. I straightened myself in my seat, wriggled and sat up taller. I coughed and took a small sip of my drink.

"Are you okay?"

I nodded, swallowing. "Yes. Of course. Sure."

"What's the matter?"

"Nothing. I'm fine. Oh, here's our food." The waiter was coming from across the room. "Good, I'm starving." I shoved my salad and bread plate back to make room for the other food, "busy work" to give myself something to do.

"Tell me more about yourself," I said. "Do you have kids?"

"Two. Five and Seven. Chris and Jody."

"No kidding? Chris and Jody. Boys? Girls?"

He laughed. "Jody's a girl, she's five. Chris, the boy, is seven." His voice was softer than it had been at any time before.

"Do you see them often?"

"Sure. They live with me."

"They live with *you*? How come?"

"Marabelle, my wife, didn't want them. She's got her lover living there now. Vera. And Vera's very young. Marabelle felt Vera couldn't handle raising children." Now he got busy, pulling a piece of bread from the bread basket, buttering it, breaking off pieces of it, letting the crumbs fall into his glass, or wherever, even onto his lap.

"Oh." I was momentarily jolted. I hadn't expected him to confess to any vulnerabilities.

"It's not like we had a perfect marriage. I've been struggling . . . trying to figure out . . . I don't know . . . what was wrong . . . for years. How much is me, how much is her. I still don't really know exactly what happened. I mean, for example, her being with a woman. Is that the ultimate rejection of men, of me? One question is, has she always been a lesbian? I don't know what to think. Did I *drive* her to it? That sounds pretty egotistical, and I don't believe it. But who knows what I may have done wrong . . ."

235

The waiter was setting up a stand for his tray. Jim half stood, brushed the crumbs off his lap. "I'm glad to see the food," he said irrelevantly. "Anyway," he said, sitting down again, "I'm glad I've got my kids, at least. I couldn't have stood losing them or even having them only part-time."

"How do you manage?" I asked him, somewhat stupidly, when the waiter had gone. "How do you run a household by yourself, with two kids, and handle such a demanding job?"

"Don't *you* do it? Everyone asks me that! It pisses me off. Women do it all the time. Why can't I?"

"Well, they're so young, your kids," I said lamely.

"Actually, I guess I can do it more easily than a lot of people. For one thing, I work nights. I can get the kids ready and take them to school because I'm home all morning. Then I have a babysitter who comes in when I leave and she picks Jody up at school. Chris comes home by bus. The babysitter meets the bus, makes them dinner, puts them to bed . . ."

"Oh, I see. Women do *that* all the time."

"Ah, don't. Believe me, it's just as hard with a babysitter. I still make all the decisions, stay home when anyone is sick, rush back for emergencies, shop for food. I do just about everything you do. I leave strict instructions for the babysitter. And the kids know I'm there for them."

236

The Amboy Duchess

I was starting to wonder how he'd gotten his bad reputation. My view of him as arrogant and flip was changing.

He drove me home, stopped in the driveway and waited, his hands gripping the wheel, the engine running.

"Would you like to come in?"

"I thought you'd never ask." He shut the motor, pulled out the key and opened the car door. "Coming?" He looked back at me, still sitting there wondering what I was getting into.

"You sure now?" I laughed, getting out of the car finally.

In the house, he grabbed my arm before I had a chance to turn on the light, turned me around to face him and looked into my eyes for a long intense moment. Then he leaned his face into my hair, pulled me closer, and sighed. It felt so good. I put my arms around his back and snuggled into his chest. Then I lifted my face to him. His lips were warm and soft. I slid my tongue into his mouth and pulled him closer, suddenly wanting him.

We made love first in the living room still without any lights, both of us hurrying, frantic to get our clothes off. Then we went upstairs to the bedroom and we made love again, this time more slowly. Afterward we lay entwined, stroking each other, silent for a while.

"Can I stay for the night?" he asked.

I sat up on my elbow. "What about your kids?"

237

"They're with Marabelle tonight. I asked her to keep them there and spend the day with them tomorrow. I was hoping you'd want me to stay."

I smiled at him, his blond hair strewn on the pillow, fanned out like cornsilk. He really *was* too good-looking. I leaned down and kissed him, lightly, on his lips, his forehead, his cheek, touched his hair with my fingertips, so unfamiliar.

I tried to imagine the morning, getting up together. My morning rush didn't include coffee with a stranger.

"I'm sorry, Jim. I can't let you stay. Not yet. My morning is too crazy. And I'm not sure I'd get any sleep with you here."

* * * * *

The bouquet I found on my desk Monday morning was so impressive I could sense everyone in the bank talking about it. A huge bunch of spring flowers cascaded around two dozen yellow roses standing straight and proud in a Chinese vase. The switchboard operator had taken them from the delivery truck first thing in the morning because she was the first one in after Gus. Everyone's eyes were on me as I stopped a foot from my desk to take in the effect. The aroma was palpable, thick enough to swim through. I reached for the card.

"I hope this is conventional enough," it read. No signature.

I looked around, felt my face grow warm as if everyone would surely know what I'd done to deserve this, and Alison smiled. "Is it your birthday?" she asked.

I smiled back. "Just a present," I answered.

I wondered if Stu was in yet. When I checked with Margaret, I found out he wasn't expected until late in the afternoon. I told her about Jim's offer to interview us and asked her to set it up for us.

* * * * *

Later in the afternoon, Pam Freeman appeared at my desk.

"Hi!"

I whirled around. I hadn't seen her come in and I was startled, more by who was standing there than by the surprise. I still felt guilty about having stolen her idea for the seminars for women business owners even though she'd forgotten about it long ago—if it had ever even bothered her at all. She was smiling, holding on to the chair next to my desk.

"Mind if I sit down? The most exciting thing just happened!"

She told me all about it. She'd gone downstairs to pick up her mail this morning and she'd suddenly had a premonition. *Something good is about to happen,* she told herself.

When she opened the box, it was empty except for one official-looking envelope. She reached for it, scanning the return address as she slid it out. It said: Minority Enterprises Small Business Investment Corporation. *MESBIC.*

Her heart started beating very fast. She couldn't wait to get upstairs and open it.

"What did you think it *was*?" I asked.

"It was that application I told you about that I sent the SBA, it seemed like only days ago! I was afraid to open it even though I really wanted to rip it open right away."

She told me again about her plan to use her investment company to fund minority businesses, especially those run by women, starting with her own three companies. One of the perks offered to small minority-owned businesses was a program that let them get as much as four federal dollars for every dollar they put up themselves.

In the elevator, all the way up to the penthouse, Pam said, she had held the envelope as if it might burn her.

"When I was a kid, I used to play a game; I'd close my eyes when I got home from school, hoping there'd be a surprise for me when I opened the door. Once, my mom bought me a doll I'd wanted and she'd set it on the couch between the pillows so I'd see it as soon as I walked in. I used to try to will more surprises, but that was the only time it happened. But I still play the game. And today it worked again!"

She told me she'd unlocked the door this morning, and she'd gone in slowly, put the envelope down on the sideboard in the foyer, forced herself to go to her bedroom and kick off her shoes, then change into a pair of shorts before letting herself open the envelope.

"Okay," she had finally told herself. "Now I'm ready."

Back in the foyer, she'd picked up the envelope and carried it to her desk. She'd set it down and stood there looking at it. Was her future about to open up? Finally, she'd opened the top drawer and pulled out the silver letter opener. "Stop stalling. Open the goddamn thing!"

The ripped-open envelope lay on the desk and the letter was in her hand. She scanned it quickly until she got to the part she was looking for.

" . . . and so it is with pleasure that we inform you that your license will arrive within ten days . . ."

She was in! The Small Business Administration was licensing her company, The Women's First Investment Corporation, to act as a conduit and apply for loan applications for women who wanted to start their own businesses. Now those corporations she had set up could be funded.

"And so, I'd like to open an account for my investment firm."

She had a nice large deposit all ready. She was the first of my women customers to match many of the men when it came to the size of her account—and the scope of her plans.

* * * * *

Stu came in just as I was getting ready to leave for the day. He waved and I saw him take in the fact that those flowers overwhelmed my desk.

I wondered if he knew about the huge account Pam Freeman had opened earlier.

Maybe he would leave me alone now, I thought.

Eighteen

Label
1946

They arrive in the middle of the night, a phone call in the dark, their Yiddish unfamiliar. "Maybe you don't know us, but we are your cousins."

A new challenge for Label, who by now is sure he can take care of anything. A driver is summoned to get them from the city and bring them—immediately—to Scarsdale. Then the call goes out to the rest of the family. This will need a meeting, a communal decision.

Now they sit, a week later, in the center of Label's couch, after sleep and food and bathing. In their European clothing and hairstyles—the dark clothes of poor people, their blond hair reminding everyone of war movies, straight, pulled back, simple—they lean against one another for support. They are worn out, yet strong in some deep way no one fathoms; a semicircle of Tannen eyes behold them with bewilderment, curiosity, awe.

243

He, grizzled, the man, past forty, nearing fifty maybe. She, very young, maybe early twenties, no more, though she looks much less, so fragile and pale, so thin. It is Eva with Ruben, Sender Tannen's son. Survivors of the war.

Label can't take his eyes off her.

Eva and Ruben met in the Polish underground where Ruben was stationed. The two worked together in field hospitals, and after the war, thanks to Jan Berendt, were among those who made it to America, and finally to Label's living room in Scarsdale.

They brought Asher the news he hungered for, yet feared, about the rest of the family. Sender, his wife and their younger children were among those murdered in one of the worst slaughters of the war. Though he had helped shape the dream, Sender Tannen never got to see his Jewish traditions transplanted to Mediterranean soil.

As resisters, Ruben and Eva had learned what happened to the "deportees." What they learned, and now told the family in my uncle Label's living room, was that no one from Roznov had survived, and few did from Czernowitz or the surrounding Bucovina area. In the section of Warsaw that Eva had come from, resisters waged a fierce war, were defeated, the ghetto destroyed.

But Eva and Ruben survived.

The Amboy Duchess

As they tell their stories, Eva can feel the Tannens' baffled scrutiny, as the two survivors lean against each other, holding one another up, like Raggedy Ann and Andy.

What to make of this pair, these reminders that survival is not a foregone conclusion, reminders of all those others who did not make it to America? What to do with them? How to think of them? How to make it up to them for the survival, the flourishing, of this part of the Tannen clan?

The Amboy Duchess

Nineteen

Eva, Warsaw
1939

She called herself Wanda. Wanda Helena Honatyka. Just
for the war. It was his idea, the jeweler she met right after her
escape. His name was Jan Berendt.

The escape was not the sort one boasts about, she felt, an
exploit, an adventurous escapade; it was, simply, a slinking away,
a fearsome walk to nowhere. She wasn't so much fleeing as
slipping into the unknown, wandering as far as she could from
that overcrowded train—the purpose of which had suddenly
become so clear to her—and, finally, from the rifle aimed at her
back.

Out of the ghetto she was alone, a fourteen-year-old
alien in her own city, unfamiliar with the streets, acquainted with
no one. Where she would eat, go to the bathroom, lie down, she
had no idea. Even her favorite doll lay abandoned on the bed she
would never see again, her parents and Chanah, her older sister,
herded away by booted soldiers while she was around the corner

247

at her aunt's house. She had gone after supper from Ogrodowa Street, where the family had sat on blankets, used as beds, to her aunt's house at Dzilva Street #7 for the candy her aunt had promised.

When she came back, wooden barricades blocked the street. German soldiers and the Jewish police, the ones without guns, told her that everyone was being shipped to the work camp. She ran back to her aunt's house, but they, too, were gone. Eva ran, then, to the station as fast as she could; she didn't want to be left behind.

They were just loading passengers when she got there, and she ran back and forth alongside the train, frantically craning her neck to see behind all the standing bodies, each jostling for a few more inches of space. She was hot and thirsty. There were thousands of people. Where were they, she wondered, her Mamma and Pappa? Already she missed them, felt the pain of aloneness in her chest, the panic, the terror. Germans, not Gestapo, she could tell because they were old, maybe forty, were counting heads, shoving people aboard the different boxcars. She stopped at one to see if Mamma, Pappa, and Chanah were on it. Were they in the back? She stood on her toes to see. Finally, she climbed on board Number 15 with a woman who held a screaming infant to her chest.

"Shhhh shhhh," the woman tried to comfort the baby. Then she saw Eva climbing up with her. A pair of the Germans on the platform had stopped shoving people onto the train and were pointing at Eva and talking about her.

"Look at that blonde hair and those big eyes," one said. "So blue. Beautiful. She doesn't look like a Jew."

"You!" the other one yelled at her. "Are you Jewish? Where is your armband?!"

The woman with the baby put a hand on Eva's arm. Eva, mute from the panic and the loneliness, willed the tears not to fall. She had refused to wear the yellow armband with the Star of David that would signify she was Jewish. It was nearly as demeaning as stripping with everyone in the same room, which they made the Jews do to be sure they had no lice, or shaving her head, as she once had to do, also, last year. Her mother always yelled at her, frantic with fear, "They'll put you in jail!" when she defiantly refused to be marked by the shameful insignia. She had told her mother she didn't care, she wouldn't wear such a thing. Now she was terrified. What would these men do to her?

"I ... I haven't got one ..." she started to whisper.

"Get off the train," the woman with the baby ordered, giving her a shove.

"I have to find my parents . . ." Still whispering.

"Your parents!" the woman hissed. "You will never find them. We're all dead people here. Get off. *Schnell*! Save yourself! Tell them you're not Jewish! You were just visiting a Jewish friend and got stuck here. *Schnell, schnell!* We're all going to the camp and there they'll kills us. All of us. Save yourself, little one!"

She felt herself being shoved toward the opening, then off the boxcar and down onto the platform, even as she grasped at the woman's skirt. She held on with her fingernails as if this would be the last bit of comfort she would ever know. Falling onto the wooden slats, she watched as the two soldiers who had been appraising her came closer. She stood up slowly and brushed off her skirt.

The younger of the two came closer. *"Ja? Vie gaidst du?"* She met his gaze. "Home."

He smiled at the beautiful young girl. "Home? And where is that?"

She was silent. How could she say where she lived? She had never stepped foot out of the ghetto. She pointed, her finger making an arc toward the mysterious world out there, the world teeming with everything alien, her eyes looking down toward the ground.

"What are you doing on this train? Only Jews are here."

"I was looking for my friend. I thought she would be on the train. I . . . I wanted to get something she owes me."

He circled her, lifted one blonde braid and let it drop down her back again. He nodded.

The Amboy Duchess

"Go home, then!" he said after a moment, lifting his rifle as he spoke, getting ready to take aim.

She stood, paralyzed. Perhaps after she started walking he would shoot her in the back. She had heard stories like that. And, anyway, where would she go? If she left now she would miss the train to Auschwitz. And then maybe she would never find her parents.

"*Go!*" He tapped his feet in a mock run, running in place so she would see he meant business.

She moved slowly at first, then more quickly, waiting for the gun to go off, the bullet to pierce her between her shoulder blades, wondering what it would feel like, if it would hurt for very long, or if she would die before feeling it. But no gun went off.

Now it was Wednesday. She was at the train station on the Aryan side for two days, wandering around in the crowds during the day, sleeping on a bench at night, watching the people, hoping to see someone leave some food on a bench. Her stomach long ago started to feel as if it were turning inside out. More than anything she was thirsty. She knew she couldn't survive there much longer.

She walked back toward the ghetto, afraid to be on these streets without the papers she knew she was supposed to have. But, after all, what could they do to her? If they picked her up she would simply say she was Jewish and then maybe they would send her to Auschwitz and she would find her parents.

As she walked she looked at the stores she had never seen before. A jewelry store on the other side of the street had a sign in the window: "We buy gold jewelry." Maybe they would like her watch.

Maybe they would! Maybe they would buy it! Then she could buy some food!

She went into the shop and timidly approached the man behind the counter.

"I want to sell my watch," she said in a loud voice.

"Your watch? What kind of watch can you have, little one?"

She held her wrist up so he could see the watch. He took her arm, adjusted a little black microscope that he held between his nose and his eye, and examined the watch.

"Is this yours?" he asked when he was finished.

"I didn't steal it," she said, tilting her chin up boldly.

He took the microscope out of his eye and scrutinized her, his soft gray eyes seeming to see things she would rather keep to herself.

He dropped her arm and told her to come to the back of the shop. She followed him because what else could she do?

In the back, he motioned to her to sit down at a table.

"Are you running away from home, *kint*?" His voice was gentle. It reminded her of her father's voice. For the first time in days her eyes watered and she could feel the sobs coming that she unconsciously held back. She shook her head, no.

"No? Then why does a lovely young girl try to sell her watch? Is your poor old mother sick and you are trying to help her?"

Now his voice was sarcastic, as if he would not believe her if she would tell him such a story.

Again she shook her head, no.

He sat down on the other side of the table, opposite where she was sitting, leaned his arms on the table and, with his head very close to hers, said in a soft, but ominous, voice: "What do you want?"

"I want something to eat," she said, the words coming out with sobs. "I'm thirsty. I have no place to go. My family—my family—is—is gone. They took them away."

"Who took them away?"

"The Germans. The soldiers."

She felt the tears wetting her face, a cascade of them running from her eyes, dropping to her hands. Looking at him through them he was blurred, but she could see him waiting to hear more, waiting calmly, unmoving. He didn't look shocked or frightened or angry. He didn't jumped to his feet, run to call a soldier, put his hand to his mouth. She had to trust him. She had no choice.

He sat back, nodded, appraised her and said, gently: "Tell me your story."

"I'm Jewish."

Eva told Jan Berendt her story and he told her his. A Christian member of the Polish underground, Jan, along with other Poles, helped Jews resist the Nazis.

He took Eva home, but kept her hidden, bringing her food, because his family didn't know of his extracurricular activities. After a time, he brought her to meetings. When she was sixteen, the Polish resisters trained her to be a nurse and she worked with underground forces in field hospitals until the end of the war.

Part Two

The Amboy Duchess

Twenty

At the time Jan Berendt was rescuing Eva, I was still a little girl in Brooklyn.

In Europe, Hitler had become Chancellor, having spent a good deal of time training for the job, honing his barbarism, pondering and writing *Mein Kampf* and becoming a master politico.

On the western continent, Jewish traditions were changing. Avi fell in love with my American-born mother and married her, thinking the family would look up to him as they did to Label, not for wealth, but for being more American. But his girdle territory diminished during the Depression. When I was born, my parents thought I would bring them luck. They named me Winnie, hoping it was their time to win something. But then, when I was two, my mother had an aneurysm and died. My father was left with the reminder that luck is always conditional.

He'd promised Stella he would never work for the greenhorn hoodlums she hated, just as he had refused to take

257

even the smallest part in Label's and Asher's thriving business. But now he needed money more than ever, partly for the housekeepers who took care of me. He started to do odd jobs, and occasionally drive, mostly for Benjie and his "guys." I knew, even before I was old enough for the housekeepers to stop coming, that the jobs and the driving were for missions that he'd rather not be part of and about which he wanted to know nothing.

He and Benjie cemented their business relationship, though, and Benjie relied on him more and more. When I was six, I was often left to fend for myself. I became street smart, shot marbles after school with the boys on the empty lot, watched the older boys shoot craps in the alley, listened to the boasts of even older kids who ran numbers, and did other favors for some of the "guys" who hung out in the back of the corner candy store.

For Jewish holidays, we'd go to Montreal, me and Avi—I called him that, like everyone else. The whole Tannen family— aunts and uncles and cousins and cousins of cousins, and other *mishpuchah* whose connections to each other were often too obscure for me to fathom, except that they all came from the same part of Europe, though no one could agree on whether it was Poland or Austria or Romania, just that it was "the Bucovina"—would gather in my grandparents' long, dark dining room in their narrow little house. I could never follow the political changes that made the study of geography in that part of the world a little like keeping track of a jigsaw puzzle made of Silly Putty. All I understood was that they had, most of them, known one another in Europe, having come from the same town or from nearby villages, and they regarded each other as family, though the word "*mishpuchah*" seemed to have a much wider meaning than the word "family" did in English, including in it even former neighbors and present business partners.

The men would sit around the long table after dinner, sipping their schnapps, and they would passionately feud about world politics, the wisdom or folly of having left their home, the dubious safety of those they left behind. Or they would quibble about the finest of logical questions in some arcane religious debate, their *yarmulkes* slightly askew, the sleeves of their crisp white shirts rolled up, revealing their furry, muscular arms, their fists pounding the table to emphasize some point. Once in a while, one of my uncles would lift me for a moment to plant a wet kiss on my face, and I would get a whiff of his hairy maleness, his unshaven black-sandpaper cheeks reeking of tobacco and stale, yellow Talmud pages.

The women would wander from kitchen to dining room carrying trays of fruit or *rugelach* or sponge cake or tea, and back again, the trays now loaded with overflowing ashtrays and dirty plates, though they would never quite clear the table for fear of disturbing the sacred discussions. Sometimes they would sit lining the walls as though waiting to be called upon. Sometimes they would chat, exchanging gossip or recipes, but most of the time they would fade silently into the scenery, backdrops to the main show.

The children, though, were never silent. We would race, girls and boys, chubby red-cheeked toddlers and wily, wiry five-year-olds and gawky pre-teens, through the house to the tiny yard out back, then in again through the kitchen and down the narrow hallway to the dining room; we would hide under the table, fight on the steps outside in front, play competitive games that required nearly as much yelling as the earth-shaking conversations of our fathers, more or less ignored by the grown-ups. I was often befuddled about the point of the din, but I know I joined right in.

A noisy, passionate clan, the North American Tannens. But I never knew, nor even heard of, the Tannens who were still in the Bucovina. I would hear names, strange foreign names, Zeyde Moishe Yussel, Uncle Naftulim, Uncle Sender. Their sound drifted over me like the smoke from the cigarettes and cigars my father and uncles consumed.

I was more than dimly aware of the war. On Saturday mornings, I would be shipped off to the movies, where I would watch war newsreels along with the double features and the serials. Hitler was Chancellor of the Third Reich, and I would see his booted Brownshirts, step-kicking in unison, like the Rockettes.

But I was too young to understand that the names that floated over me with the smoke were of relatives who lived in other lands. I didn't know, no one ever told me, about the more than ninety thousand Jews who, early in the war, still lived in the Bucovina, many of them Tannens. Nor was I aware that pretty soon that number had dropped to fewer than eighteen thousand. Members of the Zionist organization that Sender Tannen had helped build were fleeing from Europe and Russia to the Middle East, but not fast enough. Some thirty thousand of the fifty thousand Jews in Czernowitz were "deported"—to so-called "work camps"—including Sender and his family. Sender's son Ruben, the one Sender had worried so much about swimming to Darabani with Asher's older boys, was now serving in the Russian army after medical school, having escaped that particular Eastern European punishment for being Jewish, the "camps." Many of our *lantzmen* from Roznov and other nearby towns were marched off with Sender to the forest of Cosauti, some sold along the way to those who shot and robbed them. Some crossed the Dniester, balancing on a narrow bridge, struggling to keep their footing as Romanian soldiers whacked at them with rifle butts.

There were those who made it to the edge of Odessa, the road lined when they got there with corpses of women, children, the disabled, those who had been unable to keep up. Mass killings followed. Machine guns rat-a-tatted in at them from outside four blazing warehouses; inside they, Sender among them, turned to cinder, even as hand grenades landed at their burning, ulcerated feet. Those who somehow survived were condemned to a ghetto in the southern counties of Trnansnistria—Oceacov, Berezovka, Golta—and left to die of starvation, disease, and misery.

No matter how he tried—and he did—Asher was unable to find out until after the war that his brother had not managed to escape the conflagration, had not managed to realize his dream of relocating to Palestine and taking part in building a Jewish homeland.

Twenty one

Benjie
1940s

Benjie stayed in the Canadian woods until the following December, until the weather again started to freeze up. When he returned to New York, it was just past the first anniversary of the day the Japanese had bombed Pearl Harbor. The United States was now at war, and Benjie felt the need to help. He had listened to all the news broadcasts on the small radio Dovid had brought him, and now he wanted to join in the U.S. war effort.

A few years earlier, Benjie had taken part with one of the old neighborhood guys, Meyer Lansky, in a number of raids on Nazi bund meetings in Yorkville, the very section of Manhattan where Tannen's Restaurant was located. Benjie had been outraged when he first heard that Nazi thugs were meeting right here in New York. At first he felt helpless, gripped by the terror of his boyhood flight from Roznov during the pogroms. It couldn't happen here! But then he realized he was no longer that boy. Now he could fight these hoodlums.

263

When he heard about the raids being organized by Lansky, Benjie was happy to volunteer, he and the Brownsville boys along with a bunch of their cohorts from the Lower East Side. One time, Benjie and fifteen other Lansky helpers triumphantly broke up a major pro-Hitler rally at which a celebrated American Nazi, Fritz Kuhn, was scheduled to speak. When they got there, Benjie had paused only a moment at the sight of the flaming red backdrop on the great stage, its menacing swastika nearly room-high. He and Lansky's other boys got busy. Enraged even more now by the symbol than they had been when they had first heard of the homegrown Nazi meetings, they incited a small riot, picking fights with the thugs in the brown shirts and tossing firecrackers around the hall. The featured speech by Kuhn was called off.

Thanks to the Brownsville boys' activities, the Tannen family gained an unasked-for benefit: the brown-shirted thugs in the neighborhood never threatened Label's restaurant.

Now Benjie Kalmowitz, back from his enforced vacation, wanted to take part in the real war effort. He had heard, from Dovid, who had gotten the information from a cousin who worked for naval intelligence, that nearly three hundred merchant ships had been destroyed by German U-boats in the waters off American shores. Naval intelligence agents, infiltrating the docks to find out who was helping the enemy, had little success when the Italian longshoremen stonewalled their efforts. Benjie didn't know what he could do, but he felt he needed to somehow lend a hand. He let it be known through the still-active grapevine that he was available.

His return marked a major change in his career—and another swing in the Kalmowitzes' fortunes.

It happened that he came back at just the right time. What Benjie did not know was that Frank Hogan, Tom Dewey's successor, had turned to the city's racketeers for help in getting some of the longshoremen to talk to the intelligence agents. Hogan recruited Meyer Lansky to seek the help of Lucky Luciano, who was at the time serving a thirty-to-fifty-year term in Dannemora. Luciano had cut deals through the years with labor bosses along the docks, and his help, Hogan thought, might loosen a few tongues.

Luciano was transferred to Comstock prison, which was closer to New York, so that Lansky could more easily visit him. Lansky, an old-time buddy of Luciano's, was to turn up there, meet with Lucky and persuade him to help the government by getting word out that it was okay to talk to the agents. What the agents hoped to find out was where and when suspicious characters had landed clandestinely on American soil, how they had arrived and where they had gone from the time of their landing. Tight-lipped longshoremen would have such information; they just had to be persuaded it was all right to talk.

Lansky agreed to give it a try. It took a few visits, but Lansky and Luciano made a deal. Luciano would help—on a condition of anonymity. He didn't want his *paisanos* in Italy coming after him when he showed up in the old country after his release from prison. The state government, and the feds, agreed.

Benjie was recruited to help out once the deal was made. His recent retreat in the Ontario woods—and the fishing lessons he'd had from Dovid—came in handy. What he was asked to do was go out with the fishing fleet off the shores of New York and help identify the places where German secret agents had come ashore.

The upshot of the effort was that eight German agents were arrested in New York and Chicago. They had landed by U-boat with cash, explosives, maps and plans for a two-year campaign of attacks on defense plants, railroads, waterworks and bridges from the Eastern Seaboard of the United States to the Midwest.

Benjie's payoff was approval by the State Banking Commission of his application to open a small bank in Brooklyn. Lansky supplied the funds.

Allerton Bank was extremely small when it opened. The main office, and in fact the only branch at first, was on Court Street. The board of directors was comprised of a union executive from the LGWU, someone from the city's sewer department, an aide from the office of the Brooklyn borough president, an assistant from a state judge's office and a few of the boys from Lavonia Street.

They all had enough contacts to bring in a list of impressive clients—contacts from their labor dispute days, from the days of Prohibition, from other "business" dealings—and the list grew quickly. Two more Brooklyn branches opened in the next few years. The Kalmowitzes moved again, this time to an eight-room apartment in an old Central Park West building. The bank's growth kept increasing and the directors talked of opening another branch, this one in Manhattan.

Benjie became the chairman of the board.

The Amboy Duchess

Twenty two

Eva
1974

Eva and I sat in her living room, drinking tea. I'd called
her as soon as I got home from the bank the night I realized who
Benjie was, and she invited me to her home the following
Sunday. Imprisoned by her own reclusiveness, she was glad for
the company. Still beautiful at forty nine, Eva nevertheless
looked older, or maybe ageless.

Her face wasn't lined—it was smooth and lovely—nor
had her body gone to flab—she still caught men's eyes. She
seemed, rather, to be dissolving into age. Her aging was internal;
it showed in her haunted eyes. Something in those eyes gave her
an air of dark, deep, mysterious deterioration, as if she were
becoming particles of matter, completing the cycle from pre-
birth to post-life. She was the sort of woman of whom people
might say that only a fragile shell remained.

In the shadowed corner where she sat, she seemed
almost translucent, facing into an alternate, darkening universe.

The Amboy Duchess

The afternoon sun sank, dusk fell, and she kept the lamps turned off. Light frightened her, she told me, ever since the days of the Polish resistance. She couldn't explain why, but she often still huddled like this, she said, in the darkened house. She didn't like to go outside to the yard. Something about the darkened house made her feel safer.

So many years had passed since that evening she and Ruben showed up in Uncle Label's Scarsdale living room, yet as we talked, the memory of their arrival filled me again with the feelings of strangeness it had evoked then. The image was indelible: the two of them, Ruben and Eva, still ragged from the war, leaning against one another in the middle of the couch as the family circled around to hear their story.

Now she told me more. How they were forced to marry, how it was never good. The family had insisted on their marrying, threatening not to help if they didn't. It wasn't right, Zeyde Asher pronounced, for a couple to stay together unmarried. Only Label had uncharacteristically kept quiet. He had other plans for Eva, which he mentioned to no one, and marriage or no, marriage didn't matter to him.

He helped them find an apartment in Brooklyn and a job in a factory for Eva, while Ruben studied American medicine so he could pass the tests and practice here. Then, in her twenties, Eva, who had never before menstruated, began to put on weight, turn beautiful. She became pregnant with their first child, a daughter, Lisa.

The Amboy Duchess

Label helped them find a house in a Queens neighborhood populated by Poles, Jews, Italians. The neighborhood was working class, but the house was Tudor, brick, large, and Label helped them pay for it. It was a one-family house with a small apartment on the side, perfect for a medical office. Ruben treated the mainly immigrant residents of the community and became very popular. They furnished the house, still with Label's help, with cut glass and mahogany. To the world, they were like any other family, entertaining friends and relatives, raising their little girl. They even started to have hopes for the future.

Eva and Ruben began to fight, mostly about his drinking, and the drugs he was starting to rely on, which he kept in the small glass-doored cabinet in the office. She would walk through the crowded waiting room, she told me, into his office and find him injecting himself in the thigh.

She relied on Label more and more.

By the time Scott was born, even my Aunt Golde knew that Eva and Label were involved with one another, though it was officially a secret. Eva thought life was finally giving her something, the kind of love and stability she had longed for since that day during the war when she had left the Polish ghetto and wandered around the Gentile sections of Warsaw alone and frightened. The feeling lasted until the late '50s, when Label's body was found on the beach in Rockaway, where he was

271

spending the summer, drowned. Drowned. The strong swimmer from Czernowitz.

He'd gone for an early evening swim during the start of hurricane season and never came home. Someone walking along the beach the next morning had seen his things, his famous white shoes and white duck pants, his undershirt and his keys, lying on the sand in a neat pile, just as he had apparently left them.

Bereft once more, she resigned herself to raising her children the best way she could, hiding the past from them and also parts of the present; she could only hope for better things for them.

Then her son, Scott, went away to college and came back married to a girl who wasn't Jewish, and Ruben, over Eva's protests, pretended they had no son. He insisted they sit *shiva*, mourn for Scott's death. All they had left now was Lisa.

I knew Lisa. Thirteen years younger than I, and beautiful, she had been the flower girl at my wedding. Later, when I was a young married woman, raising my own children, she used to visit me; we'd sit over coffee and talk and she would tell me how bewildering it was to grow up in that house, always dim, always silent with secrets. She loved her father, though he frightened her; she felt responsible for her parents' happiness, if such a thing could ever be possible, and, in any case, for her own. She owed them that, at least, her own happiness, she said. Or else life was truly hell on a rolling planet going nowhere.

The Amboy Duchess

The last time I'd seen Lisa alive was only a few months before; she was in her mid-twenties, and troubled. We'd sat together at another cousin's wedding, two single women.

A friend of the groom had asked her to dance and she'd come back to our table in a rage. I took her hand and led her outside. We talked, but nothing she said explained the rage. What she'd talked about that day was what she always talked about. Her parents. Her brother. The tension at home. The silences, the secrets, the darkness. She'd moved around restlessly as she spoke, sitting, standing, ambling from the steps of the synagogue to the large oak tree on the lawn, leaning against it for a time, then ambling back again, sitting on the steps only minutes, then rising again and pacing once more. The sound of crickets had given an edge to the soft evening air.

As she told me she was involved with the father of one of her friends, she'd sounded like a mechanical doll programmed to mimic a girl. Her plans to go away to school in two months for a master's degree in physical therapy had seemed like plans made by someone else, she getting ready to carry out instructions, without pride, without pleasure, without questions. In fact, Ruben had pressured her into a medical career, her only rebellion a refusal to go to medical school.

Her tone had changed when she told me of her visit to her brother and his Gentile wife. "I saw my brother," she'd said softly. "I feel so guilty. I can't even tell my mother he's all right, though I know she'd like to know."

273

All her passion, total and mutilating, had gone to her lifelong quest, trying to understand the enigma of her family. She knew that the war had scarred her parents, the loss of their first families, the anguish of the field hospitals, the camps, her father a broken man now, his eyes fallen deep into their sockets, watching always for apocryphal signs of doom.

She couldn't figure out why understanding didn't exorcise her pain.

In the next two years, while she worked for her master's degree, I didn't see her. When her father died a year later from emphysema, I was ill and couldn't make it to the funeral. She called me though and wept about how she hadn't been able to save him.

When finally she got her degree, she decided to take a vacation, to celebrate her achievement, I supposed. A medical student friend found her in her hotel room.

We all wondered at the mystery of her death, never explained to us by Eva. But then we learned that her friend had discovered a *New York Times* article tucked into the corner of her wallet. "Children of Holocaust victims," it said, "often suffer from depression; some commit suicide."

But Eva would not talk about Lisa. We talked instead about my children. I told her how they spent four months with Richie now, how much I missed them even though we talked to each other every day and they wrote me once a week. I talked about my new job, the coincidence of working for Stu, Moe

274

Lewenthal's son, and of Benjie's presence there. She knew a bit about Benjie. Label had spoken to her often of the family and other *mishpuchah*. She knew how Tannen's had become a speakeasy during Prohibition, how Benjie had helped Avi. She also knew of Benjie's growing resentment toward the Tannen family; after all, Label had been married to Benjie's sister and even Benjie had known about Label and Eva.

She warned me to be careful at the bank.

"You don't want that man lurking in your life. I never trusted him. Who knows what he knew when your father and your uncle died. Or even what he may have done."

The Amboy Duchess

Twenty three

The knock on my door was gentle at first, so gentle I wasn't sure I'd really heard anything. The second knock was louder and he called me as he rapped.

"Winnie? It's me, Stu. I need to talk to you."

I was stretched out on the couch. After dinner, I'd been too tired to go through the papers I'd taken from work the night before, but I wasn't tired enough for bed. I had just been thinking about going downstairs to the den to watch some TV. I looked at the clock on the mantle. It was nearly ten p.m. Oh, well, I could still watch the news at eleven.

He was knocking again.

"God, you're impatient. Hold your horses, I'm coming!"

The night was balmy, humid. It felt as if it might rain and in fact, just as I opened the door, a loud boom of thunder frightened me so I nearly fell into his arms. Embarrassed, I extricated myself.

"Sorry. C'mon in."

He grinned. "No problem." He followed me back into the living room. "What have you been doing?" He sat down in the middle of the couch, spread both his arms out over the back and stretched out his legs, crossing one foot over the other. He looked around as if he might get some clue about how I'd been spending the evening. "You're alone?"

I was still standing in the living room doorway, amazed at this intrusion.

"Am I alone?"

He nodded, still craning his neck. What did he think he was going to find?

"Yes. I'm alone. Who did you expect to find?"

His attention came back to me. He sat up, putting his arms between his legs, folding his hands, looking down at them. That intensity tightened his eyes, shrinking the corneas to a near-dot.

"I . . . I don't know. Whoever sent you those flowers, I guess. Whoever it was who was here last night. Though I didn't see his car this time." The confession tightened his voice.

I sat down on the bent-wood rocker near the bay window, the curtains blowing in as the wind kicked up outside. I tried to lean back, look relaxed, but it was impossible to relax with him sitting there so taut that every muscle in his arms bulged out. I stopped trying and sat forward, gripping the arms of the chair.

"You were watching my house last night?" My voice threatened to squeak if I wasn't careful.

"No, of course not. I was out taking a walk and I passed by. I guess I wouldn't have given it much of a thought, though it's a pretty fancy car. But then I saw the flowers on your desk . . ."

I kept quiet.

"I guess I'm jealous," he finally admitted.

This man always took me by surprise. "Jealous! How could you be jealous? I mean, what right . . . ?"

He stood up and started pacing. "I know, I know. Of course. Don't think I'm a total fool. I can't help it. Feeling this way." He wasn't even looking at me. He might have been talking more to himself than to me. "I didn't plan this. It started the day I helped Marilyn move in. The day you dropped all the groceries. I don't know why."

"Is that why you hired me?" What a stupid question. He certainly didn't hire me because of my qualifications.

He glanced up at me as if he'd heard my thought, a smile lighting his eyes, and he didn't even attempt an answer.

"Look, by now you know how I feel about you. I don't want to hide it. I guess I see it as . . . I see *you* . . . as an opportunity."

"What kind of opportunity?"

"A chance to feel something new, something different. An opportunity for something unknown, exciting."

"Stu."

He looked at me expectantly. I didn't know what I wanted to say. I shook my head.

"I don't . . . I don't know. Go home. I don't want you here. I don't want this conversation. I don't even know what you want. I haven't given you any reason . . ."

He moved toward me and I could see he meant to touch me. I didn't want to make him angry, but I took a step back. He was my boss. Moe Lewenthal's son. And though I didn't want to let him know it, I was furious.

He stopped and stood very still.

Unexpectedly, tears started coming down my face, making me even angrier.

"No, Stu! Get out of my house! I don't want you aiming your feelings at me! They're not my business. I don't want anything to do with them."

I ran to the door and opened it.

"Please, get out. I don't want you here."

He came toward the door, stood so close to me I could feel his breath, and then he firmly shut the door. He put a hand on my shoulder, gently. I thought for a moment that he'd figured out that I needed some tenderness. But he tightened his hold and leaned forward, pressing himself into me at the same time he grabbed my other shoulder.

"For God's sake, Stu! Are you crazy?"

I tried to shove him away. But he was stronger. As I struggled, he put his arms around me and lifted me just a bit off the ground, enough to carry me toward the couch. His grip loosened and my feet once more touched the ground, but I couldn't get free. I could feel him get hard against me through all our clothing. His lips were on mine, but I twisted my face away. "Stop it! Stop, Stu. Leave me alone!" He grabbed my face in one hand, pressed my cheeks so I'd have cried out in pain if he hadn't put his mouth on mine again. He tried to force his tongue into my mouth.

I tried to kick him, tried to get my knee under him to knee him in the groin, but he had me locked in.

Finally, I opened my mouth enough to let his tongue in and I bit it as hard as I could. He let go. "Shit!"

Then, as I tried turning away, tried to increase the distance between us, he grabbed me again and threw me down on the couch. He was on top of me before I could prevent it, opening his zipper, pulling down my slacks.

I dug my nails into his back, felt his shirt rip, hoped I'd draw blood. But I couldn't get him off me. Wriggling, trying to squirm out from under, was no good, I felt him, hard, against me, while with one hand, he pried my legs apart.

His release was nearly immediate, but he stayed inside me for a few minutes, pinning me with his hands on my shoulders as he raised his upper body in a semi-pushup. He thrust his head back, let out a sigh loud enough to be a cry, and I saw tears in his eyes as he pulled himself off, zipped up, turned and ran out the door.

I couldn't get up right away; the shock had paralyzed me. I felt exhausted, as if I'd been working out for a couple of hours; everything ached. Finally, I stood, pulled up my slacks and ran to lock the door.

I leaned back against it, my heart pounding. I waited to calm down enough to get up the stairs to my bedroom and ran into the bathroom. My heart felt like a stone trying to make its way to my stomach. The feeling I had was dread, though I didn't know why. I ran a bath and submerged myself.

While toweling myself, I started to cry, but the tears didn't bring catharsis. In fact, the heaviness increased and it took all my energy to get my nightgown on and get under the covers. It wasn't until I lay in bed, finally falling into a stupor, that I began to get a glimmer of what the dread was. I felt guilty, for some reason, searched myself to discover what I might have said or done to make him attack me. But the dread had more to do with something else.

The evening had been surrealistic.

And for some reason I felt like a failure. A fake and a failure.

What I dreaded was being jobless again.

* * * * *

When I got to the bank the next day, I was bleary-eyed. I hadn't slept all night worrying about how I would face Stu. I couldn't face what had happened. Rape. I had been raped. But the word didn't come to me. I thought of myself as having been "attacked." "Rape" was too strong a concept. If I'd once faced the situation head-on, I could never have gone to work.

He was impossible to figure out, was how I thought about it. The only thing I understood was that he was into power. Mess with his perception of his power, and, boom, you were gone. Did he think attacking me would increase his power? I was already at his mercy, needing the job, needing his good will. How could attacking me add anything to that power?

I was still confused as I settled in at my desk. As my best line of defense, I got busy. First I went through my messages and found a note from Margaret; she had told Stu about Jim's interview plans and he had made an appointment for both of us for tomorrow. That only confused me more until I realized he had no idea that Jim was my lover.

I finished all the paperwork I needed for the next loan committee meeting. I had four applications to present. Then I tried to jot down some notes for my talk next week at the Woman Executive dinner. The page remained blank; I couldn't figure out what to say. I didn't even know why I was still planning to go. I'd thought I'd plug the seminars. But now I was starting to feel that promoting the bank was a bad idea.

When I realized I was getting nowhere fast with my speech, I flipped to a new page on the yellow pad to make two lists: one for things I'd found out about Allerton that I hadn't learned from the *Voice* articles, and another for things I still needed to know. That was when I noticed Margaret's memo; it had been lying under the pad.

Stu was holding a meeting in the conference room downstairs at ten thirty, the same room where board meetings— and my seminars—were held. The clock on the wall behind the tellers told me I had five minutes to get there. As I approached the room, I smelled coffee—gratefully, as I hadn't had time for any before leaving this morning—and I heard the buzz of anxious voices.

I wandered to where Melba and Bobbie stood in a huddle near the coffee urn. "What's going on?"

"That's what everyone is wondering," Bobbie said, handing me a cup of coffee. "Stu told Margaret to get everyone together. He's doing some reorganizing. Just like when he first got here."

"What did he do then?"

"Made me a vice president—who still goes around to the two Brooklyn branches to water the plants! Maybe now he thinks I've done such a stupendous job he wants to give me a raise for being the best plant-grower Allerton ever had. Give me a break.

I'm not a vice president. I'm a bookkeeper. Which is fine with me, but don't lie about it." This wasn't the first time Bobbie had complained that her title meant nothing.

"What else did he do?" Maybe if I found out how he had reorganized things, I'd know more about his part in the funny business.

"He put Harvey in charge of personnel, a definite demotion, even though he told Harvey he was being promoted. Harvey has less to do now than he did before when he was a loan officer; now he has no portfolio. Such a small bank doesn't need anyone in charge of personnel. The comptroller takes care of payroll and benefits—along with me, the vice president-slash-bookkeeper. Stu does all the hiring and firing. He doesn't even get the board's okay. And he goes through a great pantomime with the board when he goes to them for loan approvals. The truth is, he makes all the decisions here—about everything! They're not all popular decisions, either!"

Maybe he *had* been appointed by the banking commission, not by the board.

"Shhh! Here he comes," Melba warned.

Stu and Margaret strode into the boardroom, each carrying a stack of file folders. Stu went to a seat at the head of the long conference table and Margaret pulled up a chair next to him. "Let's get started," he said to the room at large, looking down at his papers. Everyone straggled to the table, coffee cups in hand, and took seats.

Stu waited until the room was quiet.

"I've been going over some records from recent months," he began, with no "good morning," no preamble to ease everyone into the reason for the meeting. For a startling moment, I thought he was going to openly announce that the bank was engaged in illegal activities. "I'm doing away with what the press has been calling our 'women's program.'"

I sucked in my breath, a loud, involuntary noise. He didn't even glance in my direction. Why was I upset? I was planning to cancel them this evening anyway. But I didn't like being pre-empted. And I sure didn't like being publicly humiliated.

"None of the accounts or loans generated by the seminars that Winnie has been running has brought in enough revenue to warrant the expense."

The expense! We had coffee and donuts. We had gotten ten new accounts, all of them below $100,000, it was true—except for Pam's, the one for $400,000, and the new one. And we'd made three loans to my women clients, one for expansion, one for Martha's film, and one to a jewelry store, and that one was guaranteed for 90 percent by the Small Business Administration. Didn't that pay for coffee? The seminars were announced in the paper, at no cost to us, and, in fact, those announcements—and all the articles that had been written about us—were such good publicity they should have *cost* the bank many thousands of dollars. Instead, we got them for the cost of an urn of coffee.

This wasn't about money. It was about sex.

And hurt feelings. And power.

". . . that's why I'm assigning Winnie a new position. Her desk is being moved to the platform right now and she will continue the job as loan officer. But she will also take on some other promotional tasks. The board of directors needs to be thanked for the good work they do. It will be Winnie's job to schedule cruises and other activities for them. We also need some other promotional ideas. Winnie will be in charge of public relations."

The board of directors needed to be thanked?! *Those crooks?!!*

"Excuse me, Stu." Bobbie's arm was sticking out across the table, as if she didn't want to provoke him by actually raising it, and she didn't want to just speak out. She waited until Stu grudgingly acknowledged her with a nod, no smile.

"We spend quite a lot of money on advertising and public relations already. The Greer Agency gets . . ."

"I know what they get, Bobbie. Thank you."

She pulled her arm back as if he'd slapped it.

" . . . I want you all to know that's why Winnie's desk is being moved from her corner—what some of you have referred to as the 'women's corner'—to the platform. Please give her every courtesy and welcome her to her new spot. Thanks."

He closed the folder in front of him, though he hadn't once referred to it, and then he stood up, nodding to Margaret. She stood and the two of them strode out as they had marched in, quickly, their eyes looking straight ahead, no amenities, no smiles.

I couldn't even stand up. My breath came in small gasps. No one except Bobbie looked at me as they filed out. Bobbie gave me a half-smile and a half-wave, shrugging a little as if to say, "I tried." Actually, she did say, "See you later," very softly. Only Melba waited to talk to me.

"Are you all right?"

I nodded, afraid to speak. I might show my fury. Or worse, cry. She was standing across the table from me, hands on her hips, looking nearly as angry as I was.

"What's he doing? Has he gone totally bonkers? Those seminars are the best thing that's happened to this bank in . . . ever."

"He's pissed at me . . . because . . ."

I told her what had happened last night. Maybe she wasn't the one to talk to, but Melba and I had become friendly, and I just found myself confiding in her. And once I got going I couldn't stop. I told her about all his moves on me. And I tried to explain my theory of how it wasn't just sex, how he was into power.

"I'll tell you what it is, honey. It's that good ol' male ego thing. *He* wanted to be the star of this bank. He came in here like the Lone Ranger, thinking he was going to save the bank and get lots of press for doing it, and you came along and stole his thunder."

She plunked herself down in her seat, spread her hands out on the table. "This bank is in big trouble, Winnie. It's run by a group of hoods from Brooklyn. I don't know if you know the things the papers were writing about Allerton just before you got here."

I nodded again. "Yes, I've seen the articles." I wanted to tell her what else I'd seen, but she kept talking.

"So you know we've gotten bad press. But there are things going on here that even the papers didn't know . . ."

"I know."

Her head jerked up. She stopped talking and waited for me to go on.

"I . . . found . . . some papers. A few weeks ago. In the storeroom. Payroll sheets . . . and . . ."

"So that *was* you! I've been wondering if you were a shill."

"A what?"

"I thought you might be in on the shenanigans with all the boys, kind of a runner for them, grabbing the evidence before I could get to it."

I stopped talking and stared at her. *She* was the one who had left them on the file cabinet! "What were *you* doing with them?" I finally managed to ask. "I thought Bobbie had misplaced them."

"She hadn't misplaced them. I sneaked them out of her office. I meant to copy them and bring them right back upstairs. But then . . ."

"Why did you take them?"

"Honey, you know I'm an auditor. From the State Banking Commission. I'm here to investigate this bank. Whatever it takes. These boys are in hot water and all we need is a little more evidence . . ."

"I have it. I have the evidence. At least, I think that's what I have."

"What do you mean?"

"Haven't you searched the files near Harry's office?"

"Not yet. I've been doing it systematically. Starting with the ones in the upstairs offices. I haven't gotten downstairs yet. Why? What did you find?"

"I found some papers, memos, letters, notes, invoices, in the files . . . Kalmowitz was looking for them one night and I saw where he was looking . . . so I came back and got them and made copies . . . I have them at home, I've glanced at them, but I haven't gone through them all carefully yet. I'm planning to do that over the weekend, before I go away. But I bet I almost have enough to convict Kalmowitz and Allerton Bank of serious crimes."

I was going too fast for her. "Slow down, slow down. What are you talking about? Why were you looking for papers?"

I shook my head, to clear it. "When I found the payroll sheets, I got scared. I thought, 'What kind of bank am I working for?' Also, I wasn't sure what they meant. You know I was brand new here and I didn't know everyone. Maybe those people *did* all work here. I just had to know more. Then when I started to be so, so visible, I needed to know what kind of bank I was promoting as a bank for women. And when Stu came on to me, that made me mad and I wanted to find something that would hurt him . . ."

I stopped. Was that what I was doing?

"Stu isn't involved. He was appointed here by the State Banking Commission. Same as I was. We're supposed to be working together. Me and the Lone Ranger. I guess that makes me Tonto." We both giggled.

Well. Okay. Now I knew that.

"But if these guys are paying people off—I think I have stuff that shows they're paying off judges, politicians, city government officials of all kinds—how do you know they aren't paying off the commissioners, too?"

Her eyes widened at that. Maybe I'd said too much. Maybe *she* was being paid off, too.

"Don't look at me like that, Winnie. I'm not being bought. And I don't think Stu is, either. He and I sort of dance around one another. We don't like each other very much. The man is too . . . too . . . well, look at what he just did. He's cold and hard and has no idea how people feel. Look how he treats Bobbie. He doesn't understand human relations. Present company a case in point. *The* case in point. If he's 'in love' with you as he claims, this is a pretty strange way to treat you. You'd think the man would want to protect you, help you, be attentive, send you flowers. In fact, weren't those flowers you got from him?"

I shook my head and felt my face go warm. "Uh-uh. Someone else." I couldn't help smiling at her look of surprise.

"Well, you should know that Stu let everyone here think they were from him . . ."

"*What?!*"

"What is *wrong* with that man? Honey, you got to *do* something. You can't let him get away with . . ."

She stopped because I was shaking my head slowly, back and forth, back and forth, trying not to let the tears that were welling in the corners of my eyes fall. I couldn't afford to lose control.

"Honey, he raped you."

I whispered: "Melba, what can I do? Have him *arrested*? My *boss*? What would I do, go on welfare when he fires me? And you know how the cops treat rape victims, and the courts, too. *You* become the criminal. I'd be a slut, almost a prostitute, a whore, who'd asked for it. They'd say I did it so I could keep my job. I did it for the money. He's the president of a bank, for god's sake! They'd go looking for other people I slept with just to prove how depraved . . . and . . . and . . . illegal . . . I am. And I'm divorced! You *know* how they treat divorcées! My picture would be in the paper . . . Then I'd *never* get a job!"

I was getting hysterical, not making sense. We were both getting very upset. Melba changed the subject.

"Maybe you're right, I don't know. In any case, you'd think Stu would treat you even nicer if he wants to win you from someone else. And shouldn't he be glad you're doing well *here*? Look how much good you've done for *his* bank!"

She handed me a tissue and tried to dry my eyes with it.

"Don't worry, Winnie," she said. "We'll talk about all that again later. Now," she patted my hand, and leaned in closer to me across the boardroom table. "Tell me more about those papers you have. What, exactly, do you think they prove?"

"I'm not sure, Melba. But it looks like this bank is tight with rackets, a little too tight, in my opinion, with government officials . . . From what I can tell so far, the papers I found prove everything that the *Voice* articles insinuate, and more."

She didn't like the fact that I was going on vacation next week, but we agreed to meet as soon as I got back to talk about what we'd both found and what we—or rather, what she—needed to do about it. Meanwhile, she was heading up to Albany tomorrow. I promised I'd drop by and put copies on her desk of everything I had before heading for the airport Sunday evening.

I spent the rest of the morning moving things from my old location to my new one, even though the effort seemed futile. I knew I wasn't going to be here very much longer. I looked around at all the other desks. If Melba agreed with me about what those papers could prove, and she took action against the board, they might all not be here much longer. I couldn't help their potential unemployment. If the bank was closed down, it wouldn't be my doing. It was Benjie and his crooked board.

My new desk was in the center of the platform and closer to the window. I had a nice view of Rockefeller Center, especially now that Stu had taken down the bizarre chartreuse sign with my name on it.

I kept staring out the window and fantasizing about how Melba and I were going to get them all.

Twenty four

I couldn't listen to music, couldn't eat, couldn't fall asleep. I was depressed and agitated, but didn't know what to do about either.

Pacing around the house, opening the refrigerator door, peering in at all the unappetizing leftovers, watering the plants in the kitchen window, tripping downstairs to the den, opening the back door to see if it was any cooler outside, closing the door again, slinking upstairs to the living room, slumping down on the couch.

I wished the kids were here. They'd bring me comfort. But I was also glad they weren't. They'd be with Richie till winter break. Until then I had only myself to take care of; I wondered how we'd live if I became jobless again.

I considered going into Stu's office and . . . and what? What would I say?

"You can't do this to me." Oh, really.

And he would say? "Get out. I'm sick of you." Or maybe worse. Maybe he'd take my being there at all as giving in.

I could never go back to Allerton.

But I had a lot of work to do. I was still getting some applications ready so the Small Business Administration could put their ninety percent guarantee on a couple of loans we wanted to approve. In the late morning, a woman who owned a mail order book dealership was coming in. She told me on the phone that she had applied for an SBA-guaranteed loan at another bank and had been turned down for espousing an ideology; her business was called the Feminist Book Mart. An ideology. Women's equality. She wanted my help. Stu would never lend her nine thousand dollars to expand if the SBA had turned her down. But I would write it up and leave the application for him.

Another woman, a doctor who'd had her own practice for nine years, had also tried unsuccessfully to get a ten-thousand-dollar-loan; hers was for new equipment. She was nine months pregnant and no one wanted to take a chance on her. I'd wanted to fight for her, but now all I wanted was out. Still, I had to at least leave some paperwork on her behalf.

The women from Liberation Limited were coming in the afternoon to apply for fifteen thousand dollars to open a retail store downstairs next door to the dildo man. I wondered what chance *they* stood.

These women needed help and they thought Allerton was the place to get it. Capitalizing on them, Stu had placed some ads this week in a number of newspapers. "We are the bank that's good to women." If only they knew!

Tomorrow was the day Stu and I were being interviewed at NBC by Jim Battle. Margaret had gotten his okay and made the appointment for us. I didn't know how we would be able to even talk to each other. But maybe we didn't have to. We could just talk to Jim. And the camera.

Pam Freeman was coming by tomorrow, too, to put more money into her account, the one she had opened last week for her investment firm. I knew she had taken out most of the $400,000 she'd opened her account with. Now she was putting in more. She said it would be a large amount, $650,000, and she wanted me to make sure everything went smoothly. At least *one* woman was operating on a grand scale.

That dinner she wanted me to speak at was being held at the Waldorf the week after next, after my vacation. She wanted me to talk about the seminars Allerton was offering women business owners. What should I tell them? Should I say Stu is a rapist—Melba got me to realize I'd been raped!—always coming on to me and punishing me when I turned him down, and when punishment wasn't enough, using force? Maybe I should tell them about the board's funny business, too. Some bank for women!

Maybe I should go up to the dais and continue the pretense. Calmly tell the audience about my work, how I'd discovered *Majority Report* and the lists of women business owners, how I'd sent out invitations to everyone on the lists to attend some seminars, and how I'd been deluged by women who needed help, big time.

The more I considered what I'd like to say, the madder I got. But I would do it! *Damn it!* I was going to go to that dinner and talk to that audience just as if I were a crusader fighting for them, for myself—like Avi had been!—and I would spur them to action.

All of a sudden, I felt very sleepy. Tomorrow was going to be busy.

* * * * *

Stu and I got to the NBC studio at the same time, ten thirty a.m., though we'd both gone straight there before going to the bank. I couldn't bring myself to look him in the eyes, I just nodded in his direction as we both approached the security desk. Stu told security who we were and they directed us to the ninth floor. I walked a little behind him, as if this were the Middle East, and let him ring for the elevator. The ninth floor receptionist called someone to take us to Studio B. There we were met by the makeup crew, who seated us next to one another in high barber-style chairs and covered us shoulders-down with sheets.

I wondered if I would get to see Jim before the interviews. I hadn't seen him since before the horror scene with Stu; he didn't know what had happened and I wondered how I'd tell him. I felt shamed, as if the whole thing were my fault. Maybe he'd feel that way, too. I tried to get rid of that thought, but I couldn't dissolve it; it stayed just beneath consciousness, nagging at me, threatening my equilibrium. I wished I could talk to him, but we were both going to be busy all weekend, and then I'd be visiting Aunt Golde and Uncle Dovid in Montreal all week. I wouldn't get to see or talk to him until I got back from my vacation. Maybe by then I'd figure out how to tell him about Stu.

"How would you like your hair?" My designated beautician intruded on my thoughts. I liked my hair the way it was. I had especially fixed it just for the show before leaving work. I was stumped.

"What's wrong with the way I have it?"

He combed his fingers through my hair, pulling it straight up in the air, and looked at me as if I couldn't mean what I was saying.

"Well, it was okay when it was combed." I was beginning to feel belligerent, not the best feeling for an interview, unless being on edge would somehow make me smarter, or safer.

Finally, we compromised on a style that wasn't too artificial and, once he was done with that, we argued some more about my makeup. I wore very little of the stuff and saw no reason to present myself any differently on television. "You have a very different look on TV," he explained patiently, as if to a six-year-old. "You don't want to look pale and washed-out." I felt vaguely insulted, but I gave in at every step of the process: foundation, rouge, powder, eye makeup, even mascara. Stu was far enough away so I couldn't hear how he was doing. I was pretty sure he wouldn't feel happy, either, with this goo all over his face.

I wondered how Stu had rationalized doing this. Wouldn't Stu realize that Jim would ask him about the *Voice* articles? I figured he wanted fame so badly he would even take it as notoriety. He wanted to be seen on TV. Simple as that.

Next they took us to an area where three chairs were set up, living-room-like, in front of the camera crew. Stu was to be first. He was led to one of the chairs on the left and someone from the crew came over and clipped a microphone to his jacket. Jim would face him. Stu looked calm and comfortable. It hit me that he was under the illusion that he was in control of the situation. He must have thought this would be like a loan interview, where he had all the questions, too, as well as, in this case, all the answers.

Jim came into the studio, holding a sheaf of papers, and walked to where Stu was seated. Before sitting down, he put his hand out to Stu.

"I'm Jim Battle," he said. "Nice to have you here. I appreciate your doing this."

Stu half rose, put out his hand to take Jim's, shook it, nodded and sat down again. Jim sat opposite him. "Is there anything I can prepare you with? Do you have any questions for me?" he asked Stu.

Stu shook his head. "I think I'm fine."

"Good. I'd like you to talk about the women's program that's made your bank so visible. But first I want to ask you some questions about those *Voice* articles that came out a few months ago. I understand you were appointed president of Allerton Bank by the State Banking Commission only recently?"

"Right." Stu nodded.

"All right, then. Good. That's how I'll introduce you when this airs. So, let's just start. Remember, this is only a tape. Don't be nervous. No one's looking at us yet. We can fix anything that bothers us." Jim motioned to the camera crew, then turned to Stu again. "Ready?"

Stu nodded. No smile.

"Ladies and gentlemen. Allerton Bank, with four branches, three in Brooklyn and one in mid-Manhattan, is one of the banks Newfield refers to in his articles as one that's been investigated by the State Banking Commission, the IRS and the FBI. Allerton has also been in the news lately for something quite different: 'being nice to women.' This is a new development, isn't it, Mr. Lewen?"

Stu nodded. "Yes, Mr. Battle. We've been running the women's seminars for a few weeks now and they've been received very well."

What?! Of course I knew he wouldn't announce his intention to cancel the women's classes. But I didn't think he'd sit there and publicize them like that!

"You, yourself, have been at the bank for how long? About eight months?" Stu nodded. "You arrived just a short time after the articles appeared in the *Voice*. Was there any connection between your arrival and those articles?"

"Yes," Stu said. "The banking commission thought I could help put to rest any suspicions the public might have about Allerton's so-called mob connections or about any possible wrongdoing there."

"Is that right? How?"

"My reputation has been as an honest, if sometimes ruthless"—at this he smiled, finally, but just barely—"banker. I don't condone fraud, and that's what Newfield seemed to be hinting at. Hinting at," he said pointedly. "Not proving."

"Do you deny the things he . . . hinted at?"

"There wasn't enough to deny. If there were we'd be suing him for libel. All he did was describe certain crimes . . . money laundering, for example . . . and say that some of the money in Allerton's accounts was city money. Nothing there to deny. But the way he wrote it, he made it *sound like* we might be hiding something. We're not."

"I see. What about that city money? I see here"—Jim again lifted the papers from his lap—"that the city makes an unusually large deposit every day into some interest-free accounts it keeps at Allerton. Would you say that's true?"

"Allerton, like some thirty five other banks in the city, holds city money in interest-free accounts. That's true. The money is used by the city for its daily cash flow. It isn't unusual, and I don't know that Allerton's share is an unusually large amount."

"Why don't I explain to the audience what we're talking about. In fact, I'll read Newfield's explanation: 'Non-interest-bearing demand deposits are like gold to a bank.' " Jim looked into the camera. "I'm quoting now from Newfield. 'A bank can easily invest this interest-free money in treasury notes or municipal bonds, or lend it out to customers, and make a 9½ percent profit for themselves on money that actually belongs to the public.' Right, Mr. Lewen?"

"Well, that 9½ percent profit, of course, depends on prime rate."

"Yes, of course. At the moment, as I understand it, any bank can, in fact, make that much. Right?"

Stu nodded.

Jim nodded back and continued reading: "Newfield goes on: 'Most of the city's daily cash flow of four to seven hundred million dollars is kept in six large, respectable clearing banks. . . . Traditionally, about twenty million dollars—half of it interest-free—has been deposited in about thirty five smaller banks. Of this twenty million dollars, two notoriously badly managed, often investigated, and very political small banks have consistently received a disproportionate share.' And he names, as one of them, Allerton Bank." Jim looked up. "Right?"

Stu shrugged and shifted in his seat.

"A little further on in the article, Newfield accuses Allerton of making payoffs to a number of well-known elected officials and to a known mobster in the form of loans and mortgages on what he calls 'generous terms.' " Jim looked to Stu for a reaction.

"Yes, he certainly does *imply* that certain loans and mortgages granted by Allerton are *payoffs*. The fact is they are simply that: loans and mortgages. We're in the business of granting loans and mortgages to creditworthy clients. It's what we make our money from. I'd like to clarify for the public that there is absolutely no proof in Newfield's articles that Allerton is making *payoffs* to *anyone*."

"There's another allegation here. He says some of the public funds from the Lindsay administration deposited in your bank, and I quote: '. . . may have financed heroin transactions by organized crime.' "

"Again, '*may have*.' Hardly a substantiated accusation."

"Another accusation he makes—and this one seems to be well-substantiated, he quotes an FBI investigator—is that a convicted felon, Sal Grizzi, who served time for making illegal loans to the mob at another bank is now working for Allerton, 'at the same branch,' he says, 'where the mobsters are getting all their easy cash—both loans and mortgages.' Mr. Lewen, do you deny this?"

"Grizzi is working for us. He's the stockroom attendant in one of our Brooklyn branches. He has nothing to do with making loans or mortgages. But I do vehemently deny that any mobsters get 'easy cash' from Allerton. I don't even know what that means."

"I think the easy cash he refers to are some of the defaulted loans that Allerton stockholders are suing the chairman of your board for. Benjamin Kalmowitz, I believe, is his name. Kalmowitz, I believe, once served time for rum-running, and he was one of Abe Reles's drivers. Reles, who was killed in 1941, was the head of Murder Incorporated."

Suddenly, Jim leaned forward and his voice became tight and urgent.

"Mr. Lewen, are you doing anything to clean up Allerton Bank?"

"Mr. Battle, no one at Allerton has ever been formally charged with any of these so-called crimes, no less convicted of them. Our board of directors is comprised of some respectable government officials, one show business personality, and a number of well-respected business people. We're a good bank. We look for groups of people other banks ignore or won't serve— like women—and we cater to other minorities, as well. And, unlike some of New York's top banks, we don't make loans to South Africa, where the abomination called apartheid is being supported by many American business interests."

Jim smiled at this. "Mr. Lewen, really. I believe Allerton is too small to make loans to foreign countries. You seem to have your hands full—and your pockets, as well—supporting quite a few abominations other than apartheid right here. But I am interested in how you happened to come up with the idea of catering to women. I wouldn't think Mr. Kalmowitz would be especially interested in supporting the women's movement. Would you tell me, Mr. Lewen, how your women's program happened to get started?"

Now Stu smiled. A real, broad, friendly smile. "I'll be happy to. I hired a woman, Winnie Charles, to run the women's department. She started working for me at the beginning of the summer and got the program off the ground in record time. Within weeks, she was signing up women business owners for a series of seminars she developed. We're very proud of her."

He was taking credit for the idea of the women's seminars, pretty much what I'd expected him to do. Well, I guessed I couldn't complain; I'd taken the idea myself from Pam Freeman. But he was doing it only hours after he'd told us he wasn't going to let us run them anymore. Now that was chutzpah!

"It sounds like she developed those seminars in record time, as well. They've been running for months, haven't they?"

"That's right. And we have several months' worth of classes going forward in the works."

Well, that was interesting. Was he planning to move my desk off the platform and back to the "women's department"?

"Just how did a bank with Allerton's reputation come up with the idea of catering to women business owners?"

"Being a bank that serves minority interests is a good way of counteracting bad publicity—*undeserved* bad publicity. We deserve the publicity we're getting now as a bank for women."

"I see. And is the women's market a good one? Have these seminars brought you much business?"

"Unfortunately, Mr. Battle, women have not yet begun—in any great numbers, that is—to run the kinds of businesses that command high profits. But we've acquired some good, solid customers from the seminars. And I'm betting that, with the right bank to support them, these businesses will grow. In fact, that's the bet we make *when* we support them."

"Why don't you tell us something about the seminars. How they're run. Who attends them, what sorts of businesses, that is, are represented at them."

"Winnie can tell you more about the classes than I can."

"Yes, why don't we get her up here with us? Miss Charles?"

Both Jim and Stu turned toward where I was sitting. A member of the camera crew, a young guy in jeans and a T-shirt, came over to me, touched my elbow and pointed to the "living room." I tripped up there, my heart tripping right along in syncopated time, and I sat next to Stu.

"Hi, Ms. Charles," Jim greeted me, half getting up and extending his hand. I shook it.

"Hi, Jim. Please call me Winnie." I shook it, unable to suppress a gleam in my eyes; I was glad to see him, feel his warm touch, even though that nagging feeling hadn't gone away.

"Winnie it is. We'd like to hear about your seminars. What do you do in those classes?"

"Let me give you a little background first, Jim. When I first started at Allerton, Stu, Mr. Lewen . . ." I turned toward Stu and smiled. He didn't smile back. He knew what I was going to say, and it didn't confirm what he'd said about hiring me to run a women's program. "Mr. Lewen was training me in what he called New Business Development, sales actually, and he said it would be a good idea for me to find a group—I think he meant a kind of business, like jukeboxes, or something—that other banks aren't good to and to offer that industry segment Allerton's services. I came up with the idea to go after the women's market, and Stu okayed it."

Jim nodded encouragingly.

I went on. "I discovered a small newspaper that caters to women business owners. It's called *Majority Report*. The paper listed the names of women-owned businesses in New York, and I started calling people from the list.

"Some of the women asked for help managing their businesses, some were just starting out, so I got together with a few women I know, a lawyer, a financial consultant and an insurance agent, and we developed the classes. We talk about incorporating versus sole proprietorship or partnership, insurance, taxes. We also talk about cash flow, leasing or buying equipment and so on. A series runs for four weeks, and we do have seminars booked for the next few months. Our phones have been ringing off the hook."

Even though I was planning to cancel them this very afternoon, I couldn't resist plugging the classes.

"And have the seminars proven to be profitable for Allerton Bank?"

"That's Mr. Lewen's department, profit. But I think he'll tell you that we haven't been doing this long enough for it to have been very profitable yet. No new business can count on profit for at least the first year or two. And we're like a new business. We haven't even begun to scratch the surface of our market yet."

"Were you aware before you began to go after the women's market that Allerton has a reputation of some notoriety?"

"No, Jim. But I discovered the *Voice* articles after I started working for Allerton. I have to admit to being a little confused at this point about what it means—for me, my career, for the women I've met who have become my clients. Stu seemed to think that if we do good things now, go after women and minority groups, we can make up for the crimes the *Voice* implied Allerton committed. Maybe, I don't know. But I'd want to be very sure the bank isn't involved in anything illegal *anymore*. As Stu said, so far nothing illegal has been proven. If that should change, well, I would have to see." I took a deep breath. I suddenly realized how I would feel at Pam's dinner in two weeks—in front of an audience!—saying things like this.

"Yes, well, we have a lot of smoke, it seems. And some of it seems to be camouflaging what may or may not be fire. Well, thank you both for being with us tonight."

It was over! He cut it off just as I was getting started!

Jim stood up, nodded at both of us and started to walk off the set.

Standing there, his hands hanging limply at his sides, Stu looked worn out. He turned and strode toward the door. By the time I got to the elevators, the corridor was empty. But when I got downstairs, Stu was waiting for me in the lobby.

I kept walking and he walked right along with me. "What kind of story is he doing?"

"How should I know? Didn't you think he'd ask questions like that?"

He was silent. Then, "Can I give you a lift home this evening?"

Uh-oh. No way, Jose!

I shook my head. "No. Actually, I'm not sure I'm going home." It wasn't a very good lie, but it was the best I could come up with on such short notice. I wanted to ask him if he was crazy; in fact, I wondered if he was suffering from some kind of disconnect. Didn't the man know what he'd done?

"How come?"

I could feel my left eyebrow go up. What? How come? What was wrong with him? I had to get away from him. Was it the feeling of power? Did he think he could just do anything he wanted?

What gave him the idea that what I did was any of his business, anyway? Before I could ask a more polite version of those questions, he blurted out: "I'm in love with you, Winnie."

I stopped, completely floored. God, the man took my breath away! Was that inappropriate or was there something wrong with *me*?

"Oh, bull, Stu. You don't even know me." I turned toward him. "In fact, that's a fact. You don't know anything about me, or my past."

"I know you well enough. Your past doesn't matter."

This was sounding like a scene from Thomas Hardy. What did he think I'd meant? That I'd slept with other men? This wasn't the 1800s.

"Stu, you're so weird. What I'm talking about is . . . remember what I told you about growing up in Brooklyn?"

"I know. You told me. You really grew up in Montreal."

"Yes. But only from the age of eight on. Before that I lived right across the street from you. I used to watch your mother feeding you."

He stared at me. "What are you talking about?" Was Stu finally unnerved? Had I actually disoriented him?

"I was younger than you, am younger than you, by a few years. Your father was a cop. Moe Lewenthal. Right?"

"How did you know that?"

"My father was Avi Tannen." I watched him carefully to see what effect that would have.

"Tannen? Not Charles?"

"For god's sake, Stu, Charles is my married name. You know that." I *had* disoriented him!

"You're Avi Tannen's daughter? The one whose body was found near the Half Moon?"

"By your father."

"Right. That's what happened. My dad found him." He was nearly whispering, as if he had to show respect for the dead. "That was your father?"

"Yes, Stu. That's right. My father was the one your father found."

"Let's go somewhere for . . . coffee, or dinner, or something. Have you eaten?"

We started to walk in the same direction again. "No, actually I'm starving." Was I going to *eat* with this man?

"Let's go somewhere nearby." His voice was the softest I'd ever heard it. "I'd really like to talk to you. There's a small bar around the corner that makes good burgers."

I still didn't know if I felt safe enough to even go some place around the corner with him. My anxiety now had two sources—his sexual aggression and his father's possible tie to my father's murder.

Right now I was scared—of everything. Should I even be talking to the man? He wasn't making me feel any calmer, that's for sure. But I *was* hungry.

"Okay." *Did I say 'okay'?!*

We settled into a booth and he leaned across the table.

"Why didn't you tell me any of this sooner?" His voice was gentle, not accusing.

"Because . . . I thought, I think, your father . . ."

"What?"

"Stu, your father was a crooked cop."

He leaned back, his hands gripping the table. He nodded.

"So some people thought. I doubt it, though. No more than any other honest, hardworking New York City cop. But that doesn't explain why you didn't tell me you knew me."

"My family thought, and I think, I guess, that he was somehow in on my father's death."

There. I got it out.

"In on? You mean you think Avi was still alive when my father . . ."

"No, fool. I think your father was involved with . . . whoever . . . killed him." Silence.

My stomach was starting to hurt. I was losing my appetite. Why was I saying these things? Wasn't I in enough

trouble? What was I thinking? I wasn't. That was the trouble.
Maybe, I thought, I should get up and just get out of here.

"Why would you say something like that?"

"He was the one who found him. And . . . I don't know."
I'd believed it for so long I'd gotten to the point where I just took
it for granted. But I had no reason to think Moe had killed Avi.
No reason other than that I also thought he was a cop on the
take—like thousands of other cops in the city. "I don't know," I
repeated, watching Stu's face.

I had to hold on to the thought that this man who was
claiming to be in love with me might himself be a crook. Though
that, too, seemed less and less likely. All he was was what Melba
called him: a lech.

"Winnie, my father couldn't have been the one who
killed your dad. Avi had been dead for several hours by the time
he found his . . . body."

"I know that! I think he was covering up the fact that he
knew who did do it."

"He was at the Half Moon nearly the whole night."

"So we heard. He was on duty 'protecting' Abe Reles."

"That's not true. He was being honored that night. There
was a dinner at the hotel the evening before, and it lasted until
early in the morning. Then, because they drank so much, a few of
the guys, his cronies, you know, decided to stay at the hotel. They
rented a room—nowhere near Reles. All the excitement with
Reles woke them. My dad decided he wanted to go home. He

found your father on his way. It was very early in the morning. While the ambulance was still at the hotel. So many people were with him, so many people saw him, he couldn't possibly have had anything to do with Avi's death. He didn't even know your dad."

That was true. Amazing, but true. Two people in New York could live across the street from one another for years, even see into each other's windows, and not know each other. I hadn't known about the dinner, though it didn't prove anything, one way or the other. But I was starting to see that I really had no reason to believe that Stu's dad had had anything to do with Avi's death.

I suddenly saw, with great clarity, that Stu probably had no idea why my father was killed.

Or by whom.

* * * * *

We got back to the bank at noon, just in time for my lunch meeting with Melba.

The phone rang as I got to my desk.

"Winnie. I have to tell you something."

I held the phone on my shoulder as I watched the tellers come out from behind their windows. It was noon on the dot. I waved to them.

"Winnie, are you there?"

"Hi Melba, yes. I'll be right down."

"Winnie, wait a minute. We've got another problem. I've been going over the accounts all morning and I found something

315

weird. Pam Freeman withdrew all the money she just deposited. That's the second time she did that. Made a big deposit—$650,000—and then withdrew nearly the whole thing."

"What's wrong with that? It's her money."

"No, you don't understand. She took almost the whole thing, but left the account open. She took it in a check made out to another bank."

It took me a minute to realize what Melba was talking about. Then I understood: Benjie wasn't the only crook. She had opened her account with a check from another bank. And she'd made this deposit, too, with a check from another bank. We'd have to talk to the other banks, but this didn't look good. Someone opens accounts at two or three banks and uses the float time of available funds to create fraudulent balances.

She pretends she has money at three different banks so she can borrow money she doesn't actually have—a Ponzi scheme that could net her millions!

I couldn't believe it! My only client with some *real* money, and her money was less "real" than anyone's.

"Omigod, Melba. What are you going to do?"

"I got in touch with the state office and they're looking into it. Looks like your client's been kiting.

Twenty five

Stu wasn't in the bank the next day. Margaret told me he was out of town for a few days. Good, Monday I'd be at Aunt Golde's. I was leaving from LaGuardia Sunday night. By the time he got back, I'd be gone.

The first thing I did was call Melba. She wasn't there, but she'd left a message for me. She'd begun the investigation to see what was going on with Pam Freeman. If her suspicions were on the mark, then my only substantial client was more air than substance. My other clients, small as they were, were at least honest.

The day went quickly. I spent a good part of it between appointments and phone calls and during my lunch hour, jotting down notes for the Woman Executive talk.

When I woke up Saturday morning, it was dark and cloudy. The radio predicted rain all weekend. A perfect excuse for staying in to study the papers I'd copied at the bank the other night. Copies of the copies, actually. I'd made copies of everything and put a set into a safe deposit box at the Blue Wood

Bank. This stuff was combustible. I had to be careful with it. I'd make another set for Melba before leaving tomorrow and stop at the bank on my way to the airport.

I got going early, spreading everything out on the living room floor, my morning coffee on the table next to me. I started making piles by category: one for each director on the Allerton board, one for Stu and one for each officer. After a while, some of the piles had to be divided up. Kalmowitz got his own pile. Stu's also grew pretty high. There were papers from auditors, various people on the State Banking Commission, city and state officials; I finally put each of these into its own pile, as well, no matter to whom they were addressed.

This took most of the morning. Annie, my adopted kitty, kept doing running slides into and on top of the piles. She seemed to think I was constructing a playground just for her. I finally had to pick her up, carry her upstairs, nuzzling her soft fur as I went, put her in my room and shut the door. She scratched and banged—I could never understand how she managed to make such a loud sound. But at least I kept the paper piles separated.

When everything was sorted, I began to read. Everything I'd told Melba I suspected was true. The bank I was working for, the bank I had turned into *the* New York bank for women, was being run in an odd way. On Allerton's payroll were the names of relatives and friends of government officials and, in fact, of all

318

the directors. On a separate sheet of payroll paper, in back of one folder marked "Private—Allerton Staff," were names of the people I knew at the Manhattan branch, without any of the alien names, and another list of people in each of the other two branches, different, smaller lists than the one Melba said Bobbie had "mislaid." Surely here was evidence of payroll padding.

Loan applications—approved by Allerton's board of directors—to well-known crime bosses all over the city were in a pile; many seemed to my admittedly amateur eye uncollectible. In addition, in the same folder I found letters to officials on the State Banking Commission, as well as to a number of people high up in both city and state government positions, thanking them for their help; stapled to some of these were bookkeeping sheets showing assets, with several very large accounts held by city agencies holding a good chunk of those assets. These accounts alone totalled eight million dollars—all of it interest-free. Well, now I knew where Allerton's extra funds for payroll padding were coming from.

And what had Allerton done to deserve such "help"? I wondered.

I suddenly felt tired and needed to stretch and walk around, so I went into the kitchen for lunch, fed the cat, and then put on my raincoat and took a walk to the nearby brook. I often came here to sit on the large, nearly flat rock that overlooked the water. Even today, with a fine rain gently pelting my face, I felt soothed here.

I mulled what I'd found.

Padded payroll, bad loans and, maybe most important, interest-free accounts holding millions of city dollars—and listed as Allerton assets. The things this bank was doing were probably serious enough to shut it down and put all the directors away—and I was holding the evidence.

I had found more than I'd bargained for. Here, indeed, was a chance to avenge my father's death. By exposing Allerton Bank's criminal activities, I would also expose Stu—either as someone involved, or at the very least, even if he was innocent himself, as Melba said—but which I didn't believe!—as the president who hadn't put an end to the wrongdoing.

I knew I shouldn't conflate the son and the father. One could be a bad guy and the other one good. Maybe I was getting a little carried away, but my fury at Stu made me want to get even—with the whole Lewenthal family.

But I didn't really want to see the bank closed down. This bank was the only one right now doing business with women business owners. I didn't want to stop the women's classes, either. Nor did I want to lose my job. I was just starting to like it. But there wasn't any choice. These guys were stealing from all of us, everyone, at least, who lived in the city. I couldn't let them keep on doing these things. Maybe I would find another place to run my women's program. Maybe the Women's Bank would be interested when it opened.

If only I could find something that would implicate Stu, leave no doubt about his guilt. Oh, how I wished I could get him, hurt him, see him tortured by shame! Not only for what he'd done to me, but for all the years of being fatherless. Not to visit the sins of the father on the son. But my need for revenge was greater than logic, greater than my social conscience, greater than anything right now.

The rain had stopped a little. Some of my neighbors were out for walks, kids were dancing around the basketball hoop at the corner house. There was only the finest mist coming down now, but I was feeling chilled.

Time to go back and finish sorting those papers.

On my way I noticed that the leaves that had turned rusty weeks ago were growing sparse; soon the trees would be bare. I loved fall, and already missed the flowers that had just started showing up but were now gone: the blue snowballs, the yellow and orange chrysanthemums, the end-of-summer roses. I sighed. Was this job like a summer romance, soon to end, too?

I stood on my front steps a few minutes, thinking about getting some wood from the garage and making a fire in the fireplace. It would feel so cozy. But it wasn't that cool. Not yet. I let myself in and went back to my paper-sorting.

I went through paper after paper, getting more and more bleary-eyed. But by midnight, I'd found enough evidence to put Allerton out of business and throw the entire board and many public officials with whom they were colluding into jail for a long time. City officials were daily feeding Allerton enormously large, interest-free deposits. The *Voice* articles had speculated that this might be so—and here was the proof!

It isn't unusual for banks to keep deposits of this sort for the city, though Allerton was getting too big a share of this. Even more incriminating, though, was another investment Allerton seemed to be making with this money. From the well-known gangland names on some of the letters and on various invoices, it seemed that Allerton might be financing heroin transactions for some of the city's best-known organized crime families. I'd been reading, not only in the *Voice*, but in other papers, as well, that some of the city's other banks might be involved in these deals.

I still had no proof of Stu's involvement. I decided to look through his desk and his files when I stopped at the bank tomorrow on my way to the airport.

Twenty six

I left Steven's kitten with Marilyn Lewen for the time I'd be away, got into my car and drove into the city. I parked on Sixth and walked the half a block to the bank. The platform was in shadows, deepening in the approaching dusk; the rear of the bank was already dark. I pulled out the flashlight I'd shoved into my bag, but didn't turn it on until I got to the staircase. The last thing I needed was a curious tourist peering through the glass, wondering why a light was on.

I headed downstairs to Melba's office, hid the copies I'd made at the Blue Wood Copy Shop in a place we'd agreed upon and went back upstairs to the office shared by Stu and Benjie. Melba was probably right, but I couldn't let go of the thought that I might be able to get Stu with the same evidence I was using against Benjie and the board.

I started with his desk. The center drawer held only a few paper clips and a couple of pens. The left top drawer was jammed with the yellow legal pads he used for notes when grilling potential lenders. Under it, in the left bottom drawer, were files. I thumbed through them slowly at first, surprised at the separate folder he kept for the applications of the women who'd come to Allerton after attending my seminars. They were marked "Women," as if women and men must be different kinds of borrowers. The other folders were broken down by industry. "Jukeboxes." "Auto dealers." "Real estate." The one that surprised me was one headed "Minority businesses." Was Stu planning to tout the bank as "good to all oppressed groups"? As far as I knew, no one at Allerton was going after the business of any minority groups other than women—and crooked politicians.

That drawer, too, yielded nothing.

On the right, the drawers were messier. Folders piled on folders, some not marked. Going through them I found handwritten notes on sheets from the legal pads, small slips of paper with phone numbers, envelopes marked "Personal." The first few of those turned out to be from women he'd apparently been dating. There seemed to be several women in his life currently. I knew my creeping rage was unreasonable. But going out with a number of women—some of whom seemed smitten!— made his moves on me seem even more smarmy.

Underneath everything was a date book for this year. I put it aside, starting a pile of things I would take.

The file cabinet behind his desk was mainly for bank operations, bookkeeping records of profit and loss, payroll records, maintenance and supplies. These were the sorts of things I wanted, though most were copies of records kept upstairs by Bobbie and downstairs by Harry. I turned anything that looked new to an upright, vertical position to mark the spot; later I'd pull out everything I'd marked and go downstairs to copy it, then I'd return everything to the drawers they'd come from. I'd read it all on the plane or in Canada when I got to Aunt Golde's. When I reached the bottom drawer, I found copies of the *Voice* articles. Copies of the payroll records I'd discovered downstairs were in another folder. Wow! If he wasn't in cahoots with the board, he sure knew what they were doing. There were also letters in this drawer; thumbing through them I saw letterheads from the Federal and State Reserve boards and other official-sounding offices. I marked those, too, by turning them vertical.

Suddenly, I was aware of sounds I hadn't heard before. I quickly shut the flashlight and pressed myself against the wall. It was the sort of thing you might see in a movie. Pressed against the wall, I was no less visible than if I'd stood in the middle of the room. But I felt safer.

Someone had just come into the bank.

I heard footsteps tapping their way across the platform. Was Benjie coming to his office? No. The sound was now coming from the staircase going to the basement. As soon as they got to the bottom of the stairs, I pulled out all the vertical papers and quickly shut the drawers, then I shoved my flashlight into my bag and hurried across the platform to the front door.

Damn! Of course. It was locked. I knelt to put my key into the lock at the bottom of it when I heard the footsteps coming back up. My fingers started shaking and I couldn't get the damn door unlocked.

Hurry, hurry. Here he comes. Omigod.

Just as the lock clicked open, Benjie reached the top of the stairs. We locked eyes across the amphitheater-like platform as I thrust the front door open and stepped outside.

"Hey!" He was running across the platform, I could see him through the glass. "Tannen, you! Tannen!" he shouted.

I ran up the block, hugging my bag to my chest, hoping I could get to my car before he caught up with me. Nearly to the corner, I allowed myself to look back. Benjie wasn't following. He was standing next to the bank, holding the glass door open, looking after me.

I didn't love the look on his face.

Twenty seven

Getting to the airport, I kept checking the rear-view mirror. It didn't hit me until I got to the Triboro Bridge that Benjie had called me "Tannen." He knew who I was! Would he have me followed? Would I be able to tell if someone was following me?

The thought was surreal: That old man in the flashy suits and shoes following me? It was ludicrous. Nor could I imagine him running to the phone and calling a henchman with instructions. "Don't let her out of your sight!" That's the stuff of bad movies. In real life it's bizarre to think that the chairman of Allerton's board would have me followed for stealing some papers. Fired, yes. But followed?

I got to the airport in time to check my bags and race to the gate. No one seemed to be running after me here, either. I boarded, found my seat and wriggled into a comfortable position, peering out the window to see if anyone out there seemed to be perusing the windows for a face like mine.

Maybe he'd called someone to go with me on the plane. I examined the faces behind me and the bits of body parts I could see in the rows in front of mine before I realized he couldn't possibly know where I was. I hadn't told anyone at the bank where I planned to go on my vacation. When people had asked, for some reason I myself couldn't fathom, I'd felt secretive about going home to Aunt Golde.

When Harry, Melba and Bobbie had asked over a bridge game one lunchtime, I'd actually lied and said I was going to Jamaica. I felt guilty afterward, but I didn't say, "Just kidding." Now I was glad I'd been so paranoid.

Of course, I was probably being even more paranoid now.

I put my bag under the seat in front of me, belted myself in and opened my newspaper, took a breath and tried to relax. The newsprint blurred as I tried to read. I put it into my lap and glanced out the window again. This was going to be a tense ride.

I was wrong, though. It was uneventful, and by the time we arrived in Montreal two hours later I was so relaxed I was nearly in a stupor. The two bloody Marys probably had something to do with my zone-out.

I grabbed a cab and gave the driver the address: "*Le Mieux, cinquante sept, cinquante sept, s'il vous plait.*"

I settled into the seat and started to look forward to my vacation. I planned to visit old Montreal, my favorite place in the city, to shop everywhere I could, to see two old friends from high school who were living traditional married lives, which in Montreal was of the Donna Reed variety. Propriety here still ruled family arrangements and all social life. But I looked forward to the stability of the expected. Lunches with old friends. An afternoon at the tennis club. A sisterhood dinner at the synagogue. I also planned to spend a few days alone in the cabin up-country where Uncle Dovid and I had gone on our fishing trips.

But mostly I looked forward to visiting Uncle Dovid. I wished he could go there with me now. Spending some quiet time alone in the cabin had its attractions; I planned to read the stuff I'd taken from Stu's office to see if I could find anything incriminating. I wouldn't be able to do that here, as I certainly had no intention of telling Aunt Golde what was going on. But being in the woods with Uncle Dovid, fishing, cooking together, drinking some schnapps and reminiscing would be more fun than spending even the much-needed quiet time by myself. As the cab zipped through familiar neighborhoods I thought about different times I'd walked or driven here with him, laughing at his raucous jokes, listening to his take on life, on family, on love. The Uncle Dovid I would visit at the nursing home wouldn't be the Uncle Dovid of my memories.

Aunt Golde was waiting for me in front of the red-brick building, sitting with some of her ladies in her black-and-white fold-up beach chair. She remained seated while I paid the cabdriver and got out of the cab. Then, for the millionth time, she formally introduced me to each one of her friends, reminding me which one's son practiced medicine in Vermont, which one's granddaughter had earned a scholarship for music. And reminding them of my achievements, my two sons who, according to her, were brilliant, good-looking *and* thorough gentlemen. When the amenities were accomplished to her satisfaction, she stood up and bent to fold her chair, waving away my offer to help without looking up at me.

She had dinner prepared and the table set, wouldn't let me help, made me sit and tell her "everything."

"I want to know what you're doing, who you're doing it with. The boys, what do you hear from them? Are they enjoying?"

I filled her in on the children's letter-writing and its lack of useful information. "Mostly they ask me to send them things, cookies, Steven's baseball glove. It's the things they don't say I'm interested in. When I spoke to the camp director the other day he told me Paulie keeps disappearing into the woods with some girl. They've both been given heavy schedules and responsibilities to keep them busier, but they have to have some free time. That's what I'd like to know about. What goes on during free time?"

I told her, again, about some of the work I was doing, and about the stirrings of something the newspapers were beginning to call—derogatively—"women's lib," about all the women who were speaking out in every field. I tried to explain it, how it had happened, all at once, all of a sudden, that women in America, middle-class women, seemed no longer satisfied with things her generation had thought "natural."

She shook her head. She didn't understand, but I continued; I was on a roll.

They were writing things, women in America, pamphlets, books, trying to explain their feelings, the social situation, meeting in little cells in people's living rooms, sharing experiences, surprised at the overlap, the statistical burgeoning, and they were writing about that, too. They held meetings and were starting to plan conferences to categorize the overlaps, to discuss the problems they were having in their lives with husbands, bosses, parents, as not just "personal," not theirs alone, not their fault, not for the couch, but as "political," as susceptible to change, to social action.

"Who are these women?" Aunt Golde wanted to know.

"There are more of them than people think. Some are women who marched against the war, the Vietnam war, former student protesters, some from Civil Rights days. They realized they were talking about social justice and the men were still asking them to make the coffee. Some are older, the generation that gave their jobs back to the guys who came home after World War II and then they spent their days dancing around the kitchen with floor polishers. And there's the group in the middle, the suburban Bloomingdale ladies, Friedan's bunch, who'd been drinking their days away in silent, lonely misery."

Aunt Golde smiled, her silent little closed-mouth smile and shook her head. She wasn't sure she knew what I was talking about, but she just went ahead and ladled the soup into our soup

331

bowls. I got up to carry them to the table. "No!" she practically screamed at me. "Sit! You're on vacation."

As she carried first one bowl then the other to the table, I tried to protest. "Auntie Golde, carrying a couple of bowls of your soup won't ruin my vacation. In fact, it's part of my vacation."

She gave me that famous wave again, the one she gives without looking at me. "Sit," she ordered again. I had no choice.

"So, tell me more."

"My job at the bank is really interesting. I didn't think I'd like it, but it's exciting."

I told her about the seminars and the chartreuse sign on the window of the bank with my name in huge letters glaring out across Rockefeller Plaza. And I explained about the hundreds, maybe thousands, of women starting their own businesses, and how creative they were, how daring.

I told her how a woman might come into the bank and there'd be nothing but a thought in her head one day and then, a couple of weeks later, there'd be, from practically nothing— because even Allerton wouldn't lend her the millions it sometimes handed out to some of the men—from practically nothing, there'd be a store on Broadway selling exotic jewelry from Africa or a someone with an idea for her own dress line, then actually designing them, sitting and sewing them, producing them, carting them around by herself to all the high class department stores, and then suddenly having the money—

thanks to Allerton!—to actually promote them and her name on the way to becoming a household word.

"An idea. Then"—I snapped my fingers—"a reality!"

"So, who's watching all their children?"

We both laughed.

"Oh! And Auntie Golde, you'll never guess who I'm working for! Stuey Lewenthal. Remember who that is?"

"Lewenthal? The cop?"

"His son. He's the president of the bank. Allerton, it's called. Allerton Bank."

She slammed her spoon onto the table. "Kalmowitz." She pronounced his name without inflection. No punctuation needed. The name itself spoke volumes. As if she'd said, "Hitler."

"You work for Kalmowitz."

"How do you know that?"

"What, I shouldn't know from Kalmowitz? All his doings? He lived here once."

"What?!"

"Well, not here. Not in this apartment. Not in our house, neither. In the cabin. Up in the woods."

"Benjie Kalmowitz lived in the cabin? When?"

"You were here then. We just came back with you a few weeks before. You were a *kint*, only eight years old, an orphan." Tears sparkled in the corners of her eyes. She lifted her napkin and touched them, each one, gently, tapping it dry. "He came in the evening, one night we just came from *shul*, he was in trouble.

Someone in New York had been killed and he had to leave because the police were questioning everyone. Who knows what he was mixed up in, that *momzer*." I'd never heard Aunt Golde call anyone a bastard before. "He was afraid," she continued, "so mine Dovidl helped him. He didn't know I knew it, I was in the bedroom when he came, putting you to bed, and Dovid didn't know I heard where they were going. I kept quiet. What could I say? He owed him. After all, he helped your father that time with the union. And he went with Dovid that time . . . *Oy*, you shouldn't know these things!"

She jumped up, grabbed the empty soup bowls and put them in the sink, then she brought the roast chicken to the table on her good platter, surrounded by tiny roasted potatoes and garnished with carrots and onions.

"*What* time? When did he go with Uncle Dovid? Where?"

She shook her head. That was the end of the conversation. If I had learned one thing in the years I was growing up it was that Auntie Golde was stubborn. If she set her mind to something, nothing, *nothing* would change it. If she decided the conversation was over, it was over. *Genug!* Enough! I knew I wouldn't learn any more from her. I wondered if Uncle Dovid would be willing, or able, to fill in the gaps.

I went to visit him the next day.

We understood each other, my Uncle Dovid and me. He saw me walking up the hallway and that knowing look came into his eyes. The disapproval was there; he would never bless my right to live without my husband. But the adoration was unqualified. He always knew something about me that I would spend my life reaching for.

He looked so gaunt, my poor uncle, aging and needing a shave. I knelt by the wheelchair and kissed him and, as I began to get up, he grabbed my shoulders and pulled me to him, gruffly, his fingers gripping me so hard I could feel his hands shaking with the effort. He grinned, nearly toothless; he had taken out his false teeth. He was happy now. His favorite niece was home.

I told him a little about my life, my job, and when I mentioned Benjie Kalmowitz he frowned. Then I asked about his life. "When are you going back home? Auntie Golde misses you. And when are you going to start walking again?"

He waved at me as if to say "Go away," but he started talking. I couldn't stop him.

The Amboy Duchess

Twenty eight

Dovid
1974

The nurses, they leave you alone here. I don't mind about nothing else. All I want is to think, to sort things out.

They got me out of bed this morning early, washed me, then put me in the chair by the window. As if I care to look outside. There's a tree reaches up to the glass, taps the pane. I hear it when I sleep. We know each other, me and this tree. We're the same age, I think.

Cars rattle by downstairs. I could see them if I wanted. Children, too. They play across the street on the sidewalk. And I could see Golde when she comes bouncing up the block, her black pocketbook hanging straight down from her arm, neat, like her house. Her cotton dress is pressed, stiff with the spray starch she uses, and her hair, nearly all white now, is pinned back in that bun she first made nearly fifty years ago when we married. Before that, it was a cloud around her head, blonde, like a *shiksa*, a Gentile woman. She comes to spend the afternoon looking at

337

my back. If I wanted I could watch for her, I could see her bob along. Today maybe she won't come because you're here, my Winnie.

I need to tell you what happened, or anyway what I know. It's time, it's time. I thought you didn't need to know, but now I think different. Soon I'll be gone and all they'll know, the children, is what the others said. It's time you hear what I have to say.

So listen good.

My father. Your Zeyde Asher. They all bowed to him. He didn't deserve it.

He's dead and he's still torturing me.

Golde tells me don't think about him, it's over; a long time it's over. I should think about her, my mother. But all I think is she didn't stop what he did. She was a Jewish wife. What else can you say about a woman?

I remember her. *Benching licht*, lighting candles, on Friday night, her head covered with a lace handkerchief, her fingers pressing down on her eyes. Then she would cut the challah, which she baked herself and call out to anyone who might be near enough to hear, "*Gut Shabbes*!"

They tell me that she wanted to leave him, did leave once, in fact, when Label and Avi were small and I was just a baby. She left Label with him, the old man, only he wasn't old then, Asher, our father was young then, but just as hard. Anyway, she left, and took just me and Avi and went back to her parents in Czernowitz, walking the nine miles from the town her husband traded in then, Roznov, Avi at her side and me slung across her breast. She kicked up dust in her anger as she walked, they said, her eyes blazing like I never saw them, crying how he would yell at her and wouldn't give her any money and how she had to scrimp to feed her babies, to put rags on their bodies, to get the food he wanted her to make for *Shabbes* meals. But they sent her back, her parents and her sister. Like they should. A bargain is a bargain. A wife is a wife. And if they hadn't sent her back, we'd be dead, her and me, and Avi would have died long before you were born, you wouldn't be, in fact. We'd have died in the war, like the others.

Oy, the others, so many. Her parents, his, too, my grandparents, all of them, and uncles and aunts and cousins and neighbors and friends. All of them, dead from the Nazis. Ay! Half of Roznov disappeared. Most of the people I grew up with, who were still there when we left, gone.

I can picture her, what she looked like young, my mother, with thick ridges of red hair, like yours, Winnele, but cut short under her shawl, though not too short—he would not allow it, even as *frum*, devout, as he was—it framed her face, her black skirt swinging around her high laced boots. She was beautiful, they said. But that's not how I remember her. I remember those eyes, faded from all the tears. I remember her kneeling in front of him, washing his feet.

She was no saint. But who is a saint? No saints, no sinners. No good, no bad. Fools, just fools. All of them. All of us.

You come here now, you young people, Label's children, you, and you bring even your children, getting older, with children soon themselves. You kneel at my wheelchair, like you're doing now, ask me questions, as if I could tell you something, as if I had some answer to what burns you. I never had any answers. You have to find your own. All I can tell you is what happened. You have to be your own judge.

They used to laugh at me. Not you, not the young people, not Avi, neither, but your uncle Label, he thought I was stupid to get myself caught. And even that Eva and her man when they came here after the war. They thought I didn't understand things like other people did. They thought I was slow. I thought so, too. I couldn't work, couldn't make any money. Especially after the disease that got me, gonorrhea, when I was working for Label in the restaurant in New York. It was that waitress what I went with to the room she kept upstairs for the men. After the disease, I could never think the same way. I could never plan or figure accounts or move very fast. They said the disease didn't do that to people; maybe not. But I was so heavy with the shame of it— maybe it was that—I couldn't work no more. It was the disease kept us from having children, though, Golde and me, even the doctors said that. But I know it wasn't only the disease. It was because of Pa, too, who never let me live. When they don't let you live, you can't think, you can't do—anything!

Where are my cigarettes? There they are, on the table. Right in front of me. Golde says I smoke too much. Bah! What else have I got left? Boy! Orderly! Come here! A light!

I *drimmel* now, daydream, that's all. *Drimmel* and smoke. And think, and remember. The orderly will push me soon to the day room. You'll come with me. We'll sit at the long table, they'll put something, mashed turnips, maybe, in front of me. I'll eat, he'll pick up the fork, the orderly, give me one forkful at a time, I'll open my mouth, like an infant, swallow, feel the food go down, let it keep me alive a little longer. It will drip down my chin, someone will come and wipe it with a napkin. I don't mind. I have this thinking I have to do.

We came here, to North America, after what they called the war to end all wars—fools!—but before the Shoah. What did they think then? They thought we would go on into the future building ugly factories and making babies, those of us who could, and collecting things, everyone wanting a car, a phonograph, a new pair of shoes every six months.

They needed money to live, even back there, in Roznov. He knew how to finagle, your grandfather. It didn't make us rich. At least not there. We managed. But it wasn't enough, there were always pogroms, taking everything away. So my brothers left, one after the other, each one, to America. But me, I couldn't leave. Me, he grabbed by the collar and pulled back. "*Wie gaidst du?*" he'd say, "Where are you going?" My job it was to help him. He was disappointed with me, I was no Label. I couldn't do what Label could. But Label left. That's what he did. The best thing, it was the best thing, though we didn't know that then.

Label swam the river with the flasks he was supposed to sell tied up around his waist. He hugged me first, I'll never forget. I watched him tie his clothes in a *schmatte*, a rag, and hang them from a stick so he could hold it over his head while he glided through the cold water. We were strong swimmers, me and my brothers. At least he taught us that, the old man. Yet, Labele died in the water, can you believe? But that was no accident like everyone said.

But that day I walked with him, held the stick while he tied the flasks around his waist, and then he turned and gave me a hug. I knew he wasn't coming back, though he never told me. Only Avi he told. They held that secret and just went, those *shtarkers*! I didn't see him again until I got to America ten years later.

Then it was Avi's turn. Label left with Benjie Kalmowitz and Avi left with his buddy, Moishe, the *trombeniks*, trouble-makers, of the town. They stole the coins the old man kept in with Ma's linens. He knew, my Pa, that she wouldn't take them. He didn't think his sons would go behind his back, neither. But he was proud when they did. I'll never forget. I worried that whole day how Pa would beat him, my Avi, when he got back. It was only later I understood that he went, too, to America, like Label. But he laughed, the old man. "*Goniff!*" he yelled, shaking his head. "Thief!" But his shrewd blue eyes twinkled. They showed him, his sons, that they learned how to be just like him, doing what they wanted, no matter who got in the way, even him.

Avi was different, though, than Label. Avi didn't go until after Etke died, screaming in terror through a pogrom and then fallen sick with no doctor to treat her. My Etke, my sister, only a child. Avi was in Vienna then. Not even fifteen and they sent him to Vienna without any money. He told me he stole rolls to eat. He wanted to go to school, so he was glad to go, but school cost more money than he could make stealing rolls, selling rags. So he came back and Etkele was gone. He cried, my brother Avi, he loved her so much. I'll never forget the tears that came on his face, only Avi would cry that way. And he blamed the old man. "You did this!" he yelled to him. He made me feel afraid. I thought the old man might beat him terrible. "Where's our education? Where's our safe home? What kind of father are you? Why don't you take us to America like a *mensch*?" It was the only time anyone ever stood up that way and nothing happened. And then he left, too, my Avi, following after Label.

Avi's words must have got to him, my Pa, because after that we went. He made us pack up, Ma and me, and we took Gitel with us, too, Ma's *schvester*, her sister, and her husband and their baby, all of us ending up not in New York, but here in Montreal, because of the quotas that year. But it wasn't Siberia. From New York they could still come to him, Label and Avi. I remember, they used to come to show Pa how much money they made, and to Ma they came when they needed to tell something. Avi came once when he was planning to get married, he got so scared of what he was about to do, scared, I think, because he was afraid he wouldn't be good enough for poor Stella, your poor mother, dead too soon, too. He ran away to Ma, but she sent him back. "It's time for a *khasene*, time for a wedding," she said, patting him on the shoulder. And he went. She was the best thing what ever happened to him, Stella, but her dying was the worst. Almost the worst.

Her you could talk to, my mother. To him they bowed. But the bowing didn't stop them from making their lives. It was enough, the little bit of running they did. It was all they needed, so they could think. Me, he held in his fists. Me, he sent to jail.

We lived, first, on Esplanade, then we moved to De Boullion. It wasn't like home in Roznov. Home we had land, trees, air to breathe. The house in Roznov wasn't big, but it was always clean and we had fireplaces in all the rooms and the main room always smelled of Ma's cooking. And anyone else's who brought a pot of *chalunt*, stew, or some *rugaluch* so they could join us in a meal. Here in Canada we were squeezed into a row of rooms, joined along a dark hallway, the bathroom in the house, two little dirt yards, one in front, one in back. There wasn't any air and the streets were concrete and the houses touched each other so you could hear your neighbors yelling at their children or fighting with each other. The only tree was the one that was dying in the back. I couldn't take it, so I left. I went to Label in New York where it wasn't better, it was worse, but I worked for him in the restaurant, that's how we did, we helped each other, always. Like in the old country. Only that's when I got the disease. When I was better, they sent me home.

"*Schlepper!*" he yelled. "*Du bist a grosser schlemazel!* Who lets a whore make him sick? Only a fool!" he hollered. I didn't blame him, he was right.

And then he put me to work.

Ay! Where is she, my Goldele? She isn't coming today? She knows when she comes I make like I'm sleeping. I think: maybe she won't stay. But she sits there, foolish woman. Don't she see I don't want her? I can feel her all the time behind me, my back burns with her accusations. "Old man," she thinks. I can hear it, like I always heard. "Old man, get up from the chair! Come home already! It's time you walked again." Don't she know I won't walk again? Why should I? You don't need to take steps to move with your thoughts. Go home, Goldele, that's what I think. We had enough years. Now it's time for you to live by yourself. But she don't hear me. Maybe that's because I don't look at her anymore when I think.

She used to hear. We never needed words. She knew everything what I wanted. Why don't she hear me now? I still hear. I hear everything. So clear. "At least get a haircut. Shave." She thinks this. "Can't you hear?" This she thinks also. Because I don't listen, she thinks I don't hear. She thinks I look like a grizzled old man. And she's probably right. That's what I am, why shouldn't I look like it? Goldele, I always say, go home. She don't listen. All she wants is for me to shave.

We met in Label's store, me and Golde. More than fifty years ago. She came to New York from Cincinnati, so I thought she was an American, even though she didn't talk like one. Then I found out she came with her brothers from a town smaller than Roznov. It was after the illness that we met. I never told her about the illness. Such a secret I had from my Goldele. But she knew it. One day she asked me, "Dovidl, is it because you was sick we can't have any children?" It was after that we got you, my wonderful Winnie, after Avele . . . Ay! I still can't think of him without crying. Ay, ay. What they did to you, my brother.

The day I first laid eyes on her, my Goldele, was when I came down to see Label with money from Pa for the bank. He gave all the money to Label. It was safer in New York, he thought, than in Canada. That was because of how he got it, the money. He thought in Canada, so close to where he was cheating, he would get caught.

In Europe, we weren't rich, but we got by on the whiskey he sold. It was enough to feed us, a family of six. Here Pa didn't know how to work, so he became a money lender at first. But that wasn't good. He didn't like it, seeing people always in trouble, coming to him and him making more trouble for them, lending money is always trouble. He liked taking care of problems for people, not making them. It was Prohibition what gave him the chance. He could go back to selling what he knew. We always made our own schnapps and our own *Shabbes* wine. Now we made more and we sold it for a big profit. Some I took to Label to sell in the back of the store, what they were calling now a "speakeasy." After Prohibition Label made the store into a regular tavern.

I came there the day I met your Aunt Goldele. She was sitting at the table in back where the family always sat. Label and me, we did our business behind the counter, and I asked him, "Who is the beauty with the yellow hair?" Right away, I knew I would marry her if she would have me.

He poked me in the ribs with his elbow. "This one you don't take to any room upstairs," he warned. I shook my head. I couldn't take my eyes off of her.

I took her to Canada after we married and we lived with Ma and Pa. Pa made her cook for everyone when he saw how good she did it. She never even complained, my Goldele. Like now. She sits there when she comes, her lips pressed together. Bah! Stay home, woman, don't come here no more. She didn't complain, neither, when I had to go to jail for the old man. She stayed in his house, cooked and took care of Ma, and waited for me to come back. Three months we were away, me and Benjie Kalmowitz, can you believe? Three months, the two of us, in jail!

Jail!

They were the bootleggers. They were the ones who cut all the corners, my brother and Benjie. Not Avi, though. Avi didn't think like them. I only did what they told me. Benjie and Label were the ones what played stickball in the street with those thugs in Brooklyn, and sat with them in the *schvitzes*, in the steambaths, too, where they did all their deals. And me, who didn't know a bottle of grape juice from a cow, I'm the one got picked to go to prison when the old man got caught. "At least you'll be good for something," he said to me. My own father. One of his neighbors turned him in. They sent us to jail for driving across the border to New York with a few crates in the back. And Benjie never forgave us, me or Label or Pa, he had it in for the whole family after that, even though I helped him after, when he was in trouble. If I knew then what I found out later, I would have done different.

Maybe Label would still be here . . .

The Amboy Duchess

The worst was how angry Benjie was from what Label did to his sister. She wasn't right for Label, no one blamed him for the women he had, even Benjie; they didn't mean nothing to him. But when he took up with Eva, that was different. Benjie never could forgive him for that. Eva was the love of Label's life and that hurt them, Benjie and Donya.

Ay, what Benjie done!

All the things he done to us. All Avi wanted was an education he didn't get and the old man to think he was the smartest, but that was Label's job, to be the smartest. Label got money and control, like the old man, and women even after he married, and he even got the old man's respect. But he didn't have it long. And me, I'm still here. I didn't get what they got, but I now got something I don't want, I got long life, time to think, too much time to remember.

When I came back from jail, I didn't live no more with Ma and Pa. I got my own house that Pa sold me for a good price. A ten-year mortgage he gave me. His own son he made money from. But we didn't care. We were so glad to be there, by ourselves. We had two bathrooms in that house, one with a toilet, the other a sink. I was working then for Auntie Gitel's boy. No more driving, no more smuggling anything across any borders.

After that was when Avi died and we got you Winnie. Pa didn't like us taking in a little orphan, a girl no less. His own grandchild. But a girl. She should go to her American

349

grandparents, he said. What for do you need a girl, to feed and dress and find a husband for? He knew only the old ways. But we settled it together, the two of us, Goldele and me, and nothing would make us change, not even the old man.

You made us have a life, Winnie. You were our luck.

The orderly is coming down the hall there now, do you see? It's good because I'm tired, my Winnie.

Twenty nine

Jail.

My Uncle Dovid in jail.

I couldn't breathe. We sat in the solarium, alone, just the two of us, a quiet, dim room, surrounded by screened windows, filled with fake leather couches and tables empty even of magazines. He talked and talked, my uncle, making up for any silences or miscommunications or failures in understanding we might have suffered through the years. He talked and I listened, riveted.

The orderly came in as Uncle Dovid drooped with fatigue. "That's enough of a visit for today, Mr. Tannen." He took hold of the wheelchair and got ready to wheel him out to the hallway. I leaned down and kissed him.

"I'm going up to the cabin for a few days, Uncle Dovid. I'll visit you again when I get back."

Outside I began to walk without figuring out where I wanted to go. There was so much I hadn't known; I couldn't absorb it all.

I'd never realized what Zeyde Asher had done to my uncle, how hard Zeyde could be. I used to think if I was invisible to Zeyde Asher it was because there was something wrong with me. All my cousins loved and respected, even revered, him. Sometimes I thought it was because I wasn't a boy. How could a girl be a Tannen? It was an oxymoron.

Tannens were male, like my grandfather, he defined the family. He loomed with his patriarchal beard, grasping the world with a greedy fist, laughing at life, his blue eyes twinkling. His voice resounded with pronouncements, political opinions, religious ponderings, tall tales, jokes. A trickster with shaggy dog stories, telling them out loud to the world or up close and intimate, either way he seemed like a god. If I was invisible to this god then it was my fault, not his. Gods don't have faults.

But if he could hurt Uncle Dovid, send him to jail, he was far from a god.

Zeyde's imperfection, somehow, reassured me. I felt stronger knowing I wasn't the only damaged one. Maybe we're all damaged. Maybe Zeyde's imperfection meant he too was damaged, maybe being damaged is what it is to be "only human." We're all damaged in some way, all imperfect. For some reason, the sudden clarity of this flagrant truth made me feel stronger.

Uncle Label and Zeyde Asher, and even Avi, were only human, but they had managed the survival of the clan.

And I could do it, too. I could make mistakes, if they were mistakes, leaving home, marrying the wrong man, getting divorced, changing jobs, even losing jobs—for I surely would lose the one I had now at the bank—and none of it meant I lacked anything crucial to being a good human being, or that I was bad or a failure or even an outsider, as I'd felt myself to be so many times in my life.

Zeyde could be hard and selfish at times, even while yelling at God to help his children, his *lantzmen*. He could take chances, sometimes dangerous ones that put everyone in jeopardy, and he could harm Uncle Dovid, but even so, he took it on himself to watch over the Roznovites, and take care of *mishpuchah*. He could love life even while the Holocaust roared its vile destruction. He could be strong and powerful, as well as hard, and he could be loved even through it all.

My father and my Uncle Label could hurl themselves into an alien environment and take chances and endure and not forget that they had obligations to others, and they could die suddenly and still young, and yet be remembered.

For some reason, my uncle's ramblings—for that was what they were—made me feel freer than I had before, and stronger. I didn't feel worried about how I would find another job, or how I would support my family. After all, I was a Tannen. I grew up with this clan, watched them, all ravenous for life, any kind of life, even one filled with pain and suffering, watched them wolf it down, with all its surprises and mysteries, guzzling it like schnapps with some salty herring.

And I was a survivor, too. It was in my genes, or anyway my *mishpuchah*. Asher helped his *lantsmen* survive; Avi helped build a labor movement; I was helping to build a women's movement.

What about Benjie, though? Uncle Dovid had said he had done bad things to us. What bad things? I understood he must be seething with resentment. And with his ambitions and his rage for who knew what hurts and denials, he must envy the Tannen lustiness.

Who knew what Benjie might have done—and might still do? He was lusty, too, but his lust was twisted; his solutions to practical daily concerns uncannily wrong. From what I had learned of him so far, his choices pushed survival beyond the pragmatic toward the dangerous, maybe even toward evil.

I needed to know more about him and about how Allerton had become the bank the *Village Voice* wrote about. Next time I would get Uncle Dovid to tell me what it was that Benjie had done.

And what, if anything, he had to do with my father's death. Uncle Dovid said Uncle Label might still be alive if he had known something. Known what? What kind of trouble had Benjie been in? And how had my uncle helped him?

I knew so little about my family's history.

I knew that Avi's body had been found in a car that had been reported stolen, parked just blocks from the Half Moon Hotel, where a notorious racketeer named Abe Reles had dropped to his death from a sixth-floor window just hours earlier. Detective Moe Lewenthal, Stu's father, promoted a few times since his days as a cop on the beat, had found him. Lewenthal had also been at the Half Moon at the time of Reles's death, so everyone in the family always said he was involved in the two murders.

Maybe he hadn't been.

He was blood-caked, my father, slumped in the driver's seat, his arm draped over the wheel as if he were just resting a moment, waiting to pay a toll, perhaps. He'd been dead, the coroner figured, only a short time, shot five times in the chest. The timing and the location prompted speculation by the police, as well as the Tannen family, about a possible connection between the two deaths, Avi's in fact, in the very style of the killers that Reles commanded.

But what connection could there be?

My father was a girdle and bra salesman. We knew he drove Benjie's car once in a while when he went on a job, and of course the family knew Benjie had been connected with Reles, especially in the earlier days. But what reason would anyone have for wanting Avi dead?

Reles, on the other hand, a self-confessed murderer, had turned himself in to the police months before and had already filled some seventy-five notebooks with his confession. He was about to name more names now, publicly, and was getting ready to prove before a grand jury that a corporate-style crime syndicate existed, incredibly coordinated nationwide and called the Mafia, and that it was the parent firm of his own organization, a group the papers were calling Murder Incorporated. His testimony would implicate some well-known racketeers in maybe a thousand murders. The sixth floor of the hotel, reserved for him and several other informers for their protection until they could have their day in court, was filled that night, the night of his death, with cops and Reles's cronies—if Reles could be said to still have any cronies after his turncoat performance.

His career, unlike my father's, had been public and violent. It wasn't hard to understand why someone would want him dead—if, in fact, his death had been a murder. A number of theories about the cause of Reles's death had made the rounds but none was ever proven. The most obvious—and most obviously false—was that he'd committed suicide. Why would Reles turn himself in to the cops, talk his heart out, then leap out a window? If he felt himself trapped, about to be caught, if he saw his time was up, why not kill himself before becoming—what he and his pals regarded as beneath contempt—a rat? Another theory was that Reles had been trying to escape and had fallen. Everyone present on the sixth floor that night—and, amazingly, there were quite a few cops among them—agreed that Reles had been drinking heavily all evening. A couple of bed sheets, tied together with lengths of wire and fastened to a radiator pipe in the room, had not held. What could be clearer, they asked. Didn't that look like a failed escape? But again, why? Why would Reles have gone to all the trouble to provide such a lengthy confession only to attempt an impossible escape before finishing the job? His wife put forth another hypothesis: He was kidding around, she said. A great kidder, he had once at a party gotten blindingly drunk and jumped out a window—only to show up at the door, laughing and surprising everyone. Maybe this, too, had been a botched attempt at such humor. Humor? Had he been so drunk the night of his death he'd thought he could fly—as well as sing, as some newspaper headlines sarcastically put it?

None of these things seemed likely.

The one that was most probable—but which couldn't possibly have happened with so many people there on the sixth floor with him—was that that someone from the killing arm of Albert Anastasia's organization, Reles's own subsidiary, had ordered and paid for Reles's death. A skilled killer—and a lot of paid-off cops—could have pulled it off. Or could one paid-off cop have pulled it off? If not Moe Lewenthal, then someone else. If not alone, then with one of Anastasia's men.

But what could that have had to do with Avi? Avi wasn't involved with organized crime. He would never place himself in so much danger. Yet his murder wasn't a robbery. His wallet was still in his pocket, in it nearly a hundred dollars, neatly folded.

Eclipsed by the Reles murder, though, Avi's case—like Reles's—remained open. The cops had more important things to do than investigate such an anonymous crime. Only the family, tortured by the implications of Avi's murder, wanted to know what had happened to bring him to that place at that time. The family wanted to know who had killed him. But eventually even the Tannens had to let go of the nightmare.

Bubbe Sarah and Zeyde Asher were aging. What could two aging people do to track down a murderer? Aunt Golde and Uncle Dovid knew Avi had gone out with Benjie that night. But even they didn't know about Benjie's disappearance until many weeks later. They were too busy worrying about me.

But they must have suspected Avi's murder, coincidentally happening at the same time and place as Reles's, had something to do with the mob. Why hadn't they done anything? Were they too scared? Did they think they might get the same treatment? And maybe they were worried, too, about me. They now had a child to raise, their surrogate daughter. Maybe they feared the mob's retribution might extend to even a child.

So they buried Avi in the cemetery in Queens where the old-country burial society had bought enough plots to inter the entire village of Roznov. They said *Kaddish*, the prayer for the dead, and went on with their lives.

But Bubbe Sarah now knew that her forebodings had been prophetic.

I walked and walked, not looking around even to see where I was going until I finally caught my breath and stopped on an unfamiliar corner. I was exhausted emotionally, but still overwrought from the adrenalin that surged through me.

Benjie had been involved with my family from the start. Uncle Label's buddy. Jealous, vengeful. Murderous?

I could never prove it. But like Bubbe Rifke, I suddenly knew the truth. It hit me with such force I nearly fell. I had to hold onto a nearby building to stay upright.

It *was* Benjie.

Benjie had murdered my father and Reles. And probably my uncle, too.

The Amboy Duchess

Thirty

The cabin was dank and musty. No one had been there since Uncle Dovid's last fishing trip which had been four or five years ago, at least. They kept the place, though, my aunt and uncle, for just such an occasion as this—the unlikely event that I would want to use it. But here I was, unlikely or not. And glad to be here. I had a lot of thinking to do.

I finished carrying my things in from the rental car, then went out and drove the car around to the side of the house. I picked up my bag, still lying open on the seat next to me, my wallet still lying next to it where I'd thrown it after getting gas. I stuck the wallet in my pocket, slung the bag over my shoulder, got out of the car and stood in the coolness, breathing in the evening air. This was just what I needed, a few days to calm down, think things through. I could see the bay from there; the boat upshore was still lying upside down as Uncle Dovid had left it, probably full of cracks by now, but maybe not. In any case, I doubted I would want to use it. I went back inside and shut the door.

The Amboy Duchess

Nostalgia hit me like a force of nature. I groped for the nearest chair and took a deep breath. No way was I going to cry. I sat there for a few minutes and looked around. The two cots against the north and east walls were still neatly made with flowered quilts bought years ago by Aunt Golde—who actually had never been here! Blankets were folded at the foot of each cot and caseless pillows were tucked under the quilts at the head. The kitchen area, against the western wall of the one-room cabin, was dim; there was no window on that wall. We used to leave a night light on all day and night, at night for my nightmares, during the day just to see what we were doing.

All my bags were on the round oak table in the middle of the room—Uncle Dovid's proud find at a house sale years ago, the table and the four spindle chairs to match. I got up and rummaged for the wine.

I sipped with my feet up on another chair, tried to wind down. I'd thought I needed something to clear my head; a long drive and a few days in the woods should do it. Or so I had thought.

It had taken a day of steady driving to get here, but instead of calming down I became more anxious, constantly looking in the rearview mirror to see if any one vehicle was with me the whole time. Now that I'd figured out—or thought I'd figured out—what Uncle Dovid had told me, I understood that I really could be in danger. I was glad I'd left all the papers from

Allerton in the bag at Aunt Golde's, even though I didn't think anyone had followed me.

I could picture Uncle Dovid now, sitting across from me in the chair my feet were resting on, his seat from the old days. I remembered the times we'd had together and I missed them powerfully. Alternately, I had disturbing visions of Kalmowitz hiding out here. What he'd been hiding from was something I didn't want to think about—but couldn't help it.

The more I let the idea sink in, the more sure I became.

Hadn't Aunt Golde said they had just come home with me after Avi's death when he showed up? Hadn't Eva told me that Benjie had been angry at the whole Tannen clan? Hadn't Uncle Dovid said "... *the things he done to us* ..."? What things? Wasn't he implying that Benjie had avenged his resentments on both Avi and Uncle Label? How had he done that? They were both dead now, and I couldn't believe what I was thinking. But Uncle Dovid had also said, "I'm still here." What did he mean by that?

Were his words just the ravings of a bitter old man?

Or were they warnings to me?

Everyone was warning me: Eva, Aunt Golde, Uncle Dovid.

About what?

Did they really think Benjie was responsible for my father's—and Uncle Label's—deaths? I was sure of it, yet I couldn't accept it.

Why hadn't they done anything about it?

Somehow I understood. Sometimes things that happen seem so incredible, so unbelievable, you can't think of anything to do that would fit your usual repertoire of actions. A woman I once knew from high school had died upstairs in her bedroom. She was having a heart attack and strangling on her own vomit—while her husband was downstairs in the kitchen reading the newspaper. He must have known, had to know, she was dying, or at least in trouble upstairs. He had to have heard something. Even if he hadn't actually caused her death—which was by no means certain—at the very least he'd done nothing to help her. People later found out about his second life; he had two children with another woman. Yet no one ever alerted the police, and his wife's death was ruled natural, a heart attack, by the doctor who arrived later, after she was already dead. No one ruled it a suspicious death. No one ordered an autopsy. Who could believe he'd do such a thing? It was beyond belief. So it was never even considered.

If you can't believe something, if it seems impossible that what you suspect really could have happened, then any action acknowledging it is also impossible. This guy had to have known what was going on upstairs while he sat reading the news. But no one would believe he'd have murdered his wife, or at the very least, let her die upstairs, so they couldn't imagine going to the cops to accuse him.

Something like that might have happened to the Tannens.

I could still see Benjie standing there at the door to the bank, looking after me when I'd fled with Stu's papers, just standing and looking. I remembered how scared I'd felt that he might have me followed. How silly my fears had seemed.

They didn't seem so silly anymore. Someone had to do something about Benjie. If he was angry with the Tannen family before, how would he feel now that I could expose his banking scams?

Still, I was safe enough here. Wasn't I? No one from the bank knew where I was. But what if he *had* had me followed? Then Aunt Golde could be in danger, too.

I decided to take a walk to try and calm down. The moon was bright enough and, reflected off the bay, it would light my way if I wanted to walk all the way around it. I swallowed the last sip of wine and put the glass on the table. I wondered if I should take a flashlight anyway, as a weapon.

"I'm being ridiculous," I said out loud, hoping my voice would reassure me. "There's no one here but me."

It was a beautiful night. The sight of all those stars gave me a jolt of longing for all the years I'd lived; I wanted them, somehow, wanted to hold onto them, keep them from disappearing into oblivion. The only thing between my past and oblivion was memory, my memory. Such a flimsy thing. I wanted to hold onto the years concretely, feel their heft in my hands, never let go of them. But even as I felt this momentary angst, I understood that even these moments, each one so intense as I lived it, fell immediately into the repository of flimsy memories.

I looked out across the bay, the reflection of the moon shimmering, and picked up a stone and cast it out across the water. It skipped a few times, breaking the calm, shimmering reflection into fragments of light. A moment later the bay was still again.

As I turned to walk along the bayshore, I heard a crackling that seemed to come from the clump of trees near the road. Feeling jittery, even though I was sure it was a squirrel or a rabbit, I moved away from the bay and into the shadows of the trees. That's when I saw the figure sliding toward the cabin.

Moving stealthily with quick, agile steps, even in shadow, he was too young to be Benjie. I watched as he emerged into the light near the cabin door. It was a youngish man, not a youth, a guy maybe in his late thirties, early forties, no one I knew. But he entered the cabin. I watched him through the windows.

He stood in the middle of the room and turned slowly, then walked to each cot, lifted each mattress, looked underneath, went back to the table where I'd left my things.

What was he looking for? I gasped when he opened my suitcase on the table and started tossing things out of it left and right. When he didn't find what he wanted, he heaved the suitcase itself onto the floor in a gesture of frustration. He went through each of my bags in the same way until all my bags, and everything that had been in them, were strewn around the cabin.

He must be looking for the papers I'd taken from the bank.

As absurd as it seemed, up here in northern Canada, that had to be what he wanted. As I stood and waited to see what he would do next, I knew I was right. What was that old line? "Just because you're paranoid doesn't mean someone isn't following you."

He headed for the door of the cabin, stepped outside and looked around as if deciding which way to go. He looked up at the moon, out at the bay, then headed straight for where I was standing. He must have realized that the only place anyone would stroll around here was where there was some light.

Now he was looking for *me*!

It didn't take more than a few seconds to realize he would surely find me if I didn't get out of here fast. But I'd have to pass him to get to my car.

The boat.

That was the only way. I was a strong rower, no swimmer could catch up with me once I got going. I'd have to move fast, though. If the boat was cracked, leaking, I'd be sunk, literally and figuratively. I wouldn't drown, I was a good swimmer, but if the boat capsized, whoever that was back there would be able to catch up with me.

The Amboy Duchess

I raced to where the boat was overturned and tried heaving it upright. It took three tries, but finally I did it. The oars were where we always left them, still in the rings of the boat, a little splintered, but usable. I pushed the boat into the water, climbed in and started rowing. I was out about half a mile when I let myself look back. He saw me.

He was standing on the shore, hands on his slim hips, looking menacingly in my direction. I headed for the nearest shore to the south. Once I got there, I'd find a place to make a call. Then I'd rent another car and head for the border. I'd call Aunt Golde later. When I felt safe.

Thirty one

I drove all night, terrified someone might have picked up my trail and followed me. But it was only at the border that I actually saw someone eying me. A tall, skinny guy, his hair matted from the cap he kept lifting off his head to wipe the sweat from his brow with a red handkerchief. He kept turning in my direction and looking at me as I waited for the border patrol to figure out why I had no luggage even though I'd been in their country for four days—which I should never have mentioned. He was up ahead, the skinny guy, parked, waiting for something. Or someone.

I'd stopped to call Melba and Aunt Golde before going through customs to let them know where I was. I told Aunt Golde to check herself into the nursing home on some pretense about having to be with Uncle Dovid. I didn't want to scare her by telling her what had happened to me, but she had to get out of her apartment and go somewhere safer. I told her just a little about the papers she had in her apartment and she agreed to mail them to Melba. She also promised to head right for the nursing home. I didn't have to go into detail; she knew Benjie better than I did.

Then I got in my car and tried to go through to the States. I was stopped by two border guards. That was when I noticed the guy with the red handkerchief. I was pretty sure he was watching me, and I was anxious to get on my way.

"I had an emergency," I repeated again to the guards who were standing at my car door. "I left everything with my aunt. I'm coming back as soon as I take care of the problem at home."

"What emergency?"

"One of my children had an accident," I lied, hoping I could keep my story straight. I was exhausted, worried about the man with the red handkerchief, too terrified by my adventure up at the cabin to think about it. I wasn't sure I could think straight enough to keep a lie coherent. "A neighbor called and told me about it. I was so upset, I just ran out of my aunt's house and headed for home."

"You said your aunt lives in Montreal. Your rental car isn't from Montreal; you got it up north. What were you doing there?"

"Yes, my aunt lives in Montreal. My aunt and my uncle. But they also own a cabin up north. That's where I rented the car.

After they called me to tell me about my neighbor's phone call. I left everything and just took off."

"What kind of accident did your son have?"

"He was playing ball, football, and he was tackled. He hurt his leg. They took X-rays, nothing is broken"—I didn't want to jinx either of my kids and give him a broken leg—"but he's in pain and he needs me."

Did I look like a terrorist? A smuggler? A dope dealer? Why didn't they just accept my story and let me go? Who was that guy who was still watching me? Did everyone look suspicious at the border? Was it my imagination? The border guards must have good imaginations, too. Surely they couldn't think I was up to anything. Me?

Could they?

This wasn't how I remembered these crossings from when I was a kid. Most of the time, they didn't even stop us. We just went right through. What made them stop me now? Everything was so wholesome then. No one ever thought anyone looked suspicious. At least, not that I'd ever noticed. Hah! When I was a kid, everyone *should* have looked suspicious. God, what was going on then! Look what I'd just found out about my own family, for god's sake!

The Amboy Duchess

Though I still wasn't completely sure exactly what it was I'd learned. I needed to be somewhere quiet so I could sort everything out.

The guards moved away from my car and talked quietly. Finally, one of them came back. He handed me my identification—my driver's license and my birth certificate—and said I could go.

I shoved them back in my wallet, lifted myself from my seat to slide it back in my pocket, then turned the key, stepped on the gas and started driving—slowly—watching the man with the red handkerchief. He was still watching me, too. As I passed him, he got into his car and took off behind me.

Omigod.

My throat felt dry. I had a pain in my chest. My hands were sweating on the steering wheel. I kept glancing at the overhead mirror; he kept a steady pace behind me. As I passed into New York, he was still there, his arm resting on the open window-frame, his hair fluttering in the breeze. I tried slowing down, thinking I'd let him pass me. He slowed down, too.

I went a little faster, passing a helmeted guy on a whizzing Harley Davidson. Red Handkerchief sped up, too, staying a car or two behind me.

I slowed down again; there he was, still a car or two behind, moving more slowly, too. My heart began racing; my hands on the wheel were clammy with sweat.

What should I do?

Should I get off the highway? Where would I go? Was I better off here, staying with the traffic? What could he do here, shoot me? I took a deep breath. I had to start thinking more clearly. This wasn't a detective novel; it was real life. The highway would be safe enough. Maybe when I got to someplace nicely populated—Lake George would be good—I'd get off and stop at a restaurant or someplace and see if he stayed with me.

That seemed a good plan. Maybe he wasn't following me at all.

* * * * *

At the first Lake George exit, he was still a couple of cars behind me. I decided to wait until I got to the last Lake George exit. But then he surprised me. He turned off at the second exit going to Lake George.

As if he were a mind reader.

Well, I'd show him! I wouldn't get off.

I wondered if getting off here wasn't exactly the thing I *should* do. Maybe I should check into a motel, take a shower and go shopping for something to wear and some toiletries. Going home was too risky right now. If someone were following me, wouldn't that be exactly where I'd be most vulnerable? Wouldn't Kalmowitz look for me there? Lake George would be a good town to stop in, and holing up somewhere was probably the best thing I could do right now. No one back home was expecting me till next week. Everyone thought I'd be in Canada till then. That's exactly what I should do, stay in a motel for a couple of days, one where no one would think of looking for me. I could get some much-needed sleep, maybe calm down.

I considered going to the cops, but I wasn't sure anyone was really after me. Except for the guy at the cabin, and maybe he was just a local burglar. I was too upset and too exhausted to think clearly about anything. And I wanted to be sure that if I went to the police, I had all the evidence I would need. I didn't want to look like a hysterical woman.

As I was making my mind up, I nearly had an accident. The motorcycle I'd been catching glimpses of unexpectedly slowed down and I nearly hit him. I swerved to avoid him and missed the exit.

Still, the idea of stopping was sounding better and better. Aunt Golde thought I was heading straight home, and she wanted me to call when I got there, but I could call her and explain that I'd stopped overnight instead of driving like a maniac; she'd be proud of me for that. No one in either New York or Canada would miss me right now. The rest of my stuff could stay up north for a while; I was glad I'd been smart enough to have Aunt Golde mail the papers to Melba. I'd get everything else later. I had the main things I needed, my credit cards, my driver's license. A nice quiet motel seemed more and more like the best idea I'd had in weeks. I could pick up some underwear somewhere and maybe a polo shirt or two, buy a couple of mysteries and read until it was time to go back to work. I could clear up my brain, think, figure out what I'd learned about what was going on at Allerton, even call Melba so she could decide what to do about it.

Could I go back to the bank after my vacation? Surely, Kalmowitz wouldn't threaten me during banking hours with everyone there. If I could deal with Stu, I arrogantly figured, I could deal with Kalmowitz. I just wouldn't go near the place at night. But what about going home? Maybe I should stay in a hotel once I got back, too. The kitten was safe with Marilyn Lewen. I wouldn't tell anyone where I was. Except maybe Melba. What else did I have to do when I got back? Those were the things I needed to figure out. I needed to stop and collect myself, think everything through. Plan my reentry.

That was it; I'd decided. I would stop somewhere and have a little vacation from my vacation.

But not in Lake George. As ridiculous as I knew it was to think that the man with the red handkerchief really had been following me and might now be right there waiting for me, I decided not to stop there. I'd go a little farther and head for a town in virgin territory, a place where no one would know me and where I wouldn't recognize anyone, either. Maybe I'd change my route altogether. Head for the coast. Find a little beach town somewhere. Even now when it was getting pretty cool up here, the beach would be beautiful.

Being near the ocean would calm me down.

At the moment, my head was spinning. I didn't have a better plan. So, that's what I'd do. I'd chance it, drive a little farther, find a beach town and check into a motel.

Thirty two

I opened the back door of the bungalow and stepped out onto the cool soft sand. I stood there for a long few moments and looked out across the ocean at the silvery slit widening at the horizon as the sun shoved its way up. The New Hampshire beach was gorgeous.

I'd taken back roads yesterday and wound my way to the coast, then driven south. The town I'd found stretched for two miles along the coast with beachside bungalows that were mostly vacant and mostly cheap. After renting one that was a little more isolated than the others, I'd had my dinner in a small restaurant that was in a little inlet where boats docked and fishermen sold their daily catch. No one paid any special attention to me; I felt reasonably safe.

I bought a bluefish for my next day's dinner, then moved—me and my wallet!—into the bungalow, and went shopping for food and toiletries for the three days I planned to spend here.

I picked up a toothbrush, some toothpaste and a bar of soap in a supermarket I passed on my way back to the bungalow.

The Amboy Duchess

I managed to stay awake long enough to watch the news, then undressed, curled up and fell into a sleep filled with indecipherable dream fragments populated mostly by dangerous men: Kalmowitz, Stu, the guy with the red handkerchief, the one in the Canadian north woods who'd searched my bungalow then watched me row away into the dark. I kept waking up, each time having to remind myself that I was in New England, not home, in a rented beach bungalow, the safest place I could find on such short notice. When I woke for good, it was dawn.

I walked toward the water now, smelled the salty air, and walked slowly along the shore, breathing deeply at last. I was sure no one would find me here.

I picked up shells as I wandered along the water's edge, my feet getting wet and cold, then I crouched down on the sand and looked out for a while at the nearly risen sun. I'd call Melba later; together we'd figure out what to do. I got up slowly and walked back to the bungalow. The sun was nearly up now and I was hungry.

Time for breakfast.

I enjoyed my first full day in my new seaside home. Still fearful about being spotted by I-didn't-know-who, I decided to stay close to "home," so I sat right outside on my own plot of beach for a couple of hours, took long walks before lunch and before dinner, then watched TV, some rerun cop shows and the news, washed out my underwear and went to bed early.

The Amboy Duchess

The next day the sky seemed to be clouding up and it was
chilly when I went out for my early morning walk. After breakfast
I turned on the TV for something to do. I switched from channel
to channel, got nothing that grabbed me: soap operas on two of
the channels, reruns of *I Love Lucy* and *The Honeymooners*,
local weather and traffic. I switched the set off and went outside
again. The sun was trying to come out but it was getting very
cool, too cool to sit out there and sun myself. I decided to take a
little drive and pick up a couple of warm things to wear, maybe
even a slicker; the guy on TV had said to expect some rain later.
I'd seen a little beach shop that was still open on my way here the
other day, and after that I'd visit the small deli I'd passed to get a
couple of newspapers and maybe a paperback book.

The clothes at the beach shop were the leftovers from the
summer. But I found a hooded sweatshirt and two polo shirts
that fit, and a raincoat that was a little too big, but had a hood
and deep pockets, so I took it. They didn't sell underwear, so I
bought a bikini for the bottoms. I figured I could alternate
washing them and my underpants out, or even re-wear things for
a couple of days.

It was getting colder and clouding up when I got to the
deli, so I slipped on the raincoat to run in and get some things to
read. The store seemed to be a local hangout, picnic tables
outside populated by two pairs of chess players, all men long past
retirement age, and a straggly group of kibitzers. Inside, a coffee

machine had attracted nearly as much attention; another man and two women sipped from Styrofoam cups as they chatted.

The newspapers were spread out on a low platform in front of the display window. I picked up the *Times* and a local daily, then checked out the paperbacks hanging on the wall next to the window. Lots of romance novels, a few mysteries, some action thrillers, a number of sci-fi, a couple of fantasy. I flipped through a few of the mysteries; as I was deciding between two of them, I glanced out the window and caught my breath. I saw something that made me nearly drop both books. Red Handkerchief was out there talking to someone I didn't recognize. When I caught my breath and calmed down a little, I looked again. That's when I saw the Harley Davidson parked a couple of feet away.

This couldn't be happening.

Was I really being followed?

By whom?

I couldn't take in and process the possibility that they might be Benjie's guys.

How had they found me?

Of course. The motorcycle.

I'd never tried to lose it because I didn't get it at first that they were together. When they'd realized I'd spotted Red Handkerchief, the Harley had taken over the chase. I'd never actually spotted *him*, because I thought I'd lost my tail.

What now?

The Amboy Duchess

I slowly put back the books, lay the newspapers down on the low table, buttoned up my coat, pulled up my collar and went to the back of the store, hoping I'd find another door there. When I did, I slipped out and got to my car without being seen. At the bungalow I threw all my things—all five of them—into the car and took off, doing eighty before I reached the highway.

The Amboy Duchess

Thirty three

"Pam Freeman is guilty of more than kiting!"

That was the first thing Melba said when she heard my voice. I was calling her from the motel I found when I got off the Thruway on my way home.

I was stretched out on the bed, exhausted from driving for five hours with half my attention on my rear. I thought I'd tell her a little about my adventure, but she beat me to it with her own news.

"Do I have a story for you!" she said before I had a chance to say much. "The kiting I told you about? Well, it seems it was only a small part of a scheme to steal ten million dollars from the feds! And she might have gotten away with it if we hadn't been examining everything in the bank so closely!"

"Ten million dollars?! Migod! How did she do it? What did you do? Did you have her arrested? Do we have proof?"

"I haven't done anything yet. I want to be sure we've got everything we need to make it stick. I've got the home office sorting everything out, uncovering new facts every day. We found all sorts of strange monkey business, but so far she's still out there operating. We'll have to plan this closely. We've got some major frauds going on here."

We both had long stories to tell, but neither of us wanted to tell them over the phone. I told her only enough to make her understand I was in danger. "I don't think I was followed here, Melba, but I'm still shaking."

We met later that evening at a small all-night diner closer to the city. I'd checked into another motel nearby. This adventure was getting expensive.

I started my story with the scary way Kalmowitz yelled "Tannen" after me when I left the bank on my way to the airport. Explaining my connection to him alone took a couple of hours. Then I went through every detail up to seeing Red Handkerchief and the Harley guy outside the newspaper store and my high-tailing it out of New Hampshire at illegal speeds. Melba nodded, shook her head and gasped in all the right places—and then insisted that I come back to her house for the night or she wouldn't tell me the rest about Pam.

We left the diner separately, Melba first. She went to her car and watched as I came out, looked around and studied each car before heading for my own. Finally I went to my car, got in and drove to the motel. Melba followed me slowly, taking off from the diner parking lot only after a few minutes of watching to be sure no one was on my tail.

At the motel, I went to my room, got all my stuff, then looked out the window. Melba had stopped her car in front of the motel office and was waiting there. After a few minutes, she blinked her brights, and I left the room, walked to the office and got into her car. We left my rental car there for the time being.

Our drive was so uneventful, she began to wonder if I just had an overactive imagination. But we weren't going to take any chances. By the time we got to her house, we were pretty sure no one was following.

Inside, she gave me a couple of pillows and a quilt and made me sleep in her bed while she camped out on her sofa. "You've had a rough few days," she insisted. "You need a good night's sleep and I'm going to see that you get it. I'll tell you the rest of the story about Pam in the morning."

Over coffee and rolls she explained Pam's elaborate scheme.

First, Pam had "developed" a number of small businesses to pretend to pool $500,000—which none of them actually had. That was so her investment firm could apply to the Minority Enterprises Small Business Investment Company— MESBIC—an arm of the Small Business Administration. MESBIC was offering private investors the chance to put together at least that much to invest in new or expanding small businesses; the small businesses her investment firm was to invest in could get up to four dollars in federal money for every dollar the investors put up.

This would all be fine—*if* Pam's investment firm had really had $500,000. And *if* the small businesses she developed—both the ones that allegedly made the original investment and the ones they supposedly invested in—really existed; but, in fact, they were all nothing but dummy companies.

No wonder I couldn't get straight what her companies did! They did exactly nothing—except scheme and plot and steal.

The Women's First Investment Corporation—which Pam had created especially for the purpose—actually borrowed, or sort of borrowed, the $500,000 from four banks, one of them Allerton, by falsifying records and by kiting. She alternately borrowed from one bank and deposited the money into another, then borrowed from that one and deposited that in a third, and so on, using the float time to move the money around. That became the money her first group of companies supposedly "pooled" to invest in the second group of companies she made up.

The Women's First Investment Corporation got $3.4 million from the SBA "to help small businesses get ahead." Then these small businesses—the *second* group of nonexistent companies she dreamed up—applied for—and *got*!—the four dollars for every dollar of the money her investment firm "invested" in them.

Four dollars for every dollar of the $500,000!

She hid the assets by buying three town houses in New York, a condominium on Long Island, and a ski lodge in Colorado.

She simply defaulted on the loans.

And this was just a small part of her scheme. Besides diverting funds for her own use and writing checks on uncollected and nonexistent funds, she phonied up her books, borrowed from loan sharks, directed her employees to doctor her financial records and led investors to believe they were buying into one company while she recorded the money in the ledgers of other companies.

Pretty tricky for an ex-high school chemistry teacher. And *I* was worried about stealing an *idea* from *her*!

But she wasn't *quite* good enough to get away with it.

Melba's detective work did her in.

After Melba and I exchanged stories, she called her home office again, the State Banking Commission in Albany, to find out what we should do next. They told her to get in touch with Benjie and me to call Pam; we were to invite them both to meet us at the bank. The banking commission would arrange for the police, the newspapers and TV networks, including Jim Battle to be there.

On the way into the city, I was still nervous. While Melba drove, I continued—just like in a B movie—to study the road behind us. No one seemed to be following.

* * * * *

The Amboy Duchess

At the bank, Melba and I went, as planned, each to our own desks. She called Kalmowitz and asked him what time he'd be in today. When she learned he'd be in right after lunch, I called Pam and told her I needed to see her that afternoon—at the same time we were seeing Benjie. Then we called a staff meeting in the boardroom and told everyone what was going on—including Stu, who was good and pissed he hadn't known all this first—and told them what the cops had said: everyone would have to stay at their posts until Benjie and Pam got to the bank. Then, in case of any trouble, the cops wanted them to be prepared to head downstairs to the boardroom. Gus stood guard at the door and stopped letting customers in just before noon.

When Pam got there, she and I took a slow walk to Stu's office, chatting about the weather as we strolled. There, Melba and Stu chatted with Benjie at his desk. He glared at me when I walked in. Both Pam and Benjie had gotten there just in time, before the media and the law arrived: cops, newspaper reporters, TV camera crews. The bank's staff—Bobbie, Stu, Harry and all the tellers, loan officers and secretaries—stayed at their posts. Everyone refused to go downstairs; this would be too good a show to miss.

If the cops hadn't been right behind us, I might have turned and run out.

Benjie's words came out spewing saliva. "You Tannens!" he hissed at me. "I thought I was rid of all of you for good."

That was all the confession I needed to be sure of my suspicions; he had murdered two members of my family: my father and my uncle. I didn't know how I could ever prove it. But if I couldn't, I figured I'd still get some justice. He was an old man; he'd be in jail for the rest of his life, anyway.

At least I had the satisfaction of knowing I'd found out the truth.

Then, before anyone could stop him, he lunged at me, grabbed me by my throat and wrestled me to the ground.

He's an old man, I kept thinking. *He can't do this to me*, as my fingers circled his, tried to pull his hands off, pulled, pulled, but couldn't get him to let go. *Let go, you fucking bastard, you fucking murderer, you killed my father, you're not going to kill me. Let me go.* I didn't know if I'd said it out loud or to myself, but I started to gain some strength. At last I pulled some of his fingers away, then bit one of them. He screamed and kicked me in the shins, but held on.

Stu and Melba pulled him from the other side, Stu's arms around his waist, Melba gripping his right arm, trying to yank him off me.

"You whore, daughter of pigs, all of you Tannens, I wish I could kill you all."

"You did it, you murdered them, didn't you?! You're a murderer."

"Not all, not Asher, not Dovid . . . but I'll kill you like I killed your father . . ."

There it was! He said it. He killed Avi.

The arrest team was swarming into Stu's office, with all the media behind them—as well as everyone who worked for the bank. *Did they hear him?* They pulled him off me, cuffed him and started out the door with him.

"Did you hear him? He killed my father!" I screamed as I ran to block their way. *"Who else did you kill, you thug?"*

". . . Reles, it was me, I killed him. Abe Reles, Kid Twist. He was about to give it all away, everything we'd worked for . . ."

I was about to say "my uncle," but here he was, confessing to one of the early "crimes of the century." Abe Reles, head of Murder Incorporated.

Now even the cops started paying attention to what he was saying.

"You have the right to remain silent . . ." one of them spoke quickly, reciting Miranda before he could ruin any chance of prosecution, in case he actually was guilty of these things. Then they dragged him away.

Another team grabbed Pam by both her arms. She wasn't surprised, she must have figured she'd been lucky to get this far with her plan; she seemed resigned and a little disgusted. She went with the cops not passively, but quietly, her head high, as if she was proud of what she had done.

Allerton Bank had never had so much good, *and* so much bad, publicity! The good news was: a wildly imaginative bank robber, Pam, was arrested on the premises, her plot discovered by one of Allerton's own employees, or anyway the examiner who worked at the bank, Melba Jefferson, before Pam had a chance to ruin Allerton along with the three other banks she "borrowed" from. But on the bad news side: the chairman of Allerton's own board was nabbed at the very same moment not only for schemes that probably surpassed in scope—though not in daring—those perpetrated by Pam Freeman, but also, it now seemed, for murder. The rest of the board was being rounded up at their homes and offices while we watched the cops put Pam and Benjie into police cars that were parked outside.

When they were all gone, and the excitement died down a little, Stu called another meeting in the boardroom and officially declared the rest of the day a bank holiday, at least at Allerton.

"We'll meet tomorrow to talk about our next moves," he promised.

* * * * *

I went back to Melba's apartment with her, got the few things I'd left there, and then she drove me back to the motel to pick up my rented car.

"See you tomorrow morning," she waved, as she drove away. I got into the car and drove to Blue Woods where I stopped first at Marilyn Lewen's house to pick up my kitten. Marilyn insisted on hearing all the details. Finally she saw how frazzled I was and let me go home.

There were still a lot of loose ends to clear up: I'd have to go back to Canada soon to return the rental car and pick up my own car in the north Canada woods. Then I wanted to spend a few days with Aunt Golde to help her ease back into her own peaceful life. And I couldn't wait to tell her and Uncle Dovid about Benjie. And Eva, I'd nearly forgotten about her! I'd call her tonight.

The most pressing thing was wondering what I would do about a job. There was no way I'd keep working for Stu. Even though he was one of the good guys at Allerton—and his father had no part in my father's death—he was a slime.

And I had to tell him so.

Melba and Stu ran the meeting in the boardroom the next morning.

"The banking commission is letting Allerton stay open while it tries to get a new board together," Melba told everyone gathered there after she'd told them the whole story about the previous day's events, given them all the details of Pam's derring-do and filingd them in on their board's illegal activities. "None of you needs to worry, though. Everyone stays at their jobs, at least for now."

"That's it," Stu stood at the head of the table. "Meeting's over. Everyone back to work."

He'd let Melba tell it all. He had nothing more to add, not even about the women's seminars. He and I would have to figure out how to let all those women on waiting lists that there weren't going to be any more classes. But not yet. For now, I had other fish to fry.

He looked over at me when I didn't make a move. Did he really expect me to go back upstairs to my desk on the platform?

I stood, a little uncertain, waited until everyone had gone back to work, until it was just Stu and me, facing each other. His expression didn't change. He didn't even say 'good job,' or 'well done.' Surely he knew that I was the one who gave Melba the evidence she needed to get Benjie and the Allerton board arrested for all the things the *Voice* had only "hinted" at?

Had I really expected praise from him?

What he said now was, "Well?"

"'Well' what? You don't for a minute think I'm still working for you?"

"What are you talking about?"

"Stu, you may be a top of the line banker, but as a human being you've a long way to go before you reach even the first rung. You're scum."

His face turned red, then he seemed to be holding his breath as if he were holding in some big explosion, then he turned white at the temples and eyebrows and around his mouth. His eyes popped a little.

He whispered. "You wanted me to make love to you. You know it."

The Amboy Duchess

I nearly choked on my own saliva. Did he believe what he was saying? "Make love? Stu, you raped me. I should call the cops, have *you* arrested. But they'd accuse me of wanting it—like you're doing. I'd become a seductress or something and we both know it. But it was rape. You're a prick. You've got a whole group of women on call; do you do the same to all of them? Do you think you love them all? Do you think they all love you? What kind of sickness do you have? Whatever it is, it's still rape."

When he didn't say anything, I continued.

"I'm going to speak at that dinner tonight, if it's still on, but I'm going to talk about women and money, not about this bank. And you'd better not come near me. Some day, things will change, they're already changing right before your eyes, right here in your bank. Some day women will be able to tell their bosses to go to hell and report them for using their power for sex.

"I can't report you, but I sure as hell won't work for you. Someone will give me a job. Maybe you won't recognize what the women have been doing here, but someone will. So I'll tell you what—I'll do you a favor, I won't tell everyone at the dinner tonight what went on here, or what you did. But your bank is finished as far as women are concerned and you'd better stay out of my way."

I pushed past him around the table and strode out of the boardroom.

My long-term future was hazy. I'd have to find another job, and soon. But my immediate future became a little clearer when I called Pam's office to be sure her staff really did still plan to hold the Woman Executive dinner even after her arrest.

"We've got some heavy-hitter speakers," her secretary told me. "There's no way we could cancel them. We're still on. And you're still speaking."

I worked on my speech all day. I was finally ready with it when everyone else began to leave for the day. All the officers and the secretaries cleared the platform. Bobbie waved on her way out. Harry, right behind her, did a little two-step and a twirl as he passed my desk. Even Gus, who usually waited until everyone else was gone, was just coming up from downstairs having already changed out of his uniform.

"You're leaving already, too, Gus?" I called.

"The wife is having a special dinner for me tonight. She thinks I helped solved this thing—and I'm not telling her any different. Got to be home early. I promised I'd help, for a change. Good luck tonight."

The bank was just about empty now. Melba was going with me to Pam's dinner. I waited for her, and we watched together as Stu left. Then we took a cab to the Waldorf.

The room at the Waldorf was jammed with round tables, each seating ten women. I scanned it. In addition to the press table right in front, photographers and reporters with notebooks lined the walls. Besides the high-powered speakers who had agreed to speak in spite of the scandal, the story of Pam's arrest had broken that morning, and the press wanted a crack at anything they could get. The buzz in the room was several decibels higher than it would normally be.

Also, this wasn't exactly a first, but it was still unusual enough for a roomful of businesswomen from a wide range of fields to meet and share ideas. Those who knew about Pam's arrest had come out of curiosity, but the big draw was still the speakers and what they were there to announce. Betty Friedan, Muriel Siebert and Carol Bellamy were at the dais. Friedan had come to publicize the upcoming opening of the new Women's Bank. Siebert, the first woman to hold a seat on the Stock Exchange, would address something more general, women and money. And Bellamy, New York's state senator, would give the audience a broad look at the women's movement now that women rated their own bank.

TV cameras were aimed at the dais, while other camera crews roamed the room, and reporters stopped at tables and shoved microphones in people's faces. My hands felt clammy and my throat went dry.

With Pam in jail, pending bail, I'd been designated by Pam's stupefied staff to give a short introduction. I'd agreed, but now I was struck with a surge of stage fright. What was I doing with such powerhouses?

I checked out the audience, looking for Jim. There he was, leaning comfortably against the wall in the corner of the room.

We'd finally gotten together the night before. I told him about my adventure first, then—and only after he'd calmed down a little—I hesitantly told him about Stu. At first, he'd wanted to go out and find "the prick" and beat him up. He pooh-poohed my own feelings of guilt after we talked and talked and talked, and I told him everything I could about the way Stu had been behaving both in and out of the bank, and my own reactions toward him.

When I told him about my adventure in Canada, he really got upset. He was still worried now that Benjie's guys might be out there looking for me. But the cops had assured me that their men knew who the thugs were and they were arresting them even as we convened here now.

Somehow my close call—and even Stu's abuse—seemed to intensify our feelings for each other, mine and Jim's. We talked about our relationship, fantasized about the future, about staying together, making a commitment, maybe in an unconventional way for now. We had a lot of fun together, and through the years ahead, we planned, we'd be able to help each other raise our four children.

He'd always be one of my closest friends.

But even though he said I was being stubborn about this, I couldn't see giving up my independent lifestyle. Maybe at some point I'd change, but right now I liked living on my own, and with my kids.

Now I saw Sarah Priest and Barbara Woolfson, the financial consultant and the lawyer who worked with me on the seminars, at a table with some of our clients. They waved, and I waved back. A woman who worked for Pam led Melba to their table; another woman escorted me to the dais. As I climbed to my seat, she turned back to stand against the wall.

When she gave me the signal, I stood and looked out at everyone. They all stopped talking and waited for me to begin.

I coughed, afraid my voice might fail me. Finally, I began.

"Good evening, everyone . . ."

My voice was clear and loud.

* * * * *

Benjie Kalmowitz and his colleagues on the Allerton board were all found guilty of racketeering and fraud, and Benjie, somehow holding up through another long trial, charged with three counts of murder in the first degree, was found guilty.

His age, though, mitigated the sentence; instead of getting the death penalty, he was in for several lifetimes.

Pam Freeman was found guilty of grand larceny, forgery, and conspiracy in a 437-count indictment charging that she had defrauded the Small Business Administration and the banks in a plot that involved more than fifty people working under more than eighty corporate names. She ended up serving nearly fourteen years in a state prison.

When she got out in the late '80s the world had changed for women.

There was finally an Equal Credit Opportunity Act, enacted later the year that everything happened at Allerton, 1974. It barred lenders from denying anyone credit merely based on their gender. Stu and his boys on the platform could no longer say—when a woman came in for a loan—"Sorry, no," and then just explain it by saying: "because you're a woman." They'd have to evaluate her creditworthiness using the same standards they used for men.

The First Women's Bank, chartered in New York State the following year, 1975, lasted only a little more than a decade. I never worked there. Instead, I went into business for myself! Yes! I took some lessons from my customers!

I became a consultant—okay, okay. No wisecracks, please. I did great! I consulted to executives in financial services who wanted to know something about the women's market, how to pitch to it, to promote the services or products produced by their corporations to people they'd never considered worthy of selling to before.

But there were some things we still couldn't do in those days. We couldn't talk about certain things that happened to us; we didn't have the language. It wasn't until years later—in 1991 when Anita Hill challenged Clarence Thomas—that the whole country had an epiphany. Hill gave us the vocabulary to describe experiences that we hadn't even been aware of having had before.

Suddenly it was Babel.

Then women everywhere were telling the same story. All it had needed was a name, and now they knew what it was.

Hill had named it.

Stu called me once during the Hill hearings. Allerton Bank no longer existed by then; he was president of another bank, one that gave loans for community development. He was helping the disadvantaged now.

That gave me a chuckle.

He'd called to say he thought he saw a resemblance between his behavior toward me at Allerton and Thomas's behavior, as described by Hill, toward her when she and Thomas had worked together. He asked me if I saw it too.

He didn't apologize to me, though.

We didn't have the language for that yet.

Epilogue

Benjie
1941

Benjie was at the desk in back of the candy store at Lavonia and Saratoga that afternoon when Dukey wandered in and sat opposite him, casually unbuttoning his coat.

"Hey, Bennie, how ya doin'?"

This was no casual visit. The Duke worked full-time for The Boss; if he wandered in and found Benjie in back of the store, it was because he was looking for Benjie; no other reason. Benjie nodded.

"Good. I'm good." He was alert, waiting for orders.

"I gotta take ya to The Boss."

They went to the Waldorf in Dukey's limo. Dukey stopped in front of the hotel and a doorman in a brass-buttoned uniform opened the car door to let Benjie out. Dukey told him to go up to the glitzy dining room; The Boss would meet him and they would have some supper together. They had a simple meal: filet mignon, baked potatoes, salad, and champagne. The Boss talked as if he was filled with sorrow at what he had to ask Benjie to do.

"We gotta do somethin' about the Kid, Bennie. If we let him keep on talkin' we're all t'rough, ya know what I mean?"

Benjie knew. He nodded as he lit The Boss's cigar.

"I got it all set up for ya. The cops will lie low whenever you let them know you're comin'. You know what to do?"

Benjie understood what he had to do.

November 12th, Benjie parked a borrowed car in front of Avi's house on Avenue P and went up the stairs. Avi was home, and Dovid and Golde were visiting, as Benjie had suggested. But none of them knew where Benjie and Avi were heading.

Avi got his coat and his hat from the front closet, he bent down and gave his little girl a great bear hug and kissed her, one of his famous wet kisses, which she wiped off with the back of her hand.

Benjie got up from the comfortable chair in the living room where he had been discussing the situation in Europe with Dovid. He held his hat in his hand on his way out. At the door, he turned to say good night to Golde.

"Take care of yourself, Goldele. You look tired. Avi may be late tonight. Don't wait for him."

The two men went downstairs and got into the 1938 Ford sedan, Avi at the wheel. Before driving to Coney Island, they went to Flatbush Avenue and stopped at Junior's for a *meal, lox and eggs and onions with bialys and coffee. They sat in the restaurant for a couple of hours, shooting the breeze. Finally, Benjie looked at his watch. It was past midnight.*

"Okay, Avi. It's time. Let's go."

Avi knew better than to ask Benjie where they were going. He didn't drive his lantzman *around often, but when he did his driving ability was not his only valued trait; Benjie hired him also for his silence.*

"Go past the Half Moon, Avi. Park on that street down near the beach and just wait for me. I won't be long."

Avi parked the 1938 Ford sedan on the deserted Coney Island street and Benjie got out of the car.

Avi leaned back in the driver's seat, the window next to him open. He enjoyed feeling the brisk air on his face, hearing the waves break against the shore, one of his favorite sounds, and he let his thoughts roam randomly. He pictured his eight-year-old daughter asleep in their small Flatbush apartment; he worried about the bad news from Eastern Europe, war wreaking havoc in what he still thought of as his homeland even after more than two decades in New York. He thought about sports, about how he missed the baseball season each year when it ended. The salty sea air dampened his brow. He pulled his handkerchief from his jacket pocket and pressed it against his forehead. He hummed softly to himself, a song he had learned only recently, ""Bei Mir Bist Du Shein." As a boy in the Bucovina he had loved to sing. He was the Tannen family's entertainer, telling his brothers and his cousins stories and jokes, singing songs for them. Now he often crooned to his little girl, Winnie, sometimes sad songs, feeling sorry for her because her mother had died when she was so young. He flicked on the radio to see if he could catch some music or maybe some breaking news.

A few blocks away, Abe Reles also listened to the radio. As Avi daydreamed, worried, pondered life, the short, squat head of the Amboy Dukes, now known as Murder Incorporated, the man with the huge hands and spatula-like fingers, rested on his bed in room 623 of the Half Moon Hotel, the half-finished bottle of Canadian rye on the table beside him. He was getting drunk while listening to the European news. Six New York City detectives were just outside the door in another room of the ten-room suite, rented just for this purpose, to protect Reles from the threatened racketeers who might want to do him harm. The window was open and Reles, like Avi, was lulled by the sound of the surf, the clanging of a buoy. He closed his eyes.

Outside his room, Reles heard one of the detectives say to the others: "Hey, I got this covered. I know you guys want to go down to the ballroom and watch the rest of the party. I wish I could go see Moe given the award wit'

chyouse, but I don't mind, y'know? He's out cold in there. I
don't need no help. G'wan, gettoutahere."

He heard the other cops shove back their chairs,
shuffle around the room as they got out of their seats, heard
the door open, heard them leave.

What happened next, what remained a mystery to
most of the world, was known only to the cop that stayed—
and to Benjie.

Benjie went into Reles's room, and, surprise on his
side, knocked him unconscious. Then he pulled the sheets off
the bed, knotted them and tied them together. He twisted a
four-foot length of radio lead-in wire to the sheets and tied
the free end of the wire to a steam valve under the window.
He let the sheets down the hotel's east wall, two windows
north of the hotel's boardwalk front, pulled Reles out of the
bed and dragged him to the window. He tied the sheet under
Reles's arms and around him, just tight enough so the man
would dangle a few minutes before crashing to the ground.

"Okay, Kid. You gotta climb out on that window
ledge and lower yourself down," he whispered to the Kid as
he lugged him to the window and shoved his limp body over
the ledge.

Reles came to and began to flail, grabbing hold of the
sheet and swinging in and out, maybe believing he could
swing himself to the window on the fifth floor, open it and
climb in. Benjie watched as Reles clung to the sheets with one

hand while tugging at the screen and the window on the floor below with the other. Reles managed to raise both the window and the screen about six inches.

As he worked, the knot on the steam valve upstairs loosened—with Benjie's help—and the sheet started to come undone. Reles kicked toward the fifth-floor window ledge desperately, but all he managed to do was scuff his shoes. The wire broke loose of the valve, the sheets gave a jerk out the sixth-floor window, helped a little by Benjie, and the 160-pound gangster plunged to the concrete roof forty-two feet below.

As Avi waited a few blocks away in the car, still listening to the radio, the hotel's occupants continued to party or sleep or listen to radio broadcasts or play cards. No one at the Half Moon heard the noise of Reles falling to his death.

Minutes later, Benjie, in his dark coat and hat, came up beside Avi, leaned against the car and casually pulled the gun from inside his jacket.

"What . . ." The startled Avi had no time to wonder what was happening. The gun exploded five times, blood splattered on the seat, the window, and Avi slumped forward over the wheel of the vehicle, dead before the second shot hit its mark. Benjie walked slowly away and took the subway to Manhattan, got to the train station and calmly bought his *ticket to Canada. He was rid of one Tannen, though not the right one.*

Meanwhile, the 1938 Ford sedan sat on the deserted beach street as the dim light glowed in the east, the sun beginning its rise. All around, on more populated streets, sounds of the November day began, people coming out of their houses, clattering down steps as they ran for buses, the hotel staff a few blocks away getting the day started.

Soon, Moe Lewenthal, coming from the Half Moon on his way home, approached the car, noticing the slumped man inside, reached inside his jacket, pulled out his gun—but he didn't fire. Instead, he slowly pulled open the car door, saw Avi's bullet-riddled body, then walked the few blocks to the hotel to call the station. In a few minutes, the police arrived, along with the coroner who declared Avi dead.

Vicki Moss is author of two other novels, *Solo Flights* and *The Lust Chart.* Her books *Alien On the Road, a poetry memoir,* and *Blood Memories, a collection of short stories,* are published by Horsetooth Press. She has written five children's books. She teaches literature at the Fashion Institute of Technology of the State University of New York.